"She was a wind shaper?"

The stranger nodded. "One of the strongest I've met."

"You've met a lot of shapers?" That meant he likely came from Ter or Vatten. Maybe even Ethea, but if he was from the capital, it seemed odd he'd be so far out here and all by himself.

"Many."

"Where? Ethea?"

They climbed down a steep slope. The man followed him easily, moving with a limber grace that told Tan he wasn't a stranger to woods like these.

"There. And other places," he said.

Tan grabbed a thick sapling as he started down another slope. "Ever meet any warriors?" Cloud warriors, the most prized shapers, could shape all of the elements. That was how the last Incendin war had been won.

The stranger laughed. "There aren't any warriors. Haven't been for nearly a decade."

*Others Available by DK Holmberg*

**The Cloud Warrior Saga**

Chased by Fire
Bound by Fire
Changed by Fire
Fortress of Fire
Forged in Fire

**The Lost Garden**

Keeper of the Forest
The Desolate Bond
Keeper of Light

**Assassin's Sight:**

The Painted Girl
The Durven
A Poisoned Deceit
A Forgotten Return

# CHASED BY FIRE

## THE CLOUD WARRIOR SAGA
BOOK 1

ASH Publishing
dkholmberg.com

# Chased by Fire

ISBN-13: 978-0692309322
ISBN-10: 0692309322

ASH Publishing
dkholmberg.com

*For Sam and Mia - may you shape your future.*

# CHASED BY FIRE

## THE CLOUD WARRIOR SAGA
### BOOK 1

# CHAPTER 1
## *Tracks and Smoke*

THE SUDDEN HOWL SENT A SHIVER through Tan. The terrible sound echoed several times during the day, and each time he reacted the same. He checked his bow reflexively, feeling the reassuring weight of the smooth ash. Whatever was out there didn't belong in his forest.

"There it is again!" Bal cried. She started up the slope until Tan grabbed her.

He still couldn't believe he had found her wandering this high up in the mountains alone. "Not the first time I've heard it," he said, wiping an arm across his forehead, smearing away sweat from the unseasonable heat. Tracks piercing the dry earth traced up the slope, winding between massive oaks growing along the steep hillside. Farther up the oaks thinned, leaving the rock bare.

"What do you think it is?"

Tan studied the trees around him. They were mostly oak and pine,

thin the higher they climbed. "Not sure. I don't recognize
ks." Bal's eyes widened. "Not wolves," he said to reassure her.
crossed their tracks a couple of times already."

"You've seen wolves?" She looked around, as if the huge mountain wolves were worse than whatever had made that horrible sound.

He pulled her back down the slope, keeping his hand on her wrist. "What were you doing up here anyway?"

Bal glanced over her shoulder before meeting his eyes. "I don't want to say."

Tan snorted and shook his head, unable to suppress the smirk coming to his face. Typical response from Bal. He waited for her to answer rather than pressing.

"I…" She bit her lip as she hesitated. "I followed someone," she finished in a rush.

Tan frowned. Who would Bal have followed into the forest?

The harsh cry came again, keeping him from asking. He listened carefully, stretching out his awareness of the forest as his father had once taught him, focusing on the sounds of the forest, smelling the air. Closer. Much closer than the last.

The sound meant more than one of these creatures.

"We should go," he said.

The hike back would take most of the day, and Tan dreaded seeing his mother when he returned so late. Since his father's passing, she was short-tempered any time she couldn't account for him. The death of his father was the biggest reason he remained in Nor rather than leaving and taking an apprenticeship outside the village.

Bal bit her lip. "What do you think you were tracking?"

"I've never seen anything like it," he admitted. "Maybe Cobin will know." Cobin had lived at the edge of the forest for longer than Tan had been alive, and if any in town would know, it would be Cobin.

"You think my father will know if you don't know?"

"Maybe, but even if he doesn't, we should still head home."

Tan started off, moving back down the slope. Sweat poured off him and he wished he had brought more than just the single flask of water with him. The upper streams were infrequent here, and with the stifling air, he went through what he brought.

A sudden gust of comforting wind touched his arm, providing a brief relief. Galen was normally a windy land and the heat over the last few weeks was worse for the uncharacteristically stagnant days.

Bal trailed behind him, strangely silent.

"What would you have done had I not found you?" Tan asked, glancing back as they made their way down the slope. No trail worked through this part of the forest and they were far from Nor. Bal could have wandered lost for days.

"Followed my tracks back down."

Tan sensed the hesitation in her voice. "Bal, who did you follow?"

She wouldn't meet his eyes. They moved much farther downslope before she finally answered. "I didn't mean to follow him. Just sorta got away from me. I thought it strange he'd come up in the hills. Not like him. Too dirty for his type."

"Bal?" Tan already thought he knew who she meant.

She looked up at him, defiance in her eyes. "I followed Lins."

Tan laughed and shook his head. "You know what he'll do if he knew you followed him?"

"No worse than he does to you. Besides, just because he's Lord Alles's son doesn't mean he can do whatever he wants. If the king knew some of the things he does…"

Tan swung around a stump and pointed so Bal didn't trip. "The king doesn't care much what happens in Nor. And Lins…well, Lins will eventually inherit his father's house, so best we don't anger him too much."

"Why do you say that?"

Tan frowned. "About Lins?"

She shook her head. "The king. Why wouldn't he care? We're right here next to Incendin. And Ethea likes our iron plenty."

Tan shook his head. The only time the king seemed to care was to summon them to service. Like his father. "Ever seen a shaper here? If Nor is so important, seems we'd be better protected."

Bal slipped on some loose dirt and Tan grabbed her wrist to keep her upright. "Wish we *had* a shaper. Wouldn't be so blasted hot."

"It doesn't work like that, Bal."

She jerked her arm away from him. "Like you know. You've seen exactly as many shapers as I've seen."

Tan laughed and let her get ahead of him. Besides, she was right. Maybe shapers could control the weather. The only help Nor got were sensers, and there weren't many of them. Fewer since Tan's father died.

"Did you see what he was doing?" Tan asked. Bal had gotten too far in front of him and he didn't want her to get lost again. Talking slowed her down a little.

She turned and put one hand on her hip as she glared at him. Dirt somehow stained her brown shirt. "Who?"

"Lins. Did you see what he was doing up there?"

She shook her head. "Just saw flashes of him when he got too far ahead. Then I lost him."

Tan started to say something, but motion at the edge of his vision startled him. Tan should have sensed it, but his ability was weak. Nothing like his father. He waved a hand at Bal, motioning for her to remain still. He crept forward, his awareness focused like his father had taught him while walking these hills. Doing so made him feel close to him again, however briefly. Long moments passed where he detected nothing.

Then he saw tracks again.

Tan hadn't followed them down the slope, choosing an easier hike down than the one he took up the mountain, but the tracks appeared anyway. Marked by three toes and in a shape he didn't recognize, there hadn't been other signs of these creatures except for the painful cries. Until now.

The forest seemed strangely silent, but Tan didn't sense anything else in the woods. He had practically grown up wandering the forest and hills of Nor, which made the vague sense of unease settling into his chest even more unnerving.

The odd footprint had initially just sparked his curiosity. The climb had begun as a diversion, a way of avoiding his chores for the day. Several sheep had gone missing and Cobin was convinced the wolves took them. So far, Tan saw no sign of wolves in the valley. It had not taken him long to find other prints as he had made his way upslope. Eventually, even tracking became difficult, forcing him to use his weak sensing to find the next print.

The creatures didn't follow an easy climb. In some places they moved quickly up sheer rock. Other times he went dozens of paces before finding another print. When he had come across Bal, he took it as a sign to turn back.

"What is it?" Bal whispered, edging up to him.

He stared through the trees. Was there something there? Was it Lins? Tan wouldn't have any easier a time than Bal if he ran into him up in the mountains, but at least he'd have a reason to be here. "Not sure. Thought I saw something."

"What?"

Tan studied the ground as he crept forward, searching for the strange print he had been following. "Nothing, I guess."

Had his mind played tricks on him? He slid forward, eyes focused, ignoring Bal as she spoke to him. There had been something here—he was certain of it. He only had to find proof.

Then he found the next print.

Tan glanced behind him and then turned, looking upslope from where they had come. Bal stared at him, a worried look to her face. Had the creature truly been this close to them? Tan turned, kneeling to look at the print, unable to tell how fresh it was.

"There's another print." Tan pushed on Bal's shoulder, moving her downslope. "I think you should get back to Nor. Follow the tree line to the next stream. You can use it to make your way back to town."

"What are you going to do?"

"I'm going to follow this a little further."

She shook her head. "Not without me."

"We don't know what this is. I'll have an easier time moving in the woods without…" He trailed off before finishing. Bal didn't need him to insult her too. And she would take anything he said about her slowing him down as an insult.

"Without what? Me pestering you?"

Tan sighed. "I was going to say without worrying about you."

"Well I wouldn't want you worrying about me, Tannen Minden!" She stomped off down the slope, making enough noise to scare away anything he might have been tracking. She glanced back at him once, her eyes flashing anger, before disappearing.

He sighed, hating to anger Bal, but it was for the best. He would worry about her and she *would* slow him, but it still pained him to upset her. Part of him debated chasing her. Like her, he should return to Nor, but he still hadn't figured out what made the tracks. It gnawed at him that he hadn't.

Tan climbed upslope, watching for more prints. After a dozen paces, he saw another. Now that he'd found them, he could clearly follow the tracks. The prints wound across the face of the slope, never moving completely upslope or down. No further howls echoed but the sounds of the forest still didn't return. Nothing resonated with his senses. Gradually, the sun dipped below the tree line. Soon he would need to abandon his tracking.

Then he found a second set of prints.

They were as unusual as the first, though in a different way. Long, almost as if made by a man, but with a strange dimple near the heel on each. When the print led over a rocky stretch of ground, he realized the dimple came from the nail of a sharp claw that had left scratches along the stone.

The uneasy sensation twisted his stomach and sweat slicked his palms. The original tracks mingled now with the new prints, as if they traveled together.

Was he the hunter or the hunted?

Tan looked around, the area unfamiliar. He focused on slowing his breathing, controlling his emotion, and extending his senses into the forest as his father had long ago taught him. Nothing moved in the forest around him. Something to that feeling bothered him.

Turning toward home, he felt an intrusion upon his senses like an itch at the back of his mind, a sense he'd learned to trust over the years, and froze. Any sudden movement might frighten the animal—either to run or to attack. He didn't want to take any chances. Starting forward, he moved cautiously, and the sensation intensified. Tan scanned the forest for the source of his unease, but saw nothing.

Then the strange cry suddenly rang out through the forest, nearer than before. Near enough that the sound hurt his ears.

He ran. His steps were careful at first, but after another sharp braying sounded even closer, he tore through the forest. Nearing a rocky outcropping, he climbed up for a better vantage as the terrible howl came again.

It sounded almost upon him. Tan hurried up the rock and scraped his knees in his haste. He swore softly, knowing better than to press his luck tracking so far from home armed with only his bow.

The creature howled again, this time from behind him.

How did it get behind him?

That meant two of the creatures. Or more. Could this be a pack?

The idea terrified him. What of Bal? She should be far down the slope by now, but he knew her well enough to know she might have turned back to check on him. He prayed her anger carried her all the way back to Nor.

He couldn't run. The steep slope and the treacherous footing made him an easy target. On the rock, he was too visible and could be easily surrounded if facing a pack.

That left up.

The nearest tree was his best option. The huge oak had no low hanging branches that would allow another creature an easy climb. Tan scrambled up the rough trunk, tearing his knees more in the process, before settling into the crook of one of the large branches. He pulled his bow off his shoulder and nocked an arrow, setting it to the string without tension. Nothing moved below him.

Tan listened, sensing the forest. He struggled against his racing heart, but sensed another presence among the trees, one he didn't recognize. Another cry came, much closer.

A low growl answered, almost below him.

His arms prickled with a chill. They had his scent.

A smoky haze appeared near the base of the tree. With it came a dry heat pressing up at him, like a fire burning. A fetid stench wafted up that he didn't recognize. A flash of dark fur moved within the haze.

He brought his bow up and aimed, loosing an arrow into the smoke. A snarling yelp told him he'd hit.

Tan waited. Maybe he could scare the creature off. With enough arrows, maybe the creatures would decide he wasn't worth it.

The heat pressing up the tree increased. Already hot, the day became unbearable. Several distinct voices howled below him, joining in a chorus. Definitely a pack.

The smoke began to obscure the forest floor. Heat left his skin feeling raw. He crawled further up the tree, hoping to get away from the fire, but the heat followed him.

Tan pushed down a rising panic as his father had taught. Steady his breathing. Use his senses. Listen, always listen. The answer would come.

This time it didn't.

The next tree was too far to offer any hope of jumping. Upper branches wouldn't support him if he crawled higher. And still the heat pressed toward him. What made the heat?

Each breath became painful. The skin on his arms turned red. If he couldn't get away, he would burn.

He closed his eyes again, forcing himself to focus. A wave of anxious nausea rolled through him that he ignored. A quiet sound whistled in his ears, slowly intensifying like a howling wind. The steady gust of wind picked up speed as it blew through the tree, a gale like the area's namesake. It blew faster, tearing through the trees.

Tan clung to his branch.

The heat blew away with it, disappearing like a candle snuffed out. Flashes of fur prowled around the base of the tree. For a moment, it seemed the heat fought the wind, then the animals howled again before streaking up the slope of the mountain and out of view.

The wind continued, its familiar pressure a relief. He shivered uncontrollably.

He climbed down carefully. Near the bottom of the tree, the

ground looked darkened and scorched. The air smelled of char and sulfur. Even though the wind had finally returned, heat still clung to the air. Tan didn't linger and started down the slope toward Nor. His heart didn't slow until he was back in familiar land.

He found Bal about halfway down the mountain face sitting atop a flat rock, staring upslope. Her jaw fixed in a stern expression and she leaned forward, trying to look fierce.

"I thought you'd be back in Nor by now." He tried to hide the relief in his voice.

Bal frowned at him, jutting her jaw forward. "Maybe I won't show you what I discovered, then."

Tan hesitated, uncertain he could stomach tracking anything else today. Whatever had happened, he felt lucky to survive. He needed to reach Nor and find Cobin. He'd lived here long enough, and he'd know what to do. Whatever creature Tan had found didn't belong here. The next time, it might not only be sheep missing.

"What did you discover? Something about Lins?" he asked.

Her jaw relaxed and a playful smile slipped onto her face. "Not Lins. Better." She jumped up from the rock and started back up the mountain. "Come on, Tan!" she shouted as she ran.

Tan looked up the slope. The strange hounds were still up there, and with the fading light they needed to return, not risk running through the woods on another of Bal's whims. "Bal!"

She didn't answer. Tan swore to himself and hurried after her, determined to drag her back to town if needed.

She stopped overlooking a slight ravine where two smaller peaks merged and turned back, a smile spreading across her face. "Well?"

Tan stared, uncertain what she wanted him to see. "I don't see anything."

She tapped her head and then pointed out toward the ravine, a narrow pass through the mountains. "How can you not see them?"

Tan strained to see through the trees into the ravine. Finally, another sound carried on the wind. A light tinkling, like many tiny bells ringing, carried softly up to them from the pass. Only then did the fear that had been sitting in his chest since he first heard the strange howls finally lift.

Though it had been many years, he recognized the sound and felt a surge of excitement. The Aeta had returned.

# CHAPTER 2
## Glimpse of the Aeta

THE CARAVAN SLOWLY RUMBLED through the lower part of the valley, moving upon a barely visible trail. Brightly colored wagons flashed through the heavy foliage. Men and women sat atop the wagons, steering them through the valley, their clothes as brightly colored as the wagons they drove. Small bells hung from posts and it was their quiet tinkling that preceded them, a distinctive musical sound, and one that sparked memories of the last Aeta visit.

Tan could count on one hand the visits during his lifetime and remembered each vividly, the last nearly five summers ago. How had Bal even known what the Aeta looked like? She couldn't have been more than four or five at the time.

The Aeta were traders and different than the typical merchants traveling through Nor. Visits were almost festival-like when the Aeta came. People from nearby farmsteads would travel to Nor to trade with the Aeta, visit with friends, or simply come to see what new exotic items the Aeta had for trade.

"Where do you think they travel from?" Bal asked with barely restrained excitement.

Tan stared, imagining the direction of their wagons. "There is nothing but mountains this way." But that wasn't quite right. Over the mountains and through the passes lay Incendin, though none in the kingdoms traveled to Incendin. The barrier between the two nations prevented all travel. "And Incendin," he added.

"Incendin? How would they have come from Incendin? Shapers stopped that long ago. That's how the war was ended."

Tan laughed as Bal lectured to him. "I know how the war ended. But no one travels there." The Aeta made the earlier fear a distant memory.

Bal smiled, the annoyance she'd had with him now gone. They crept closer to the wagons, finding the small path the Aeta followed. Foliage covered it, but enough stone remained to mark the roadway it once had been. Tan didn't know a path into Incendin ever existed here.

The light tinkling of the Aeta bells grew louder as they neared. They hid among the trees as the caravan rolled closer. The Aeta were a happy people, exuberant traders, and part of the excitement with their visits was the carnival atmosphere they brought with them. But at this vantage, a tight expression strained the dirty faces of the Aeta and a dour mood emanated from them.

"Maybe they were in Doma!" Bal whispered.

Tan shook his head. More than just a mood, but also a darkness seemed to follow them. "If they were, then it was long ago. And I'm not sure how they'd get there from here."

"How do you know they didn't just come through Incendin?"

Beyond Incendin lay Doma, with Chenir to the north. The simple geographic barrier Incendin presented kept contact with their people limited in this part of the kingdoms. The kingdoms, once the separate nations of Vatten, Ter, Nara, and Galen, had been bound together nearly a thousand years ago and ruled by the king in the capital of Ethea. Within the kingdoms, the ports of Vatten imported goods from Doma and Chenir, but rarely did they make it this far. When they did, the cost was prohibitive to all but the manor lords. It was the fancy Doman silver Bal wanted to see, but he knew his mother would be more interested in Chenir woolens.

"The barrier," he reminded her. A shaping so powerful it kept the kingdoms safe from Incendin. Not much was said to be able to pass through, at least not easily. Watching the Aeta, seeing the darkness on their faces, the edge of nervousness he'd felt higher in the hills had returned.

Bal glanced from him to the Aeta before shaking her head. "All I see are Aeta."

Tan looked away from her, wishing he could see the world through her eyes. As the caravan neared, one of the Aeta caught his eye. A woman sat straight-backed atop a bright red wagon. Her dark eyes darted around the forest. Full lips tilted in a slight frown and pale yellow hair pushed behind her ears, flowing down to her mid back. She was beautiful.

Tan stared and found himself sliding out from behind the trees. Bal grabbed at him too late. He stood openly in view of the caravan. The Aeta woman looked over and locked eyes with him.

She seemed unconcerned that he stared at her, hidden within the forest. Her lips parted slightly and the corners twitched, threatening to smile. One long-fingered hand touched the side of her face delicately.

Tan felt a brief fluttering within his chest. He'd never seen anyone like her.

"Tan?"

Tan shook himself, as if awakening from a dream, and looked over at his friend. "What?"

Bal pulled on his sleeve. "We need to get back."

He glanced at the sky. By the time they returned it would be getting dark. "*Now* you want to return?"

"We need to be there when the Aeta arrive!"

The train of wagons continued slowly past them. Tan made little effort to hide. The woman stared until her wagon was no longer visible, turning as she passed to keep her focus on him. When the wagons had finally disappeared, he said, "We should hurry."

"So we can see the Aeta arrive?"

"So you can. I need to see Cobin first."

Bal frowned at him, as if disappointed he would not be there with her as the Aeta arrived in town. "Don't tell him I was up here."

Tan shook his head and chuckled as Bal started down the slope toward Nor.

Tan followed after her, unable to completely shake the vision of the beautiful Aeta from his mind.

The hike back down the mountain went quickly. The heat of the day slowly faded and a soft breeze filtered through the trees, cooling the sweat upon his face. Weeks had passed since a steady wind had blown through Galen and he welcomed its return. In spite of it, sweat still dripped from his brow.

Tan guided them through the woods downward and to the west, knowing almost instinctively how to find his way back. Occasionally, evidence of the strange creatures he'd tracked triggered a memory of the fear he had felt following them. Each time, he felt a little flash of anxiety, a nervousness in the forest unusual for him. The sight of the strange prints only urged him forward faster.

Bal walked ahead of him, humming as she hurried toward home.

15

Every so often she would dart ahead before returning to him. Tan suspected she searched for the Aeta but they saw no other sign of them. He didn't know the road they followed, but suspected it led into town. Other than Nor, no other towns were this deep into Galen.

As the sun drifted toward the tops of the trees they saw the first signs of Nor. Areas where the woodcutters had felled the trees opened up the forest and the pale sky flashed through. In the distance to the east, above the mountain peaks, dark clouds threatened rain and occasional lightning flashes streaked across the sky. A slow rumble of thunder followed much later. Given the weather recently, chances were good that Nor would not even see any rain.

The cleared stretches of trees became more frequent. Finally Tan reached the main road. Bal ran ahead, waving as she hurried toward town. Probably to tell some of the other children about the Aeta. He had no doubt she would find him later. Since the time Tan had intervened and kept her from being bullied, she'd clung to him.

Tan continued on to Cobin's farm, pausing near the sheep pen to examine the prints there. They were the reason he'd ventured up into the mountains in the first place. Now he saw the evidence of the same beast encircling the pen, and probably at least three of them by the different sizes.

"Tan? Any reason you're crawling on the ground near the sheep?"

Cobin stood behind him. The large man was only ten years his senior but had a weathered face with gray already speckling his dark beard. Tan had known him almost his entire life.

He motioned toward the prints as he stood. "I found these prints this morning."

Cobin grunted before stepping over to him. A large axe hung loosely in his hand and his face was streaked with dirt. "Wolf?"

"Not these. Look at the toes. Too small for our wolves."

16

Cobin squatted and stared at the dusty soil, his dark eyes squinting in concentration. He grunted again. "Then what?"

"I followed them up the mountain—"

Cobin interrupted him with a deep laugh. "That explains it, then."

"Explains what?"

"The scuttlebutt coming from the lord's house."

Tan looked at Cobin before staring off toward Nor, scrubbing his face with his hand. "Mother?" He already knew the answer.

"She's not pleased," Cobin answered before laughing again. "Could be someone else drew her ire. Probably too late for you anyway."

If only Cobin were right that it was someone else. "These tracked several miles up into the mountains before being joined by another type of print. Like this." He traced the strange print into the dusty soil, remembering the heel spike.

"Did you find anything?"

"They found me."

Cobin looked up into the mountains and his face went slack for a moment. "They?" he asked. "You mean a pack?" Cobin's hand squeezed the handle of his axe unconsciously and his knuckles turned white with pressure.

The appearance of the Aeta had pushed away most of the anxiety from his experience with the animals, but enough remained. Tan shivered, thankful that he'd survived the encounter with the creatures. "There were at least three, I think."

"You didn't get a good look?"

He shook his head. "I saw only flashes of fur. I got chased and climbed a tree to get away. Everything got smoky, but it was probably dust from as dry as it's been. I couldn't see anything."

Cobin grunted, making it somehow sound like a question.

Tan shrugged, understanding his friend. "Not sure what it was. The wind picked up suddenly and scared them. I didn't give chase."

Cobin arched his brow at him. "Glad I don't have to be there when you tell your ma where you've been."

Since his father's death, she wanted him anywhere but in the mountains. Preferably in Ethea, studying at the university. Only, the idea of sitting and staring at books all day left him feeling anxious and fidgety.

"Maybe not all of it," Cobin agreed.

Tan laughed and tapped the ground. "What do you think this is?"

"Not entirely sure." He looked up at Tan. "But you want to track it again."

"I think we need to. If it's come this close to town, we should know what it is."

Cobin hadn't taken his eyes off the track, his brow furrowed as he studied it. "You're probably right. I'll get Heller to come, as well." He paused. "Don't tell your ma."

A bit of his anxiety eased. Cobin would provide support as they tracked it, and Heller, though nearly fifty, was a crafty old man and knew much about the woods. Plus, he was still one of the best shots with a bow in this part of Galen.

"Tomorrow?" Cobin asked.

"Probably not tomorrow. Might want to give it a day."

"Too long and we'll lose the track. You think your ma won't let you out of her sight once she hears what you were up to?"

Tan grunted, lifting his eyebrows. "There's that," he agreed. "And the other thing we found."

"We? Bal with you?"

Tan debated telling Cobin, but he'd promised Bal he wouldn't say anything. Cobin wasn't quite as protective of Bal as his mother was with him, but it was a close competition. "Just the lower hills. She's the one who found the Aeta."

"Where'd they come from? Nothing there but Incendin."

Tan nodded. "Came on an old road I'd never seen."

Cobin nodded thoughtfully. "An old trader road. Don't think anyone has used that path in more than twenty years."

"The Aeta did."

"I didn't think they'd be able to cross the barrier. Wonder where they came from?"

Tan remembered the darkness that seemed to follow the Aeta. "Not sure, but they should reach Nor tonight. Figured they'd get set up and trade..."

Cobin laughed. "What, you think you get to trade with the Aeta?"

Tan hadn't planned on trading anything. Not that he had much anyway. "See you in town?"

Cobin nodded at him absently, and as he left, his friend circled the pen, staring at the tracks, a troubled expression etched onto his face. Every so often he would glance up into the mountains and frown.

What did Cobin know and not share?

# CHAPTER 3
## *An Unlikely Threat*

TAN WOULD NEED TO FACE HIS MOTHER sooner or later, so he closed his eyes and took a deep breath, steeling himself before entering her room.

She looked up from her massive desk and eyed him, noting his dirt-stained face and clothes, before turning back to the stack of papers she was sorting through. A hand reached up and touched the jet-black hair pulled severely back from her face.

She ignored him while she sat stiff-backed, working through the house numbers. Tan waited quietly in front of her desk like all the other house servants she supervised, trying not to rock anxiously on his feet. Nervous energy welled through him at the thought of the visiting Aeta. Even his mother would be interested in their visit, wanting to see the items they had for trade, and he bit at his lip to keep from saying anything that might make his scolding worse.

"You shouldn't chew your lip," his mother admonished without looking up.

"I'm not," he protested weakly, looking away. The walls of his mother's office were decorated simply, just a sigil of the Great Mother hanging. A large wrought-iron lantern rested on the corner of her desk, giving the room light.

His mother looked up at him and sighed. "Tannen, you know better than to lie to your mother." She blinked a moment before setting her hands upon her desk and meeting his gaze. "Where have you been?"

Tan resisted the urge to turn away. He couldn't lie—his mother would see through him easily—so he decided on the truth. "I found some prints near Cobin's pens and followed them."

"All day?"

"Not all day. The last hour or so I was with Cobin."

"You went into the mountains, then." When he didn't argue, she went on. "What of the task you were assigned?"

Tan had forgotten about that. She'd asked him to sweep Lord Alles's barn on the edge of town. He had put it off, thinking he would have time after tracking the prints, but he had gone farther into the mountains than he had expected. Then the Aeta had pushed all thoughts of chores out of mind. "I didn't do it," he admitted, "but I saw something you need to know about—"

"I am sure you did. Cobin told Davum it was probably wolves that got into his stock. The men should know how to protect their stock from wolves, especially in this part of the kingdoms. I don't need you tracking wolves and risking yourself like that while ignoring your chores. There's a reason Lind allows you to remain in the manor house. If you ignore your responsibilities…"

"I'll get them done. Wouldn't want Lord Lind upset that I didn't sweep the stables." He sighed and nearly turned away. Cleaning the stables felt like such a waste of his time. Had his father still been alive, he wouldn't have to do it. Tan didn't know what he would have ended up doing if his father still lived, but not that. "Besides, it wasn't a wolf. I don't know what it was, but it wasn't a wolf."

His mother looked up again and pushed her papers away, focusing on him entirely. "What was it, then?"

Tan wasn't sure if she humored him or if she believed his concern. Cobin hadn't questioned. And his mother knew he was a skilled tracker and what he'd learned from his father.

"Some kind of hound," he answered, shaking his head. "I couldn't see them clearly. There was some kind of smoke or cloud of dust."

She closed her eyes and took a deep breath, visibly calming herself. "You came upon a pack while tracking an unfamiliar creature."

There was a heat to her words now. Tan needed to choose his answer carefully. "We needed to know what had attacked the flock. Father would have done the same!" Immediately, he knew that he'd misspoken.

Her eyes flashed with a quick anger. She clenched her fists before slowly relaxing. "Your father," she began, taking a deep breath before continuing, "is no longer with us."

Tan knew she intended to say something different. Almost more than him, she still suffered daily from his father's absence. Before he'd gone, she smiled easily and laughed often. All that changed when he went to war at the king's bidding. When he didn't return, neither did his mother's mirth.

"Tan," she said quietly. "I cannot lose you, too."

"I know." But she still wanted him to leave Nor. She wanted him to go to Ethea, learn at the university like his father had, but Tan wanted something different. Why should he go to the capital when everything he knew and loved was here?

She shook her head, touching a hand to her neck where a small locket hung. "How did you get away?"

He shook his head. "It doesn't matter."

His mother didn't care what he'd seen, only about his safety. But something about the creatures gnawed at his senses.

He sighed, knowing his father would have understood.

"Sighing won't bring him back."

"I know," he said softly.

She set her hands on either side of her desk and studied him a moment. Then she took a deep breath, letting it out slowly. "It's time for you to think about your studies."

Tan swallowed before answering. "But I don't want—"

"You need to understand your gifts, Tannen. Like your father, the Great Mother gifted you as an earth senser. You can learn to master that gift in Ethea."

"And have to serve like Father?"

She nodded.

After what happened to his father, he didn't understand why she pushed him to study in Ethea. "The other sensers in Nor never went to the university. Most are like me—too weak to do anything useful anyway."

"How can you know how strong you can be if you never try?"

He shook his head. His father would have understood. Had he not gone off for the king, he would've taught Tan himself. "What can I learn at university that I can't in Galen?"

"The fact that you ask tells me how much you have to learn."

He sighed.

"Tannen!"

He blinked and took a deep breath. "King Althem called Father to serve *because* he'd studied at the university. I'm just a weak earth senser. No use to the king."

"That's for King Althem to decide."

"He's not my king," Tan mumbled. He squirmed under the look she shot him. A moment of silence fell between them and he let it settle before speaking again. "There was something else." She opened her mouth as if to say something, but Tan pressed forward. "Bal saw Aeta."

"Bal was with you?"

He shook his head. "Not with me," he said. "I found her. She followed Lins Alles into the upper reaches but got lost. If I hadn't found her—"

Hopefully telling her about Bal would ease some of his mother's anger. She knew how impulsive Bal could be.

"And she found Aeta?"

Tan's frustration continued to rise.

"And where were they traveling from?"

"Came from Incendin direction. An old traders' road."

His mother's sharp eyes closed for a moment, quickly considering what he had told her. "They crossed through Incendin?"

The question took him aback and made him think of the darkness that trailed after them. "Can they cross the barrier?"

His mother frowned at him. "Another reason you need to go to Ethea. The barrier doesn't prevent all passage. Just some. You'd know that if you studied." She came around her desk and waved at him. "Come."

She led him quickly through the manor house and to the lord's office. The door stood open and she did not knock before entering, walking brusquely into the room. It was a large room with a fireplace in one corner and walls interrupted by large open windows, letting in the warm breeze that smelled of rain. Animal hides adorned most of the remaining wall space, though the horns of an elk were displayed proudly as if Lord Lind had caught the animal himself. The manor lord sat at his desk, poring over a stack of parchments, and looked up at the sound of her entrance, smiling when he realized who entered.

"Ephra," he said warmly, setting down his pen. A dark red ink smudged his hand, looking almost like blood. "What brings me this honor?"

The quiet snort was such that Tan knew the lord would not have heard it. Lind Alles had been pushing his mother for marriage since she had joined his staff with an insistence that irritated him. He was reassured that it still was obviously so for his mother too.

"My lord," she answered curtly. Lord Lind only smiled wider. "Tan brings word of the Aeta. Likely traveling from Incendin." She said the last as if it were important. She didn't mention the strange beasts that killed Cobin's sheep.

Lord Lind turned toward him and the smile was still painted across his face, yet his eyes narrowed and his shoulders tensed. "Truly?"

Tan nodded, not wanting to make eye contact but knowing his mother would be angry with him if he did not. "I spied them in the mountains." Better not to admit to Lord Lind that Bal had been with him.

Lind scratched his chin and a bit of the dark ink stained it. He turned to look out one of the large windows of his office, staring out into Nor as if the caravans would already be arriving. "See that they set up outside of town."

His mother tilted her head slightly and crossed her arms over her chest. "You know custom allows the Aeta to trade in town."

Lind turned back and shook his head once. "Not in town. They may set up outside of town only." When she didn't move, his face changed. "Do not cross me in this, Ephra."

"Why?"

Lind looked down to the stack of papers upon his desk. "The king has sent missives," he began. "There have been skirmishes on the border of Nara. Some of his strongest shapers were sent to investigate." Lind shivered slightly.

Some didn't care for the abilities of the shapers and were uncomfortable with them. Usually they had no ability of their own—not even a weak sensing like Tan. He hadn't known Lind was among them.

"The king didn't pass along details, only that he worries these aren't isolated incidents. I was instructed to remain guarded against any possible threat. So I am."

His mother shook her head. "And you think the Aeta pose a threat?"

Lind shrugged. "Probably not, but I won't chance some attacker posing as the Aeta and gaining easy access to town."

"There is little chance someone could imitate the Aeta, my lord," she chided. "There are few folk like them. And do you really think we have anything in Nor valuable enough to attack?"

Lind turned away and did not disagree.

"That's not your only reason. What is it?"

He said nothing and she pressed.

"Lind!"

He looked up at her stern tone. Tan was surprised, unaccustomed to the familiar note his mother used with the man, and suddenly uncomfortable with what it meant.

"Why must the Aeta trade outside our walls?"

Lord Lind sighed, closing his eyes as he did before turning to meet Ephra's gaze. "I don't trust them," he said simply. "Trades always seem to work in their favor."

His mother stifled a smile. "The same could be said about any merchant, my lord," she answered, her tone softening. "They are traders, and shrewd ones at that."

Lind sniffed. "There is more to it than that, I think." He shook his head. "No, Ephra. They are to remain outside of town."

His mother didn't argue, instead taking Tan's arm and leading him from the lord's chambers. She pulled him along, stepping quickly through the manor house. The occasional servant stepped out of her way, bowing as she passed. His mother didn't acknowledge them, barely slowing until she reached her quarters. Only then did she release Tan's arm.

"Why are we hurrying?" He rubbed his arm where her firm grip pinched him.

His mother paced in front of her desk, her long skirt swishing as she did, and one hand clutched the necklace at her neck. "There is something I'm not seeing," she mumbled to herself.

Tan doubted she meant for him to hear.

She stopped and closed her eyes, focusing inward, and her lips moved as if speaking. She stood like that for long moments before she opened her eyes again and turned to him with a fire in her eyes.

"Mother?"

She frowned, though the angry look in her eyes softened. She shook her head. "He doesn't know the insult he gives, having the Aeta camp outside our walls. Not that he'd care. I must see if I can soften it somewhat."

"Where are you going?" he asked.

"You are coming too."

"Where?"

"To talk to the Aeta."

# CHAPTER 4
## *Greeting Mother*

TAN FOLLOWED HIS MOTHER out of the sprawling manor house on the north end of Nor and down the cobbled street until they reached the edge of town. She walked with a purposeful stride, her back straight as always, and her hair pulled tight so the light breeze filtering through town didn't disturb it. She didn't glance back as she walked, trusting he followed, and Tan dared not defy her now that he saw her mood. There was a quiet intensity about her and an undercurrent of anger, though he didn't know why.

Reaching the low wall encircling the town, they passed through the open wooden gate. Tan had never known it to be closed. His mother stopped just outside the gate and looked up the road into the mountains. She crossed her arms over her chest. One foot began tapping impatiently while she stood. Otherwise, she stood completely still.

Tan had no choice but to stand with her. "Why won't Lord Alles let the Aeta into town?"

She didn't look over. "He's a fool."

"And you think to ease the message? Why do you need me here?" He didn't object, but was surprised his mother had brought him along.

She looked over and her eyes flashed briefly. "You don't wish to visit with the Aeta?"

He shrugged and pretended to turn away.

She snorted. "You can't fool me. Not like you did your father."

"I could never fool Father."

"He might have been a powerful senser, but he had a blind spot when it came to you." Gone a year, Tan heard how much she missed him. "Had he not, he would have pushed you to the university two years ago."

"I was only fifteen then."

"Old enough. Older than I was when I went."

Tan wanted to ask more, but his mother never spoke of her time at university other than to say that the one good thing she took away from there was his father. "And in spite of your experience, you want me to go."

She fixed him with a hard look. "I want you to go *because* of my experience." She sighed and turned to look back up the road. "It may be hard for you to believe, but there is more to this world than just Nor. You can experience only so much wandering the woods."

"What if I don't want to experience anything more? I like tracking and hunting. I like Galen. It's my home."

She looked at him again and didn't say anything. She didn't have to. Since his father died, Galen hadn't felt the same for either of them. That, more than anything, was why she wanted him to go.

"If I went to Ethea, what would you do?" he asked.

She blinked slowly, her face fixed in a mask. "I would stay and serve."

"Because of the king?"

She turned her attention on him again. "There is a price to everything, Tan. This is the price I agreed to pay."

He shook his head. She still didn't understand. "But it's not one I'm
willing to pay. I won't blindly go off like Father."

She smiled at him sadly. "If you think he went off blindly, then..."
She trailed off.

"Then what?"

She swallowed and debated her answer. "I wish he were still here
to explain."

"Me too."

They stood in silence. After what seemed an eternity, the soft tinkling of bells touched the air. Brightly colored wagons drifted out of
the shadows and rolled down the lower foothills and rumbled toward
town. As they neared, his mother glanced at him, her eyes warning
silence, before turning to face the slowing wagons.

She waved a hand in greeting and the nearest wagon driver waved
a response. The rolled sleeves of his bright green jacket revealed tattoos
on his massive scarred forearms. "Greetings," his mother called. The
man nodded but did not answer. A small smile tugged at the corners
of his mother's mouth. "I hope the winds of Galen have treated you
well and welcomed you to Nor." The man nodded again and remained
silent. "We look forward to trading with the fair Aeta, but before we
do, I request to speak to the Mother."

The wagon driver's eyes widened a moment at the request. There
was a creak and the light tinkling of bells as a door opened on a cart
further down the line. A tall woman with streaks of silver in her dark
hair strode confidently toward them. She wore a bright red dress and
large hoops of gold hung from each ear. A wide silver band circled her
throat. As she approached them, the lead wagon driver climbed down

to stand next to her. He towered over the woman, standing protectively near her. Muscles strained the seams of the jacket he wore.

"Greetings, Mother," Tan's mother spoke as the Aeta woman neared. "You are welcome in Nor."

The Aeta woman smiled and, with it, her face became radiant. "Am I? Yet you meet us along the edge of town."

Tan's mother nodded. "I serve the manor lord and the king. While here, I can attend to any needs you may have."

The Aeta woman tilted her head in a slight bow. "I am the Mother."

"I am Ephra."

The Aeta stared at her for a moment before a curious look came to her face. "That is an interesting name," she said, pausing and considering his mother. "I knew of a woman once, a powerful shaper, similarly named."

"Oh?" Her arms tensed slightly.

"Similar, though different. She traveled among us for a time. She was not Ephra, though."

She tilted her head. "And I'm no shaper. Only Ephra."

The Mother smiled, narrowing her eyes as she nodded. "Still, you serve the king. That makes you a senser of some value." His mother waited and the Mother smiled. "I thank you for your welcome, Ephra." Amusement touched her words, mixing with a musical quality.

Another approaching Aeta interrupted her. Tan's eyes widened in recognition. The girl from atop the wagon. Pale yellow hair fell gently around her face and she brushed back a stray strand. A thin band of silver, like the Mother's, circled her delicate neck. Wide eyes took everything in. A light smile turned her full lips. She was not as tall as the Mother, though she had similar features. Seeing her in the forest, he had thought her attractive; up close, she was beautiful.

Something about her pulled at him and his heart began to flutter. His mouth went dry and the back of his throat threatened to close. A soft whistling echoed in his ears. He took a deep breath to steady himself, looking toward his mother to avoid staring.

"Mother," the Aeta said, unconcerned about interrupting.

The Mother turned to her and frowned. "Amia. You were not summoned."

"I wasn't?" Amia smiled. "But I must observe."

The Mother shook her head once and laid a gentle hand upon Amia's arm, turning her back toward the wagons. "Not this time. Wait until you're summoned."

Amia resisted, turning to Tan and smiling. He felt the pounding in his chest anew. Looking back to the Mother, she asked, "How will I learn to be Mother if I can't observe?"

The Mother ignored the question and pushed her softly back toward the wagons. "We will talk later, Amia." Her tone brooked no argument. Amia considered a moment before nodding and returning to the wagons. The Mother watched her until satisfied that she was safely back within the lead wagon before she turned her attention back to Tan's mother.

"She is young," Tan's mother commented.

"She is headstrong," the Mother countered.

His mother laughed. "Probably. The young often are." His mother stared at the wagon for a moment before facing the Aeta. "It is not often that one so young is named successor."

The Aeta paused and considered his mother again before smiling tightly. "It is not often one of the kingdoms understands the ways of the Aeta."

"Perhaps." The two women stood facing each other for a long moment before his mother spoke again, glancing again to the wagon where Amia had disappeared. "Regardless," she started, turning her attention back to the Mother, "you are welcome in Nor. If your

32

wagons are burdened, know that you will find us eager traders and helpful hosts. Anything you may need is simply a question away."

The Mother tilted her head carefully, watching his mother with suspicious eyes, waiting, as if knowing there would be more.

"As you prepare to trade, Lord Lind requests your wagons be set up on the edge of town."

The Mother sniffed softly and a dark smile crossed her lips, as if expecting the offer his mother had made. Hands moved to her hips and her fingers gripped the cloth belt wrapped around her waist. "It appears we are not welcome *in* Nor," she said carefully. "Rather, we are welcome *near* Nor."

The large wagon driver frowned as well, looking over at the low wall circling the town.

"I'm very sorry. Lord Lind has received missives from our king warning of attacks along the borders to the south and east. He prefers caution and asks you respect his request."

The wagon driver laughed, incredulity clear in the low rumble, and shook his head. "He fears the People?" he asked. The Mother looked sharply at him and his laughter died as the man raised his hands in surrender. "It's an insult, Mother, and you know it. And after everything we've been through—"

The Mother shook her head, cutting the man off. "Nonetheless. We'll respect the request and remain available for trade. Maybe it's for the best. Our stop will be regrettably brief. We are able to stay only a short time. Tell your lordship we will soon depart from his lands." Her manor shifted, her demeanor brightening. "But our wagons are burdened and heavy. We'd welcome trade, especially for your Nor steel."

"You will find the people of Nor eager to trade with the Aeta."

The Mother nodded once before turning and striding back to her wagon. The large wagon driver paused a moment, staring at Tan and his mother as if about to say something, before he turned and returned to his perch atop the wagon. With a whistle, the caravan started forward, moving off the road to form a wide circle on the edge of Nor.

Tan's mother watched wordlessly, staring intently at the wagon the Mother had disappeared into, before turning back to Tan and sighing. She shook her head as she did. "He doesn't know what he's done," she said quietly, frowning.

"Who?"

She looked at him as if realizing that he had been there the entire time, shaking her head again. Hair that had been pulled tight did not move with the motion. She lightly touched the locket at her neck before answering, taking a deep breath as she did. "It's customary to allow the Aeta to trade within the walls of town."

The only other times the Aeta had visited, their wagons had circled the town square and a weeklong festival had accompanied the trading. The Mother had said the visit would be brief and he wondered now how long the Aeta would stop in Nor.

"They are the wanderers," his mother continued, "and their history is one marked with much sadness." She shook her head, staring at the Aeta now departing their wagons. "It's customary to provide shelter and give them a sense of home, if only briefly." She sighed, as if thinking of a terrible memory, before turning back to face town. "There is something off here."

"How do you know?"

She sniffed. "Tannen," she scolded, "I know you sense it. In spite of their past, the Aeta are a happy people. Something has happened that's made them somber and careful. I worry what that might be."

Tan looked back at the Aeta and saw the beautiful Amia staring unabashedly at him from behind one of the wagons. As he turned, his heart started hammering wildly again. He turned away and hurried to catch up to his mother.

She looked over, as if knowing his thoughts. "Finish your chores before you chase that girl."

"I'm not chasing—" he protested.

"I saw your eyes. And I know how young men think." A distant note came to her voice as she hurried back to the manor house.

# CHAPTER 5
## *A Pig and a Rat*

TAN CLEANED THE STABLES faster than he had ever managed before. Thoughts of missed opportunities to watch the Aeta hurried his work. But more than just the Aeta, he wanted to see Amia again. Even the thought of her made his palms sweaty.

The moon shone brightly in the cloudless night sky. The sound of laughter and hundreds of voices all talking at the same time echoed from the edge of town. Had he finished the chore he'd promised his mother before tracking the prints into the forest, he would have been free to watch the trading. Now he missed some of the early excitement.

He followed the sounds, passing the small shops at the center of town and the rough stone homes on the edge of town, until he reached the low town wall and passed through. As he did, he realized his mother was right. It felt wrong for the Aeta to camp on the other side of the wall. Why should the wall separate them from Nor, if even for a night?

The scene was much different than it had been earlier in the day. Lanterns blazed bright, illuminating wagons and traders. The wagons formed a circle, and each had a table folded down and stacked with items for sale or trade. The Aeta stood beside each table and called out to passersby, though truly most were already engaged in conversation. A large throng of people moved through the middle of the wagons, most talking and laughing. Some locals pushed carts through the crowd, selling food or crafts. Several fire pits had been erected and their wide flames lit the night.

In spite of the trading, something seemed off. Tan couldn't quite place what he felt. Most of the Aeta were quick to make a sale or traded easily for the steel local craftsmen were known for. There was not the joy upon the faces of the Aeta he remembered, nor the frantic energy from them as they pressed each transaction.

Tan tripped and bumped into someone as he moved through the circle of wagons. "I'm sorry..." He trailed off as he turned and saw Amia. The thin band of silver at her neck gleamed softly in the lantern light.

She tilted her head, considering him for a moment. "You."

"I'm sorry," he said again. His mouth suddenly felt dry. He licked his lips, trying to force moisture back onto his lips.

The corner of her mouth tilted slightly in a hint of a smile. "I've seen you before." Her voice was musical and soft, though a hidden vein of steel ran through it. Someone who was accustomed to having her way.

"I'm Ephra's son and was with her when she met with the Mother earlier today."

Amia closed her eyes and nodded. "You were, but that wasn't the first." The comment was not a question. There was an air of curiosity to what she said.

"In the forest as well," he acknowledged. He had forgotten the sounds of the trading around him, unable to focus on anything other than Amia.

"You spied upon us as we traveled?"

"I wasn't—" Tan sputtered. "I was tracking an animal that had killed some of our sheep."

"What kind of animal?"

Tan shook his head, remembering the unusual tracks upon the ground and the strange beasts that had trapped him in the tree. "I don't know."

Disappointment swept through him when Amia frowned. She glanced from him to look back toward the mountains looming behind them, a darkness shadowed against the night. "Were you successful? Did you find your creature?"

"More like they found me." When she frowned, he went on. "I followed their tracks up the mountain, following their howls." She winced briefly as he said this and Tan wondered why. "They surrounded me, chasing me into a tree."

"You're safe now." She eyed him up and down, as if appraising a horse.

He nodded. "I am. Something scared them off."

She frowned again, a sad tip of her full lips, still managing to remain beautiful. "What did you do to scare them off?"

"I didn't do anything. I shot arrows at them but it didn't do any good. A gust of wind, I think, scared them."

"I'm surprised you were able to track them."

"It wasn't easy."

She shook her head and opened her mouth as if to speak, but was interrupted by the sudden appearance of three large figures slowly emerging from the shadows to hover behind Tan.

"Minden," one sneered, "out of your element, here, don't you think?"

"Lins," Tan acknowledged.

Lins Alles was Lord Lind's son and carried himself as if he were related to King Althem himself, bullying and taking whatever he wanted. It was unfortunate his father never disciplined him. Truth be told, few—if any—of the often cruel and just mean-spirited things he did made it to his father's ears for discipline. Most were too scared to say anything. Tan had once made the unfortunate decision to complain about Lins to his mother, who promptly spoke to Lord Lind.

Lins never forgave Tan for the insult, ignoring the beating that had been the impetus for Tan's grumbling. Now Lins and his ever-present friends Rapen and Niles used every opportunity to pick on or humiliate Tan. Usually Tan had the presence of mind to steer clear of the lord's son, but occasionally he could not be avoided. He closed his eyes, wondering what humiliation Lins would think to bestow upon him tonight, and worse, in the presence of Amia.

"Lord Lins," Lins said proudly, turning toward the Aeta. Rapen and Niles remained silent, only grunting to note their presence.

"Not yet," Tan muttered, shaking his head. Maybe by that time he'd finally leave Nor. Or maybe something would happen to Lins, though that seemed too much to hope for.

Lins glared at him and turned to Amia. He offered her a toothy smile. She tilted her head carefully and studied him. Tan felt a sudden pressure behind his ears that passed quickly before she smiled a half-smile.

"And you are?" Lins asked.

Amia shook her head slowly. "No one near as important."

Lins laughed, a harsh and grating sound. "Nonsense." His tone gave lie to his words. He turned his attention back to Tan, though remained facing Amia as he did. "Finish cleaning my stable, Minden?"

"It's your father's."

"It's the same." He smiled quickly at Amia. "At least my father has something of value to pass on to me." Rapen and Niles laughed with Lins.

Amia watched him carefully, ignoring the smile Lins offered and the brutish forms of Rapen and Niles. Pressure built behind his ears again that passed quickly. She crossed her arms over her chest and turned suddenly to Lins, returning his smile with an almost feral one.

"And what have you done of value today, my lord?" Her voice retained its musical quality but carried an edge with it.

Lins's smile faltered. "I aid my father in the running of Nor."

"Oh?"

Tan suppressed a laugh. If chasing the young women of Nor and bullying the boys helped his father, then Lins indeed aided him. Lins glanced over to him and glared again.

"The horses find value in what Tan has done today," Amia said.

"The horses?" Lins asked, laughing.

Amia nodded.

"I'm sure the horses care that their manure has been shoveled."

The Aeta shrugged. "Perhaps, but they enjoyed the hay." Her smile hardened. "There's value in such work. I don't know if there's value in a pig-faced boy who thinks insulting others makes him appealing. I will ask the Mother."

Lins wore a look of shock that Amia would dare insult him. Tan felt certain he would not take it well. Rapen and Niles laughed in spite of themselves, stifling it suddenly when Lins glared at them. They both raised their hands in submission before backing away.

Lins looked from Amia, who now smiled innocently, to Tan, who had found the sense to close his mouth, his face reddening with anger. His jaw worked to speak before he finally found his words. "Minden," he sputtered, focusing his rage upon Tan, as Tan knew he would. "I will leave you with this Aeta rat and will find you later."

When Lins left, Tan sighed, fearing the truth of the statement. Lins wouldn't rest until he felt this wrong was righted. Tan was certain it would be a painful correction. "Thank you. I'm not able to speak so freely."

Amia smiled warmly at him and Tan felt his heart race again. "I sensed that," she answered simply.

She looked at him again and Tan remembered what she'd said before Lins appeared. "Why were you surprised that I tracked the creatures?"

Amia frowned. "They aren't easy to track. Few manage to do so." She paused, tilting her head and staring intently at him. "And I thank you."

"For what?"

"Tracking them. I think it scared them off."

"I doubt I scared them," he began before a question came to him. "What are they?"

"They're fearsome hounds. They followed us from Incendin." She stopped at the sudden approach of another shadowed figure that appeared out of the fading light of the lamps and fire pits.

"Amia," a stern voice said, interrupting the young Aeta as she spoke to Tan.

Tan looked up and recognized the regal features of the Aeta Mother, who stood staring at him while holding firmly to Amia's arm.

"Mother," Amia acknowledged.

The Mother smiled, though it did not reach her eyes. "Come, Daughter. You're needed to observe."

Amia considered the Mother for a moment and as she did, a rising pressure built within his ears. She glanced to Tan before turning her attention back to the Mother. "I am?"

The Mother nodded curtly. "You are. Come." The Mother turned to Tan and nodded once. "Son of Ephra," she said respectfully before turning away and leading Amia off.

Amia looked back as she followed. Tan wondered if he would ever see her again.

# CHAPTER 6
## *Stories of the Past*

TAN STOPPED IN THE MANOR house after leaving Amia, not wanting to stay and risk seeing Lins again. Lins could be cruel, especially when trying to prove himself to Rapen and Niles. He found the door closed and knocked, waiting for her to answer. When she didn't, he pushed the door open.

A single lantern burned on her desk. A stack of papers piled neatly nearby. The only thing out of order in her office was the row of books along the wall, remnants or reminders of her time in the capital, now with several hastily shoved back into place, as if she'd recently read through them.

Tan stepped over to her desk and peeked at the papers. Numbers lined the page, some sort of inventory. One of his mother's duties keeping the manor house running involved purchasing supplies. With as tidy as she used to keep their house, Tan suspected she did it well.

As he turned away, a small, leather-bound book lying open on the desk caught his attention. Written in his mother's tight scrawl, he read a few lines before realizing that it was a journal of some kind. Two names jumped out as he looked at it.

"Tannen."

He spun, a flush of embarrassment working through him. He shouldn't have been looking at his mother's belongings, not without her permission. "Mother. I was just…"

She waved her hand dismissively. "I thought you'd be with the Aeta all night. Practically all of Nor is there."

He noticed her hands were empty. She hadn't done any trading then. "I was there, but had an…issue…with Lins."

She sniffed and made her way around her desk. She glanced at the small book lying there and flipped it closed. "Lins is a fool. But he'll inherit his father's title one day. You'd best not have too many issues with him if you intend to remain in Nor."

Another dig at him, but he let it slide.

"What did you need, Tannen?" She had turned to the row of books on her shelf and pulled one out. Her voice sounded tight and tired.

He took a deep breath and then sighed. What did it matter if he told her about the hounds? She wouldn't know anything anyway. Not like his father would have. He nodded toward the book on her desk. "What's that?"

She glanced over her shoulder. "A journal. From my time in Ethea. Something from a long time ago."

Tan was even more surprised by the names he'd seen in the book. "What's in it?"

She offered a tight smile. "Don't go dancing around your questions, Tannen. Ask what you want to ask."

He frowned. "Did you know them?"

At first he didn't think she'd answer. Then she sighed. "Studying at the university, you get to know many people."

"But the princess?" How had his mother never shared that with him?

A distant look crossed his mother's face. "She…was a complicated woman. Many were saddened by her death."

"How did you know her?"

"Like me, she studied at the university." She took the book off the desk and flipped through the pages. "It's a different place than others. Everyone is equal. Until you're not. Skill and experience mean more than titles. Even for royalty."

"You were friends?"

"Few were friends with her at that time. Had she more friends, perhaps she wouldn't have died."

Tan didn't know much about the princess other than that she'd been assassinated a long time ago. But his mother seemed to know more. "What happened?"

"It was a different time. There were more shapers then. Cloud Warriors too. Not like today." She flipped open the book and looked at one of the pages.

When she didn't say anything, Tan pressed her. "Why would shapers matter?"

She looked up. "Because some think a shaper killed her." She shook her head. "The only sign of foul play was a dark burn across her chest, as if shaped, but her face was said to have been peaceful." She opened her book and studied one of the pages. Tan wondered what she'd written there. "I don't know what shaper could have done such a thing. Not Theondar, as the rumors of the time would have you believe." She seemed offended by the suggestion. "But a priceless heirloom went missing, and who other than Theondar had access to her rooms?" She said the last mostly to herself.

When he was younger, Tan's father had told stories of the warriors, so the name Theondar meant something to Tan. To most people in the kingdoms, likely. A warrior who'd stopped the Stinnis surge single-handedly. Who'd pushed back the Roke when they threatened invasion. The exploits of Theondar were some of his favorites.

"Did you know him?" Somehow, the idea that she'd known Theondar impressed him more than her knowing the princess.

"No one really knew Theondar. He was...arrogant and stubborn, but talented unlike almost any other shaper save Lacertin. A sad thing we lost them both."

His father never really spoke of what happened to the warriors after the war. And since they'd come to Nor, he probably didn't know. "Were they lost in the Incendin war?"

She flipped a few pages, reading for a moment before blinking and shutting the book. "Had they been there, the war might have turned out differently."

"Wait...you mean Theondar didn't even fight in the war?" That took something away from the stories his father had told.

"Who's to know? After Ilianna died"—Tan noted she said "Ilianna" and not "Princess Ilianna"—"Theondar left Ethea. He'd always traveled, always using his shaping for the kingdoms, but he'd always returned to Ethea. After her death, he left for good."

His mother took a seat and pulled the stack of papers over to her. She looked at the topmost page and let out a slight sigh. "Now, if there's nothing else..."

Tan hated that she still had work to do. While everyone else in Nor was free to celebrate and trade with the Aeta, his mother had to stay walled off in her office and work the inventory for Lord Lind. Had his father still been alive, that wouldn't have been necessary.

Tan turned and started for the door. He'd ask Cobin about the hounds rather than his mother. Besides, Cobin had agreed to help him track them. If they were as fearsome as Amia thought, Cobin would want to be a part of it.

At the door he hesitated. Something bothered him about what his mother had said. He turned back.

"Ask your question," she said before he had the chance to speak. She didn't look up as she did.

Once, he would have laughed at how she seemed to know what was on his mind, but ever since moving to the manor house, she'd changed so much she wasn't the same person. "You said both of the warriors were lost."

She scrawled a note across the page and nodded. "And your point?"

"What happened to Lacertin?" Tan didn't know much about him other than his name, not like with Theondar.

Her pen paused on the page. "Lacertin was forced to leave the kingdoms."

"Forced? Why would one of the Cloud Warriors be forced away?" They were unrivaled shapers, supposedly able to shape each of the elements, and were said to have the ability to dance above the clouds.

She looked up and the debate about whether she should answer raged across her face. "Lacertin was found trying to enter King Ilton's chambers after he died. No one knows his reasons, but it took three warriors and a half-dozen shapers to get him out. He fled Ethea, chased by the warriors and the furious Prince Althem."

"Why would he enter the king's mourning chamber?" Tan asked. Custom dictated that the deceased king be left alone, dressed in his robes and goblet, sitting atop his throne for seven days after his passing. According to custom, none should disturb him as the Great Mother prepared for his arrival.

She set both hands on the table and met his eyes. "You have a curious mind, Tan. You always have. With your ability…" She trailed off and shook her head. "I really wish you'd consider going to Ethea, if only to see what it has to offer you. I think you'd be surprised by what you'll find. There are others like you—others with your talent—"

"I don't have any special talent," he snapped. Tan took a steadying breath, controlling his emotions before saying anything more that he might regret. "I'm just a senser. It's a useful enough skill here in the mountains where I can track, but in the city?" He shook his head. That was one thing he'd never understood about his father—how he could have gone to Ethea to study, taking on the king's fee for his studies. And dying for it.

His mother sighed and looked back down to her pages. She didn't bother to hide the disappointment on her face. "Then get some rest tonight so you can get up and complete your responsibilities on time tomorrow."

Tan left her room without another word, not wanting to disappoint her further.

# CHAPTER 7
## *Stranger to the Forest*

THE AETA CARAVAN LEFT EARLY the following morning. Tan rose early, dressing quickly to finish his chores before Lins awoke for the day. If he managed to get everything done, he could be up in the mountains with Cobin tracking the creatures before Lins came looking. And he would come looking.

As he worked setting down hay in the stalls, the light tinkling of bells told him the caravan was moving. The Mother promised their stay would be brief. He hadn't expected it to be quite so abrupt.

Tan ran out of the stables and hurried to the wall to watch the Aeta depart. The caravan had already circled around the outer wall and slowly rambled south and east. Other than Velminth, there wasn't anything in that direction for hundreds of miles.

"They're already leaving."

Tan turned. Cobin leaned on the wall, scratching his dark beard as he stared after the wagons.

"They told my mother they couldn't stay long. I figured another day at least." He prayed for a glimpse of Amia, one last parting shot to remember her by. Only the wagon drivers sat out this early.

A slow smile spread across Cobin's face. "That why you're up so early?"

Heat rose in his cheeks. "Did you get to trade?" Tan asked, changing the subject. He hadn't seen Cobin the night before, though after talking with Amia and running into Lins, he wasn't sure he'd remember.

"Thought I had more time." Cobin looked down the road where dust followed the wagons. "Anything interesting?"

"I don't know. I ran into Lins."

Cobin grunted and spat. "Best stay clear of him today."

"That's the reason I'm up already," Tan admitted. He didn't fear Lins—not really—but Amia had embarrassed him in front of Tan. Lins wouldn't let that go.

"Want to head north? Heller said he'd come." Cobin paused and considered Tan for a long moment. "Probably ought to check with your ma first."

"Like she'll be happier knowing you're with me?"

Cobin laughed. "I think me and Grethan got into too much trouble together for that. She already thinks I'm trying to corrupt you too."

Tan forced himself to laugh. Cobin had the chance to know his father much longer than Tan ever had. And now never would. Summoned to serve the king, and for what? To keep the border of Galen free from immigrants from Incendin?

"I wasn't the only one to see them," he said. Cobin waited. "The Aeta did too. Some kind of hound out of Incendin."

Cobin's face changed, his eyes narrowing and growing hard. "Called them Incendin hounds? You sure?"

Tan tried to remember what Amia said about the hounds before nodding. "Why?"

"Just…there are stories about Incendin hounds." There was a different edge to his voice. "Not sure how they could slip past the barrier, but if these are Incendin hounds, I need a few other items before we track them again." He turned and looked up into the mountains. "Actually surprised you managed to follow them."

"What are they?" It wasn't like Cobin to be nervous, but something in his tone told Tan he didn't share everything he knew.

Cobin shook his head. "Talk about it later. I need to find Heller, talk to him again." He turned back to Tan. "Maybe this is one you should sit out. If your ma finds out I let you track hounds…well, I'm sure I don't want Ephra's wrath."

"I'm old enough to decide for myself." Tan hated how pouty he sounded, but Cobin sometimes took his view of protecting him too far.

Cobin's face softened. "I know you are. But after what happened with your father—"

"I know what happened with my father. And it had nothing to do with tracking hounds."

Cobin sighed. "Tan, believe me when I tell you that if these are Incendin hounds, you are lucky to still be alive."

Tan started away. Staying would only lead to an argument. After battling with his mother, he didn't need to argue with Cobin, too. "I'll find you later."

"Not sure I'll change my mind. This one might be more dangerous than I thought."

"That's why you need me."

Cobin grunted. "I need you to stay alive. Promised your father that." Cobin started off, leaving Tan staring after him.

Questions lingered. Had he more time with Amia, he might have asked other questions about the hounds. Why had it suddenly gotten so hot? Why had he struggled to see them clearly? What scared them off?

Thinking of her left him disappointed he would never see her again. Or could he?

It was early enough and he *had* already done the chores he'd neglected the day before. Why couldn't he follow the Aeta wagons? Maybe he'd even catch another glimpse of Amia. The wagons didn't move quickly. If he cut through the woods, he could intercept them before they went too far.

Before thinking about it too much, he set off at a slow jog. He kept the winding path of the road in mind as he climbed through the woods. His way took him up steep, rocky inclines and down hazardous ravines. It was nearly midday by the time he heard the distinct sound of their melodic bells.

Tan slowed as he neared the road, careful to remain hidden within the trees. He'd already followed the Aeta once. How offended would they be to see him after them again? When he saw them through the trees, the caravan moved slowly upon the road toward Velminth. The bright wagons rolled past him, flashes of color against the greenery.

As he watched, he worried for a moment he might have missed his chance. And then…there she was, sitting near an open window of the rear wagon. She sat frowning, one hand twirling through her golden hair. Then, as if sensing his presence, she turned to look in his direction, a smile parting her lips.

Tan ducked. She shouldn't be able to see him through the layers of leaves and branches, yet she had looked right at him. And smiled. His heart fluttered and he dared to lean forward, risking exposure. The wagons disappeared, but he thought she waved.

He sighed, ignoring the pang he felt at her leaving. He barely knew her, yet something about her pulled at him, leaving him with a sense of longing.

A harsh *snap* broke the silence of the forest.

Tan turned, fear of hounds or wolves jumping to his mind. He hadn't paid attention as he'd followed the Aeta. Could he have missed their tracks?

Quickly, and without thinking about it, he listened to the forest around him, sensing for anything off. It felt different than yesterday. Alive and as it should. Birds chirped in the trees overhead. Squirrels danced along branches. Wind whispered through the canopy.

That he'd forgotten to bring so much as a knife didn't make him feel any better.

"Greetings."

Tan stiffened. A figure emerged from the shadows of a nearby tree. How had he gotten so close without him knowing? Dressed in a heavy cloak covering his face, a sheathed sword hung at his side. One hand hovered over the hilt.

Tan eyed the man's sword nervously, afraid to say anything. He considered where he could run if needed. The road would be easiest, but it would be the same for the man. Better off through the woods. He knew these woods and had some advantage there.

The figure followed Tan's gaze down to his sword and pulled the hand away. Raising palms forward, he lowered the hood of his cloak, revealing wavy silver hair and bright eyes. "Just wandering the woods?"

Tan nodded, realizing he still wore his dirty breaches and shirt from his work in the stables. Had Amia seen him this way?

"What villages are near here?"

The question seemed odd. Most traveling through Galen knew it well enough. Near Nor was Velminth, a logging town. Beyond that lay the upper reaches of the Gholund Mountains, deep and twisty mountainous terrain few bothered to travel. The upper passes there would already be seeing the first snow. And beyond the mountains lay the edge of the kingdoms and the border with Incendin.

"Nor," Tan answered. He positioned himself closer to the road. At least he could move quickly if needed.

The man frowned. "Nor? As in steel?"

He nodded. "Not many bother to work with steel anymore." There'd been a time when the mines produced enough iron to practically supply the entirety of the kingdoms. That had been long before Tan was born. Now miners managed barely a trickle, though steel made in Nor still had value.

The man patted his sword quickly. "Still useful," he said. He turned and looked around the woods. "Hunting?" He considered Tan for a moment before shaking off the question. "Not hunting. But not expecting me. Comfortable among the trees." He spoke mostly to himself.

"The Aeta visited last night. I just watched them leave."

The man looked up the road, ignoring Tan as he did. "The Aeta?" A curious look crossed his face. "I hadn't thought of that."

Tan frowned.

An uncomfortable moment passed before the man turned and smiled again. "I didn't mean to come upon you like a wild elemental."

He grinned as if seeing one of the elementals should make sense. From what his father used to say, that might have happened once, but the elementals were even rarer in Galen than shapers.

When Tan didn't answer, he went on. "I'm looking for a woman from this area. A wind shaper of some strength. She's gone by many names so I don't really know what she's called now." He shrugged, as if names were unimportant.

Tan shook his head. "We have no shapers in Nor." Lord Lind would

54

panic if one ever did settle in the area. "We have few enough sensers here." He said nothing about his ability. What Tan did really couldn't be considered sensing, not to any real degree. His father had been a senser, but he used as much traditional tracking as he did sensing, combining them more than anything.

The man frowned. "None? There are shapers all along the border."

"We're not entirely on the border."

The man turned and looked to the east, staring into the mountains toward Incendin. "We're near the mountains. I presumed there would be shapers maintaining the barrier." The stranger waited for Tan to say something more; when he didn't, he looked down the slope of the mountain. "Can you lead me to Nor?"

Tan debated briefly. While he could follow the Aeta farther, he'd be doing so without a knife or a bow. Or even a skin of water. And the stranger could just as well follow the road into town. "You won't find your shaper there. Not much other than a few old smiths and a cranky manor lord." As soon as he said it, he wished he could take it back.

The man eyed him but thankfully didn't comment.

They started off. Tan took him on a direct route, bypassing the road. "You said you are searching for a shaper?"

The man nodded.

"What's she like?"

"Don't really know anymore. She was lovely when I knew her, but fierce. She had this dark, flowing hair and olive skin…" He trailed off and shook his head. "But it was her laugh that truly made her beautiful."

"You knew her well?"

The man simply shrugged. "Once."

"She was a wind shaper?"

The stranger nodded. "One of the strongest I've met."

"You've met a lot of shapers?" That meant he likely came from Ter or Vatten. Maybe even Ethea, but if he was from the capital, why had he traveled by himself?

"Many."

"Where? Ethea?"

They climbed down a steep slope. The man followed him easily, moving with a limber grace that told Tan he wasn't a stranger to woods like these.

"There. And other places," he said.

Tan grabbed a thick sapling as he started down another slope. "Ever meet any warriors?" Cloud Warriors, the most prized shapers, could shape all of the elements. That was how the last Incendin war had been won.

The stranger laughed. "There aren't any warriors. Haven't been for nearly a decade."

"Why?" Tan's father used to tell of how he'd seen some of the great warriors when he'd trained in Ethea, back when they'd been called into battle to defend the kingdoms. Shapers so skilled they could practically walk across the sky, shaping themselves into the clouds.

"Few enough are born sensers. Fewer still can become shapers. Warriors have to master all the elements."

They fell back into silence for long moments as they drifted toward the edge of the forest. Nor opened up in front of them, spreading far below. The stranger arched a brow at him. Tan shrugged and started down, sliding on his heels as he made his way down the steep embankment. Near the bottom of the hill, he waited. The stranger followed closely behind, not struggling as much as Tan would have expected.

"So how do you know so many shapers?"

The stranger shrugged. "Happens in my line of work."

Tan laughed. "What line of work is that?"

56

The man laughed. "You don't know?"

Tan shook his head.

"Thought you recognized the ring," he said, pointing to the silver band on his first finger.

Now that he saw it, Tan still didn't understand. He thought he'd seen it in one of his father's books before, but couldn't remember where. He shook his head.

The man grunted. "There was a time when a man recognized the mark of the Athan."

Athan. That was a term he recognized. Direct servants of the king. They spoke with his word, his voice. Only five Athan served at a time. But why would King Althem send one to Galen?

# CHAPTER 8
## *Tainted Name*

THE ATHAN WAS QUIET as Tan led him to the manor house. Tan didn't bother interrupting, especially not now. He shot occasional glances down to the man's ring, but didn't dare let his eyes linger.

Once the man caught him looking and smiled. Tan turned away, a hot flush rising in his cheeks, and glanced at the cloudless sky. The sun pressed toward the tops of the trees, unseasonable heat coming with it. No wind whistled through town. Sweat slicked his arms and back.

Bread rising somewhere made Tan's stomach rumble. He'd been gone most of the day again, though this time not tracking anything as dangerous as the hounds. But atop the scent of bread lingered a sharp stink of sweat. Amia probably had been happy to leave Nor.

Lins Alles emerged from the shadows near the manor house as they approached. His eyes were red and bloodshot and his hair disheveled. Probably just getting up now. He saw Tan and sneered before turning and staggering away, probably still drunk from the night before.

Tan sighed.

"Not a friend?" the man asked.

He shook his head. "Not a friend." How far would Lins push him now? Tan couldn't really fight back—not against Lins and certainly not when he was with his friends—but Lins wouldn't let last night's insult slide by without additional comment.

"Who is he?"

"Lins Alles."

The stranger watched Tan as they walked the last few steps in silence before pausing at the doorway to the manor house. As Tan set his hand to the doorknob, the stranger laid his hand atop his. Tan stiffened, fearful of what the Athan might say. The voice of the king could punish him with only a word.

"You empower him when you fear him."

Tan swallowed. He didn't fear Lins—not yet—but eventually he would inherit the manor house. "It's not empowerment." Tan took his hand from the door. "It's entitlement."

The stranger tipped his head, frowning.

"Lins Alles, son of Lord Lind. Manor Lord of Nor." Tan eyed the Athan, waiting for his response.

"I see." The stranger's frown deepened. "But that's not all."

Tan shook his head and laughed softly, glancing over to where Lins had disappeared. "Lins thought to impress an Aeta girl by insulting me last night."

"Did it work?" The man's tone indicated he knew it wouldn't.

"She insulted him in kind. He didn't care for it. I think he blames me."

The stranger's silver eyebrows raised and he chuckled. "That young man needs to learn a few lessons about impressing women. Particularly one of the Aeta."

"Don't we all," Tan said.

The stranger's laugh deepened and he clapped Tan on the shoulder.

Tan pushed open the door and led the man through the hall. From his frequent visits to see his mother, he knew the way toward Lord Lind's office. At this time of day, he was likely there.

"I'm fortunate you know the house so well."

"My mother works for Lord Lind. Came here after my father died. Called by the king to fight an Incendin insurgence to the south. He didn't return." Tan made a point of looking at the stranger.

"What was his name?"

Tan frowned. Why did this man care? "Grethan Minden."

The stranger didn't have the opportunity to question any further and Tan was more than relieved to let the topic drop. As they reached the door to Lord Lind's room, he knocked firmly, uncertain if the lord would even be in his office at this time of day. Then he'd have to go to his mother to find him. He didn't look forward to that.

"Enter."

The door muffled the words. Tan swung it open to reveal Lord Lind's office, intending to leave the Athan and depart; there was still the matter of the hounds and Cobin might take Heller and leave without him. When he turned to leave, the stranger placed a hand upon his back, pressing him forward.

"Introduce me," he whispered.

Tan tried to turn but could not. "Lord Lind," he said as he entered, nodding carefully. Tan had never presented himself to Lind without his mother present and he was uncertain how Lind would react. Lord Lind's feelings for his mother might not extend to her son.

Lind looked up from his desk and stared at Tan for a long moment. Then he looked at the Athan, eyeing his odd clothing and the sword at his hip. "What is this?"

A nervous sweat beaded upon his back. "This is…" he trailed off, realizing he didn't even know the man's name.

"Roine," the Athan whispered.

Tan licked suddenly dry lips. "Roine," he continued. "He requested an audience with you."

Lind sniffed, motioning toward the door. "I don't have time for this, son." He spoke with a stern sort of annoyance and waved him away.

The statement bothered Tan more than it should. "My lord—"

Lind shook him off. "If you think my relationship with your mother grants you privilege—"

Tan interrupted, feeling a surge of irritation mixed with anger. Relationship? Tan didn't think they had more than a passable working rapport, but what if it was more than that? "Lord Lind. He comes from King Althem."

Lind glared briefly at Tan before turning his attention to the stranger, seeming to consider his dress once more before dismissing him. "And you believed him? Any simpleton could claim the king sent him. You may go." He turned back to look at his desk.

The stranger set a hand upon his shoulder, pressing him back. "Thank you," he whispered. There was an unexpected mirth to his tone. Tan suspected the stranger had just learned all he needed to know about Lord Lind.

With a flourish, he pulled a rolled parchment from a hidden pocket, presenting it forward while leaning toward Lind. He cleared his throat to get Lind's attention. A gold seal was obvious from where Tan stood and from Lind's expression, he recognized it as well. But it was the ring his eyes lingered on the longest, the mark of the Athan. "I assure you I *am* sent by Althem," he said. "He sends his greetings to his loyal manor lord and requests your assistance in this matter."

Lind stood and took the parchment. Shaking his head as he unsealed it, he quickly read the words within before looking up and eyeing Roine strangely. Finally, he rolled the parchment back up and returned it to Roine. "I don't have what you seek."

Roine cocked his head and smiled, more teeth than not. "No, I did not think you would."

Lind muttered something quietly under his breath.

"What was that, my lord?" Roine asked.

"I said I did not think our king has seen this part of Galen in years."

Roine shrugged. "Perhaps not. I don't often know the mind of Althem, but speak as his Voice. He has asked for your service and assistance as I travel through your land."

Lind stared at Roine, his eyes darting again down to the ring before answering. "Of course I serve the king."

"That wasn't the question."

Lind blinked. "You will not be impeded in your search."

Roine frowned. "And that wasn't the request."

Lord Lind took a slight step back at the admonishment. "You will have what you need." Lord Lind motioned toward Tan. "Take him to Ephra. She can help him with what he needs."

It was a dismissal.

The Athan considered Lord Lind with a mixture of amusement and irritation, before following Tan away from the office. "That was unfortunate," he said as they made their way down the hall.

Tan said nothing. It didn't pay to get involved in the king's business.

The Athan looked over at him and chuckled. "You don't need to fear me. Though your Lord Lind should remember he serves at the king's leisure." As they neared his mother's door, he turned to Tan. "Whom did he send me to? Who's Ephra?"

Tan knocked and, hearing his mother's voice inside, paused before entering. "My mother."

The Athan chuckled again.

His mother sat behind her desk, her pen scratching quickly along a parchment, looking strangely like Lord Lind sitting at *his* desk. She looked up, glancing at Tan before looking back to her parchment. "A moment, Tan," she started, then caught herself and looked up again, seeing the Athan as if for the first time. Her eyes skimmed over him, catching on his ring. She raised her brow ever so slightly, such that Tan was not sure he saw it. Had that been recognition in her eyes?

"What is it?" She set her pen down upon the desk and looked at Tan, ignoring the stranger.

"Mother." Tan glanced at Roine. The Athan wore a blank look, completely unreadable. "This is Roine, Athan to the king."

"Lord Lind should meet with the Athan, not I."

"He did. He requested your help."

His mother frowned. "You have already been to Lind," she said softly, dropping the formality of the title. "How is it you present him, Tannen?" She looked past Tan and at the Athan as she spoke.

Tan decided to answer quickly. Anything he said now risked angering his mother more. "I met Roine in the forest." She frowned deeply at him. "I finished my chores this morning and followed the Aeta as they left town. It was along the road to Velminth that I encountered Roine."

"The Aeta have already left?"

It was not the question Tan expected. "Early this morning."

"Toward Velminth?"

Tan nodded again.

"And you met Roine along the road?" She said his name with a strange inflection. The stranger smiled.

"My lady," Roine said, bowing his head slightly. "You son was kind

63

enough to lead me to Nor. I have learned much from him."

His mother sniffed and then lightly shook her head before finally laughing quietly. "I am sure you have, Roine." She made a point of pushing his name with the odd inflection. She leaned forward. "What is it you need?"

Roine laughed and stepped inside the door. He tilted his head. "Ephra." He said her name with the same odd inflection. "Your son has been most helpful. He even secured me an audience with the manor lord."

"I think as Athan you would have no trouble on your own."

Roine shrugged. "I didn't refuse his assistance."

She snorted. "And what assistance do you require?"

Tan was taken aback by their banter. Like his father, his mother had studied in Ethea. That's where they'd met. She was a senser, though claimed to have lost much of her ability and never spoke of it. Neither of his parents ever really spoke of their time in the capital, other than to encourage him to go to the university.

Roine smiled at the question. "I came looking for a shaper, one of great power."

His mother blinked and waited.

"But seeing the Aeta raised a new concern. So it seems I need help."

"What kind of help?" his mother asked.

Roine pulled the rolled parchment he'd shown Lord Lind and set it on the desk. "I have searched for an item. I thought this shaper I knew could help." He shrugged. "Perhaps not. But to find it, I need to get through the mountains quickly."

His mother stared at Roine for a long moment, the silence between them growing slowly palpable. Finally, she took a deep breath. "Why?"

"I was sent by Althem."

His mother shook her head. "Why?"

"My lady," Roine began, more to silence her than anything else. His eyes darted briefly to Tan and his mother slowly nodded. Roine shrugged. "There is…an item…that must be found. Everything I can find tells me it will be within Galen."

His mother unrolled the parchment and smoothed it out. She studied it and then flipped the page over, giving it more attention than Lord Lind had bothered. "This…"

Roine nodded. "You understand the urgency. I need to get through the passes quickly."

"Why?" She let the parchment roll back up and set it to the side.

"I don't think I'm the only one searching."

"The hounds."

Roine frowned. "Hounds?"

His mother looked to Tan. "He saw them yesterday. Chased the Aeta."

The Athan studied Tan for a long moment. "Then it is even more urgent than I feared."

"If Incendin seeks this item and you need to travel quickly, you need someone who knows the mountains well."

"Better than me, at least."

His mother nodded, a resolute expression coming across her face. "You will take Tan. He's the best tracker in Nor and knows the mountains better than any."

"That's all?"

"He has some skill with earth sensing," she added.

Roine smiled. "You didn't send him to the university? Most go for the chance they may be shapers."

"I'm not going to the university," Tan said.

The smile left Roine's face. "Your father?"

Roine couldn't understand. More than just losing his father. He knew the terms of study at the university. And he had no interest serving the king after what happened. How he'd simply been summoned. Taken from them.

"Tannen—" His mother met his eyes, pleading with him. "If you won't go to Ethea, at least do this for your king. You know these mountains better than any and if Incendin searches…"

"Father knew them better," Tan said.

His mother nodded. "Perhaps. But he is gone. And he went willingly. He understood the need to serve."

Tan considered refusing but what she asked meant he'd be free to wander the forest. If he could serve the king doing that, would there be any reason not to? At least this way he got away from the city for a while, away from an already-annoyed Lins. Maybe he could stop disappointing his mother, if only briefly.

He sighed. "I'll go."

She watched him before finally nodding. Turning to Roine, she asked, "How long?"

Roine shook his head. "I don't know. A week. Maybe longer."

"Prepare for longer, Tannen. You will leave in the morning?"

Roine nodded.

His mother stood at her desk. "Then take tonight to gather what you need, Tannen. And be safe."

He nodded, uncertain how to react.

"Roine, a word?" she asked.

Tan turned and left his mother's office, pulling the door closed behind him. As he did, a snippet of unexpected conversation wafted through the door. He paused to listen and what he heard left his heart hammering in his chest.

"I know this must be important if you were sent." The door muffled her voice.

"It is."

"Your name...Roine?"

Roine said nothing.

"Reminds me of the ancient language. *Roinay*."

"Not many know *Ishthin*."

She snorted. "It's no secret I studied at the university. But *roinay*? Tainted?"

"Your point?"

His mother paused before answering. "No point, then. But with Grethan gone, Tan is the best we have. If what he told me yesterday is true, you face a danger like we've not seen in the kingdoms in years." There was a pause. "Theondar..." She paused again and Tan frowned, wondering why his mother would mention the name of that warrior. "You must protect him."

"I will do my best, Zephra."

# CHAPTER 9
## *Service and Roots*

TAN SAT IN HIS SMALL ROOM, staring at the wall. A small lantern sputtered, the oil already burning out. Had he not planned on leaving, he would have collected more lard oil. The stuff smelled foul and burned with a thick, pungent smoke. Nothing like the clean lamp oil Lord Lind used. Probably Lins, too.

The bed was shoved against the wall, but still there wasn't much space in his room. The place his mother managed to secure for him was in the servant quarters. And even then most of the other rooms had more space. They were certainly warmer in the winter than his room. At least with the heat of the summer, his room finally had some benefit.

A small trunk rested near the end of the bed. Inside was everything else he owned. Not much, really. A few changes of clothes. Some books his father had long ago given him. A necklace given to him when he'd turned sixteen that he never wore. A long hunting knife. His bow hung on a hook he'd worked into the stone, the quiver laying on the floor near it.

Emotions rushed through him. He should be thrilled his mother asked him to lead Roine through the upper reaches, but he couldn't help but feel hesitation. The only other time he'd traveled that far had been with his father. And he had nothing like his father's skill. Besides, going with Roine—the Athan to the king—meant serving the king. Did he really want to serve?

A light knock rattled the thin door. Tan jumped off his small bed. Other than his mother, he didn't have any visitors. Well, Bal sometimes, but she usually got in enough trouble that she spent most evenings in the kitchen cleaning.

Cobin waited for him on the other side. "Gonna let me in?"

Tan pulled the door open and Cobin stepped in. Since he'd moved into the manor house, he didn't think Cobin ever visited. Once, Cobin had visited often, but that had been before.

"Were you gonna come to me?" he asked.

"About what?"

Cobin grunted and scrubbed a hand across his face. "About what. You think I haven't heard?"

Tan shook his head. He should have gone to Cobin to tell him about Roine. Might be that Cobin would be better to travel with him than Tan anyway, but a part of him really wanted to get away from Nor for a while, even if only for a week.

"Yeah, I should have said something. When I saw—"

Cobin grunted again. "When you saw them. After what happened yesterday, you'd think you'd know better. Your pa would have, and I don't mean that to hurt you, but it's the truth. Didn't I warn you about the hounds?"

"Hounds? What are you talking about?"

Cobin jabbed him in the shoulder with a thick finger. Tan winced. "You went off on your own and killed three wolves. Thought you said it wasn't wolves you tracked yesterday. You're the one who got me fired up about the hounds, and then you leave the wolves. Not sure why you felt the need to burn them."

"Cobin," Tan began, backing into the wall, "I didn't kill any wolves."

Cobin's hand froze in the air. "Not you? Then who?"

Tan shrugged.

"Then what were you talking about?"

Tan slumped onto his bed. "I thought you knew."

Cobin leaned against one wall. As small as the room was, he practically filled it with his bulk. "Knew what?"

"When I went after the Aeta, I met someone."

Cobin's eyes narrowed. "Not sure I like the sound of that."

"One of the Athan. Here on behalf of the king."

Cobin snorted. "Definitely don't like the sound of that. Last time we had a messenger from the king—"

Tan nodded. "I know." He'd tried not to think about the last time. A letter sent, sealed with the king's own sigil, asking his father to return to service. And his father had gone, giving everything.

Cobin's face softened. "Of course you do, Tan. I don't mean to keep throwing that at you. Great Mother knows how hard all this must be on you. Wounds still fresh and all." He looked as if he wanted to either punch him or hug him. Either seemed awkward with Cobin. "Why did one of the Athan come to Nor?"

Tan shrugged. "Don't know. He met with Lord Lind and was sent to my mother."

Cobin coughed. "I'm sure that went over well."

"It was…strange. Almost like they knew each other."

"Well, your parents both spent time in Ethea back when they studied at the university. Could be they knew him there. What's his name?"

"Roine. Gray-haired. Older. Something dark about him, though."

Cobin frowned. "Can't say I recognize the name, but not that I would. Darkness probably comes with the job, too." He paused. "Wait—what did he need from your ma?"

"He needs help getting through the passes quickly. He's after something—he didn't say what—and thinks Incendin is after it too."

Cobin scrubbed a hand across his face. "Incendin?" He shook his head and a pained look pulled at his cheeks. "First the hounds and now this. Can't help but think they're tied together, but we haven't heard anything from Incendin here in over twenty years, and even then the passes kept us pretty protected from the war."

Tan's parents spoke rarely about the war with Incendin, other than to say how bloody it had been. Fire shapers from Incendin battling with the warriors of the kingdoms, each pushing against each other. The war was the reason they'd been allowed to study at the university. Anyone with potential had been allowed to study.

Cobin studied him. "Don't worry. Incendin hasn't had the strength to fight us in a long time."

"And we haven't had the strength to fight back in a long time. There haven't been any Cloud Warriors since then."

"We still have plenty of shapers. That's enough to keep the barrier between the kingdoms and Incendin intact. Not much can cross the barrier."

"The Aeta did."

Cobin nodded. "They're given free reign. That's how it is with their people. They can travel freely and trade so long as they don't stay too long or settle."

"Other traders aren't given the same freedom."

"Other traders aren't the Aeta," Cobin said.

Tan didn't push. There was more to the story of the Aeta but he'd never really gotten a clear understanding. Traveling merchants, but more than that. They traveled as families, each caravan connected to the Aeta whole. Most really didn't understand more than that anyway. Maybe Cobin did. Tan suspected his mother did. But now that the Aeta had departed, it didn't really matter. It'd be years before they returned.

"So who did your ma send to help?" Cobin asked. When Tan didn't answer fast enough, Cobin's eyes widened. "She sent you? Thought she's been trying to get you to go to Ethea? Now she sends you the opposite way?"

"She wants me to serve the king."

Cobin took a slow breath and then laughed softly. "That's what it's been about with you? Serving? I always thought you just didn't want to go to the capital. Plenty of folks don't, especially those who live most of their lives out here, disconnected from everything else. Barely feel like you're a part of the kingdoms, let alone think you need to go off to the capital to study. But service?" He shook his head. "We all got to serve something. Time you discover what that is."

Tan hated the way everyone seemed to know what he needed. "And you? What do you serve?"

His face took on a serious expression. "I serve plenty. Since her ma died, I keep Bal fed and sheltered."

Tan shook his head. Cobin had lost as much as any in Galen. "My mother wants me to study in the university, knowing that doing so puts me in debt to the king. Like my father."

"And your mother," Cobin said softly.

Tan rarely thought of that and wondered how she would repay her debt. Or maybe she already had and never told him about it.

Cobin grabbed his shoulder and pulled him off the bed. "I told your pa I'd do what I could to help with you."

Tan nodded, swallowing the thick knot in his throat. "I'm sorry, Cobin. I shouldn't argue with you. I know you're just trying to help. It's just…"

Cobin shook his head. "Don't need to explain. Sometimes it takes time to know what you want."

"That's just it. I know what I want. And it's not in Ethea."

Cobin's upper lip curled back in a smile. "So you know what you want?"

"I want to stay in Nor. It's comfortable. Home. And it's the only thing I have left of him."

His voice dropped off as he said the last. He hadn't really been able to put words to it before. Now that he had, he knew it was probably the biggest reason he didn't want to go anywhere. Once he left, would he start forgetting the lessons his father had taught him? Would he forget how he'd learned to sense the woods around him, to listen to everything from the wind to the groaning of the trees to the sound of the animals—squirrels and birds and mice—working through the forest, to taste the scents in the air and know when deer passed through or wolves had marked the edge of the territory? Every time he walked through the forest, he felt his father. Once he left, he'd be gone for good. At least staying, he could still remember the deep way his voice sounded, the way he praised him when he got a lesson right, chided him when he forgot something simple—never too harsh. No…Tan couldn't leave Nor.

The smile faded. "Not going to be comfortable forever, Tan. Especially if Alles stays as the manor lord. Once that boy of his takes over…"

Tan shrugged. "Could be years. And by then, maybe I'll be ready to move on."

"Or so settled you can't go anywhere. Once you put down roots, it gets pretty hard to walk." He shook his head. "Trust me, best to do it while you're young. At least then you'll never wonder what you missed."

"Like you?"

Cobin frowned. "I wonder all the time. It's worth it, though, if she grows up and can have a life of her own." Tan had never heard so much regret from Cobin before. Cobin sighed. "So are you going to take him?"

Tan shrugged. "Not much of a choice, is there?"

Cobin laughed and pushed away from the wall. "Probably not. Forget the king, you can't risk angering your ma too much."

Tan laughed. "Sorry I won't be able to help you track the hounds. Tell Heller to leave one for me."

Cobin's face darkened. "If Incendin is after the same as the Athan, then you might be seeing more of the hounds than you'd like." He hesitated, thoughts working across his face. "Maybe you'd like some company along the way. I could go with you. I've been through the passes with your father a few times. Might not have your skill with sensing, but I can be plenty useful. Your ma can keep an eye on Bal while I'm gone. She owes me that much."

Tan laughed. "I'd like that. Not sure she will." Cobin shrugged. "Shouldn't be any reason the Athan wouldn't want extra help. Especially if he really wants to move quickly."

"And if there are hounds..."

Tan swallowed. He prayed they wouldn't see hounds again. What he'd gone through the day before had been enough. At least if they faced them again, Cobin might be there. And Roine. He seemed comfortable with his sword. Not that a sword would be any better than a bow, but maybe a pack of hounds would be frightened by more of them.

"Talk to your ma before we go, Tan. Sometimes I think you forget you're not the only one struggling."

Cobin was right. He needed to talk to her. All she wanted was for him to find something that made him happy. "I will."

# CHAPTER 10
## *Responsibility*

T AN FOUND HIS MOTHER SITTING at the edge of town atop the low wall. A cool breeze gusted out of the north, whipping at his shirt and pants but somehow leaving her alone. The air smelled of rain and lightning, the threat of the earlier heat still hanging on. She stared into the mountains. Tan didn't have to question to know what she thought.

"We could return," he said as he approached. "Live in that old house again…"

She turned and smiled. Deep wrinkles at the corners of her eyes faded. Her hair, pulled tight behind her head on most days anymore, now hung loose around her shoulders the way his father had always liked it. She sighed. "Some things you can't go back to."

Tan looked over her shoulder, up into the lower hills. Their old home was up there, now left abandoned. Little more than three rooms and built solidly by his father, it had a warmth to it that was missing in Nor. "I could go back."

"And do what? Spend all day hunting? With your father…"

She didn't finish. She didn't need to. His father was a skilled senser. Hunting came easily for him. Tan didn't have the same skills as his father. "You were happier there too."

She nodded and turned back to look toward the tree line. Bright silver moonlight shone down. A wolf howled distantly, the sound strangely reassuring. "I miss him." She said it so softly that he almost couldn't hear it.

"I think that's why I don't want to go anywhere," Tan said. He climbed over the wall and sat next to her.

She took his hand. Her fingers felt strong and soft, but so small compared to his. At least in that he took after his father. "We have mourned him well, Tan. Now it's time to move on."

"Is that what you're doing? Is that why Lord Lind treats you so well?" The words came out harsher than he intended, but she looked at him and smiled anyway.

"Lind treats me well enough."

He noticed that she didn't really answer. They sat in silence for a while longer. Another wolf howled, its cry low and lonesome. Tan let his eyes drift closed and listened to the trees, tracing the presence of the wolf high into the mountains. He thought of what Cobin said about the wolves and wondered who had killed them. The huge mountain wolves mostly left people alone, but when they attacked, they could be deadly. Killing three meant strength. And if something were that powerful, it could just as well have avoided the wolves altogether. Hopefully he and Cobin could keep them away from the Incendin hounds as they made their way to the upper passes with Roine.

"Do you know him?" he asked.

She turned toward him, her face shadowed. "Who?"

"Roine. You sounded as if you knew each other."

She blinked slowly. A debate worked across her face for a moment and then was gone, blown away by the gusting wind. "I knew him once." She shook her head, and her hair tossed in the wind. "It was a long time ago. We were different people then."

"Why'd he call you that name?"

She frowned.

"I overheard you after I left. He called you Zephra. That's the name the Aeta Mother said, too."

"That is a conversation for another time, Tannen."

"Why? You want me to serve the king by leading him to the passes, why shouldn't I know?"

She held his gaze and something changed in her eyes. "Zephra was my name once. That was how he knew me."

Something dawned on Tan then, a thought so surprising that he wasn't certain it could be real, but what other explanation fit? "You're the wind shaper he sought." He always knew she could sense the wind, but there wasn't much use to that skill. Not like his father's earth sensing. But shaping? That was different.

How could she be a shaper? How could he not have known?

She looked as if she wouldn't answer. Then she sighed and nodded. "When I was known as Zephra, I served the king as a shaper. That was a long time ago."

"But he said you were powerful. One of the most powerful shapers he's ever known. How could that change?" Other questions raced through his head but he didn't ask them, questions like how she could be a shaper and not tell him, or what it was like to shape the wind, or what could she do? Could she call up a tornado? Could she push away a storm? Some wind shapers were even said to practically fly on the wind; could she do that?

She only shook her head. "Everything changed during the war."

"You were in the war?"

She nodded. "Your father too. We only settled after. Nor was your father's home, and with the winds of Galen it always felt comforting to me."

How could he not have known that she was a shaper? First learning that she knew the dead princess and now this? It was like he was learning a whole new side to his mother, a side she wanted to keep from him. "Why haven't you told me before?"

"Because it didn't matter. That's not who I am now. Now I'm just Ephra."

"You're a shaper! Why would you want to hide that?"

A sad smile twisted her lips. "For the longest time, all I wanted was to be a shaper. I struggled even catching the wind. And when called by the king, I served willingly in the war. But it changed. I couldn't do that anymore. Nor was my reward."

Tan couldn't think of anything that would make him not want to be a shaper. His sensing was too weak to ever become anything more. He'd never know the power shapers possessed. But his mother...she was a shaper and chose to abandon it. "What could change that would make you want to give up shaping?"

She squeezed his hand. "We had you."

He didn't say anything for a long moment. "Is that why you want me to go to the university? Do you think I could be a shaper?" In spite of how he felt about leaving Nor, the idea still gave him a slight thrill. Could he eventually learn to hone his weak earth sensing, turn it into something stronger? Could he become a shaper?

"I always knew I could shape. The wind called me when I was barely seven. It took years before I learned to control it. Some learn later in life. Rarely at your age."

It was a long way of telling him no. Tan wondered why he felt a hint of disappointment.

"There is more to the university than simply learning how to become a shaper. The Great Mother gifted you as a senser. Your father did what he could to teach you to use that gift, but there are others who could teach you much more about earth sensing." She sighed again. "But it's more than that. Had he not died, we still would have wanted you to go to Ethea. You've lived your entire life in Nor. There is more to this world than what you've seen. After gaining that perspective, if you decide to return, then you won't ever wonder what else you might have missed."

It was the same argument they'd had countless times since his father died. Only now he knew she was a shaper. That changed things for him somehow. "Do you miss shaping the wind?"

"Sometimes," she admitted. "It's been so long that I can't even call it consistently. That's how it is with wind shaping."

"If I go," he started, not really thinking he would ever see Ethea, "would you come with me?"

She patted his hand and sighed. "That's a journey you must take on your own. If I were to go with you, I'd only hold you back. You can't worry about your mother when you're studying at the university."

Tan sensed there was more. "You don't want to go back."

She smiled. "It's been so long since I've been in Ethea that I'm not sure I do. I'm a different person now. Not the shaper I was when I last was there. Everything would be different for me."

Tan nodded. "And Roine? Who was he when you were there?"

Some of the softness to her face faded. "It doesn't matter who he was then. It matters who he is now. And he's Athan to the king. He speaks with his voice."

"That's not how you knew him."

She shook her head. "No. He went by a different name then. But as Athan, you need to lead him where he needs to go as quickly as possible. After that, you can decide what you'll do. Stay or go on to Ethea. If you stay, you'll have to begin thinking about what you will do next. You can't stay living in the servants' quarters. Lind has allowed it for this long, but I doubt he will permit it forever. Serve your king now, but prepare for a decision."

Tan nodded slowly. "I will help Roine."

He sensed she wanted him to say more, but he wasn't willing to. Not to commit to going to Ethea as she wanted. That meant serving the king. But the idea of staying in Nor felt less appealing than before. What would he do if he stayed?

She stood and pulled him into a tight hug. "Travel safe, Tan. If Roine is right and Incendin seeks the same item as him, there could be more danger than you know."

"I'll bring my bow."

She smiled and nodded. "That'll be good. But always listen. Trust the lessons your father taught you. If something seems amiss…run. Don't try to fight off the hounds on your own."

There was a weight to her words. "You've faced the hounds before."

She flicked her eyes toward the mountains and nodded. "They are dangerous. Like so much else in Incendin, they are deadly. Bred to hunt and kill. Don't try to face even one." She took his hands. "And if their masters appear, do all you can to escape."

"Their masters?"

She shook her head and smiled. "A warning is all. As far as I know, the barrier still stands. Roine would have said if it were otherwise."

Another low howl echoed high up in the mountains. It ended abruptly.

Tan listened for it to return, sensing the forest, but the distance was too great for him to hear anything other than silence.

After what had happened yesterday, it was the silence that worried him.

# CHAPTER 11
## *Shattered Wagons*

MORNING CAME QUICKLY. After the conversation with his mother, Tan rested little that night. He tossed and turned, dreams of his mother shaping interrupting his sleep. At one point he awoke in a cold sweat, wondering why she hadn't been summoned for the king instead of his father. Another question for later, he realized.

A soft knock on his door woke him from sleep. He stumbled out of bed and pulled it open. Roine looked back at him, his deep blue eyes crisp and alert. His silver hair was slicked back atop his head. The short sword hung at his side. A tightly packed bag was slung over one shoulder. He studied Tan for a moment before realization dawned on his face.

"She told you."

Tan didn't ask how he knew as he nodded.

"That was a long time ago. We were different people then."

The words sounded so much like what his mother had said. "I still don't understand."

Roine sniffed and reached a hand out as if to pat him on the shoulder before thinking better of it and dropping his hand. It fell onto the hilt of his sword. He sighed. "Pray that you don't. But that's why I need your help. I need to ensure Incendin doesn't get strong enough to attack again."

"What you're looking for could make them strong enough to attack?"

"What I'm looking for could make them strong enough to drop the barrier."

The barrier. He knew so little about it other than how shapers built it during the war. The construction somehow pushed Incendin back and out of the kingdoms. It was what prevented the worst of Incendin from attacking the kingdoms. "I don't know anything about that."

Roine nodded. "Pray that you don't. Just know your mother—"

"It seems I know very little about my mother." Tan didn't mean to spit the last, and it came out angrier than intended.

Roine blinked. "I'm sorry, Tan."

"Me too." He turned away and grabbed his bundle and bow. "Are we walking or riding?" he asked without looking at Roine.

"Can we reach the pass by horse?"

He shrugged, still not looking up. "Equally fast either way. By horse we'd have to stick to the road. Slope is too steep otherwise. By foot we can climb straight up."

"If it's no faster by foot, then we'll go by horse. Lord Lind promised any help we needed…"

Tan pushed past Roine and made his way to the stables. At this time of the morning, it was quiet. Horses whinnied softly. The cool air held the scent of hay and dung. He debated which horses to take before settling on a pair of solid brown mares. Then he moved onto a silver dappled stallion, smiling as he did. Lins preferred this horse.

As he saddled the third horse, Roine coughed. "Only two of us going, Tan. No supplies to carry."

"I invited my friend Cobin."

Roine frowned. "I never said anything about another person coming with us. We need to move quickly. A third might slow us down."

He shook his head. "Not Cobin. He used to hunt with my father. He knows these lands better than anyone. If you're so worried about an extra person, maybe you should just take him."

"You don't want to go?"

Tan thought about what he wanted. Leaving Nor for a while, even as briefly as the week it would take to lead Roine into the upper passes, might be time well spent. And he needed that time away from his mother, time to consider what he'd do with his future.

Cobin saved him from answering. He wore thick leathers and a massive axe slung over one shoulder. He carried his bow in hand. When he saw Roine, he frowned.

"Tan said you needed to reach the passes quickly."

Roine eyed Cobin for a moment and then nodded.

"Seeing as he's only been there once, he asked me to help. Consider it a bargain. Besides, he told me Incendin hounds made it into the woods. Might be better to have an extra body if they catch our scent."

A look passed between Roine and Cobin that Tan didn't understand. Roine finally nodded. Tan kept the dappled stallion for himself and led them from the stables at a steady walk. Cobin glanced at the horse Tan chose before chuckling softly.

As they left Nor and entered the shadows of the forest, he cast a glance back. The road took them above the town and from here, the angle of the path made small houses and low wall look small. Smoke from a few fires drifted into the sky, but otherwise the town was quiet. Before he turned away, he saw Bal watching him from atop the wall. She wore plain gray pants and a loose-fitting shirt—probably Cobin's—and waved at him. Tan wouldn't put it past her to follow them.

The road Roine led them on would eventually lead them to Velminth. Usually two days from Nor by horse, if they rode quickly enough. He wondered if they would reach the Aeta again. He doubted Roine would stop. Velminth was farther south than he intended to go.

They made good time riding mostly in silence, stopping around midday to share jerky and bread Cobin had brought. As they ate, a heavy roll of thunder echoed in the distance.

Roine looked skyward, straining to see into the distance. His head cocked as if listening to something only he could hear. Another peal of thunder rumbled, sounding far away but closer than the last. The wind picked up, whipping dust from the road into their faces.

Roine looked at them. "Storms usually come in this quickly?"

Cobin took another bite of bread. "They can. Weather moves over the mountains and seems to just appear." He shrugged as thunder crashed again. The sky darkened quickly. "Looks to be a bad one. Haven't had weather like this in a while. Probably should find shelter."

Roine looked around, his eyes taking in the trees and steady slope of the mountains. "Where do you suggest?"

Cobin looked at Tan. "There's a couple of places along the road where we could find some protection. Still going to get wet."

Roine looked up at the sky again and nodded.

Cobin led them along the road quickly. The wind gusted, pushing against them. Thunder rolled regularly overhead and black clouds moved quickly in the sky. As Tan watched, light exploded in the distance, followed by a loud *crack*.

"These lightning storms can be dangerous," Tan shouted over the wind.

"That's why I'm trying to find an old mine shaft," Cobin said. "Should be one soon."

There was another bright flash of lightning followed by an ear-splitting crack. Closer now. And then the rain began. It started as slow drops, heavy and warm, but quickly turned into a hard downpour of tiny needles slicing into their skin.

"How much farther?" Roine asked. He'd pulled the hood of his cloak over his head. In spite of the rain drenching him, he rode tall in the saddle.

"Just around this bend," Cobin answered.

The rain sleeted down and Tan struggled to see through it. As they made their way up the road, he realized something felt off. He listened, sensing the forest around him, before recognizing what bothered him. Nothing else moved in the forest around them.

A scent of char and sulfur bit through the rain. "There's something—"

He cut off as they rounded the bend.

Broken and charred wreckage scattered across the road. Painted wood was splintered and debris strewn up and down the road, filling a rent in the forest floor. Random pieces of melted and misshapen steel were scattered across the forest.

It took a moment before he realized what he saw.

Roine unsheathed his sword with a soft ringing of steel. Cobin grabbed his axe.

"What happened here?" he whispered. His horse danced nervously beneath him. "What happened to the Aeta?"

Cobin and Roine sat atop their horses and surveyed the road and destruction around them. Neither spoke. Roine held his sword in hand with a white-knuckled grip. Cobin's axe twitched in his hand.

"What happened?" Tan repeated.

Roine shook his head as if reluctant to answer.

It was Cobin who finally answered. "Incendin." His voice was hollow and thin and shook more than he'd ever heard from the large man.

"How many wagons?" Roine asked.

"At least a dozen," Cobin said. "I don't know how many Aeta were among them."

"At least three times that." Tan looked past the debris, searching for any sign of the Aeta. They had to be close to the abandoned mine shaft Cobin had sought. "How far to the mine?"

Cobin looked back at Tan and met his eyes before shaking his head.

"What do you mean?"

"Too far, Tan," Cobin said. He didn't look up to meet his eyes.

"Wait...they're dead?"

Roine nodded slowly. "As good as."

Tan stared at the slowly smoldering remains of the wagons. The rain had not completely quenched whatever burned them and the now-steady drizzle left the broken fragments of wagon steaming. The small streams of rainwater runoff were lighter in color now. Thunder still rolled around them and the gray sky overhead matched his mood.

"How?" Tan couldn't fathom how this destruction was possible.

"Incendin knows only one kind of shaping," Roine answered. "And their fire shapers are quite skilled."

"Fire shapers? But how would they have crossed the barrier?"

"I don't know."

Cobin watched Roine, a different question on his face.

"I don't understand. Why attack the Aeta? They're just traders."

Roine sucked in a soft breath as he shook his head.

"Did hounds do this?" The idea terrified him, but what else made sense? Both his mother and Cobin warned him about the hounds, but how could hounds—even a pack—destroy a caravan of wagons?

"These aren't hounds. Hounds are…messier." Roine paused and looked around the destroyed road. "You said you tracked the hounds? That's where you saw the Aeta at first?" Tan nodded. "How?"

Tan thought of the difficulty he'd had making sense of the tracks. "It wasn't easy. Especially when they treed me."

"Not many men can follow their tracks." Roine paused as he surveyed the remains of the Aeta wagons. "I knew the hounds were already in the kingdoms. Possibly for days."

"Not just hounds," Tan said, remembering the other set of prints. "I saw another set mixed with the hounds."

Cobin looked at him strangely. Tan hadn't told him about those prints.

"What type of prints?" Roine asked.

A low cry echoing through the forest kept him from answering. The sound made the hair on the back of his neck stand on end. Tan recognized it; he'd followed the same sound only days before. He understood why he sensed nothing else in the forest around him, the same absence he'd felt while tracking the prints the other day.

The hound cried again, low and closer. Tan shivered, though not because of the rain. The Incendin hounds had returned.

# CHAPTER 12
## An Unusual Storm

WHEN THE BRAYING OF THE HOUNDS finally stopped, Tan looked at Roine. He sat atop his horse, rain dripping from his face, bright blue eyes piercing the gloom of the forest. He'd slipped his sword back into its sheath.

"Where are the Aeta? The survivors?" Tan asked.

Roine shook his head. The sad look in his eyes spoke volumes. "I don't think there were any survivors. This kind of attack isn't meant for anything other than destruction."

"Why the Aeta? Why would Incendin shapers attack the Aeta?"

"This type of attack hasn't been seen in…" Roine shook his head. "The barrier has prevented this for years. A dark power is needed for this."

"And they're still here?" The idea of shapers powerful enough to destroy an entire caravan made him fear for Nor.

Roine shook his head. "I don't know."

"But there must be tracks we can use to find them."

Cobin guided his horse over to him. "I don't think you wish to find shapers this powerful."

"So what? We let them roam Galen? I thought you served the king!"

"They will not remain behind. If this is what I fear, then this was a targeted attack. I suspect they returned to Incendin now."

A crack of lightning split the sky, lighting the growing darkness overhead. A deafening roar of thunder followed. In the flash of light, the clouds overhead had been revealed as thick, dark smears in the sky, heavy and floating low, as if barely skimming the treetops. The lightning had come from behind them. Tan wondered how the worst of the storm had passed them so quickly.

"This is an unusual storm," Roine said.

"We get heavy rains in Galen," Cobin said. "Especially this time of year."

Roine looked at him for a moment. "I think this is strange even for Galen."

There was another crack of lightning, followed by another in rapid succession. The trailing thunder exploded around them, growing farther in the distance each time. Rain pelted down more urgently. Thankfully, the strange odors lingering on the air began to fade.

Tan listened to the forest. A few birds perched in the trees but otherwise it was silent. Wind whipped around him, tearing at his cloak. His horse danced beneath him.

An edge of frustration crawled through him. Had the rain not come, he could've tracked the hounds as he had before. And if he could track them, he could hunt them. Maybe chase them from Galen. But the rain would wash away any tracks, especially as heavy as it fell.

Something caught his eye off the road. Several of the low tree branches had snapped free. Such breaks could have been random—the heavy winds of the storm could easily have caused that damage—but there seemed a pattern to it. Leaves and weeds covered the rest of the forest, leaving no other evidence that anything else passed through here.

Tan jumped from his saddle to investigate, studying the broken branches while letting his eyes follow the disturbance, his focus wandering as he struggled to find meaning to what he saw.

"Tan?" Cobin called.

Tan ignored him. Another strangely twisted branch caught his attention. He followed it, picking his way forward. The bent undergrowth and random changes to the forest guided him farther from the road. Tan was not sure what it was that he followed, but it pulled on him, demanding he do so.

He came to an area of the forest where the ground sloped quickly upward in a jagged rocky climb. There were no branches here, no undergrowth to follow, just the rocks. As he nearly turned back, he saw scratches on the stone. The scratches were spaced evenly and regularly.

Higher up, long prints with a dimple near the heel seemed burned into the stone. The ground was drier here, protected by a rocky overhang. The heavy rain had not washed out the markings. Tan studied them; they were the same tracks he had followed the other day.

What kind of creature could scratch the stone like that? Was this the Incendin shaper Roine mentioned?

"Tan?"

Cobin watched him strangely, relieved to have found him. Roine followed, flickering his eyes as he looked at everything around him.

Tan pointed to the scratches in the rock.

Roine frowned and climbed from his saddle. He knelt next to one of the marks, following them the same way Tan had.

"How did you find these?" he asked softly.

"I followed marks left in the forest," he said, though knew that wasn't quite right. Subtle disturbances along the forest led him to the rocky incline.

"You tracked this?"

Tan shrugged. "Sensed it, probably. I'm not as skilled a senser as my father. Mostly a good tracker."

Cobin smiled at him.

"Your mother said you had some skill. This is—"

He didn't finish. "You recognize this?" Cobin asked.

Roine glanced at Cobin before nodding. "I haven't seen these marks in years. Since before the barrier." He looked down at the prints. "This wasn't a simple Incendin shaper. Those are bad enough. Even the weakest of them knows shapings our fire shapers do not. But this…" He shook his head. "This is worse. Much worse."

"What is this, Roine?" Cobin asked.

"I should have suspected when you told me of the Incendin hounds. But why would I? We haven't seen them in so long."

"Roine?"

Roine nodded. "To understand, you need to understand Incendin. Hounds are bad enough. They are dark creatures with strange gifts that have never been well understood. When I say you're lucky to have faced hounds and lived, know that I don't exaggerate. Once they have your scent, they don't lose it. They will track you until cornered, and then they slowly tear you apart. That is the nature of the hounds."

"Can they be killed?" Tan asked.

Roine nodded. "Not easily. It takes shapers usually. A few skilled with the bow or just plain lucky." He met Tan's eyes. "Remember when I asked about shapers in Nor?" Tan nodded. "Hounds can cross the barrier, but do so rarely, and at great cost. Most towns are protected by their shapers."

Had his mother protected Nor? He didn't think so, especially since she said she had abandoned her ability since settling in Nor. Then who? His father and Cobin often hunted in the woods, but he never heard anything about hounds. And Cobin hadn't seemed to recognize the prints. "And if there are no shapers?"

"You pray they lose interest." Roine looked up the rocky slope. "The hounds roam freely throughout Incendin, no different than the wolves of this area. But occasionally they're directed."

"Directed?"

Cobin's eyes went wide. "Lisincend?"

Roine looked over to him and they shared a look. He nodded.

"You lost me. What are the lisincend?" Tan asked. What kind of creature could direct these hounds? How terrible must they be?

"They were men, once," Roine answered. Cobin raised his eyebrows at the comment. "Long ago, the lisincend were men, fire shapers all, and powerful." He paused, collecting his thoughts before going on. "Some have said they were all related to the Incendin throne. It's not known how, but they performed a shaping upon themselves, using fire to alter themselves. Now they serve fire directly, twisted by their own shaping and empowered by it in a way none of our scholars have ever understood. They are powerful shapers, made more powerful by what they have become." He voice grew more withdrawn as he spoke, and his eyes closed, almost as if remembering. "Even the hounds fear and obey them."

"And they are here?" Tan asked.

Roine pointed to the tracks and nodded grimly. "It appears so, but I should have felt them."

"How do you mean?" Cobin asked.

"The lisincend can't move undetected. Their shaping has turned them into a manifestation of the fire they serve. They radiate heat as they move. This can be felt. This is one of their few weaknesses."

"You think that a weakness?" Cobin asked.

Roine stared at him. "When you know where your enemy moves, you can either move to attack. Or avoid."

Cobin grunted but said nothing else.

"Why are they here? Is it the same thing you're after?"

Roine glanced to the sky. "I hadn't considered the lisincend would be sent. The barrier should have prevented them. That they're here…" He looked down at the tracks again before turning to Tan. "Can you follow these? Can you tell me where they went?"

Tan thought he could. Not just following the tracks, but if he focused hard enough he could sense the disturbance in the forest they made as they moved through. "The tracks start here." He walked over to the rocks and pointed down at the prints evident in the dirt. "They climbed down the rock and jumped down here." Enough of an indentation remained for him to almost envision the foot that left it.

"How many?" Roine asked.

Tan shrugged. "I can't tell. It might only be one."

Roine looked at the rock again, considering. "One is probably more than we can handle. Pray there aren't others."

"If it's the lisincend, where'd it go?" Cobin asked.

He was answered by a series of lightning strikes in quick succession, far in the distance. Heavy waves of thunder followed. Roine turned, looking back down the slope and saying nothing.

Toward Nor, Tan realized.

# CHAPTER 13

## *Return to Nor*

ROINE SQUEEZED THE HILT OF HIS SWORD, his eyes going distant for a moment, and then took off without saying another word. He rode through the forest and back toward Nor.

Cobin looked back at Tan. "Tan…" He trailed off, as if unable to say anything more.

Tan nodded. "I know." If the lisincend had attacked Nor, what would they find? Would his mother have been able to defend the city or had the wind not answered when she called? Tan knew so little about shaping. Had she told him about what she could do sooner…it wouldn't have changed a thing.

Would they find Nor looking like the Aeta caravan?

A nauseated knot rose in his stomach and he struggled to swallow against it. He'd already lost his father. Nor was home. His mother was there. Everything he knew was there. And there wasn't any reason for Incendin to attack Nor. The mines weren't even really active anymore.

It was just a mountain town like so many others.

Cobin watched the struggle play out over his face. "Did your ma tell you what he searches for?"

He grabbed the reigns of his horse from Cobin and shook his head. "Nothing. I'm not sure she knew."

"Or that she'd tell you if she did?"

Tan sighed. "Or that."

The rain picked up again when they reached the road, sluicing down, heavy and painful. Gusts of wind from high in the mountains blew at their backs, suddenly cold and biting. The sky crackled with lightning coming in rapid succession. Sharp explosions of thunder split the air. Ripples of rumbling followed, finally fading. Tan felt the silence as much as he heard it.

Roine rode far ahead of them. Tan and Cobin chased after as quickly as possible. No one spoke. The horses seemed to sense their unease and pushed forward. Relief flooded him as the packed path began to widen.

Roine and Cobin pulled up suddenly.

Tan stopped alongside them. "What is it?"

And then he looked past them. His heart seemed to stop.

Nor was no more.

A blackened crater spread out where the town had been. He saw no sign of the low wall that surrounded the town, none of the shops or homes within the town, and nothing of the manor house. The crater steamed like the charred fragments of wood where the Aeta caravan had been destroyed.

The scent of ash and soot filled the air. The stink of sulfur hung overtop everything.

Tan hadn't known what to expect, but not this.

He looked at Cobin. A pained look pulled at the corners of Cobin's eyes and mouth. Nor had been his home, too.

"I don't—" Cobin started. "Bal?" Her name came out as a pained cry.

Tan jumped from his saddle and started forward. Roine held him back with a firm grip. "I need to go see—" Tears welled in his eyes.

Roine shook his head. "Not yet."

Tan forced back the emotion threatening him. "Why? Why Nor? We're no threat to Incendin. There's nothing here…"

"I don't know," Roine answered.

"What could do this?" Cobin asked. His voice had gone high and shaky.

Roine sighed. "This…this is the lisincend."

"But the caravan…"

Roine shook his head. "That was probably a single lisincend. This is what happens when the lisincend work together." He closed his eyes. "I have seen this only a few times. The last was long ago."

"Did anyone…survive?" Cobin asked.

"This isn't meant for surviving. They cover their tracks, obliterating any evidence of anyone who might have seen them pass." He shook his head. "I'm so sorry."

When he had first seen the remains of the Aeta caravan, he had thought it a terrible fate for the peaceful people. This was worse. These were people he knew, had loved, and had lived with. People he'd called friends. His mother. Bal. So many others. All gone.

Tan turned away. He could no longer look.

"Is this because of you?" Cobin asked. Something in his voice had changed. A hard edge had come to it. "Did they do this because of what you seek?" Cobin worked to choke back a sob, staring at the emptiness around them.

"I don't know."

Anger and rage flashed across Cobin's face. "You don't know? You come to Galen...our home...and bring death with you! This," he started, sweeping his arm around him, "was your fault. You're the reason my Bal died!" He jabbed his finger at Roine with each word.

To Roine's credit, he didn't move, just shook his head. "I'm sorry. Truly, I am. It's possible they came here searching for me."

"And King Althem? What will he do?" Cobin asked.

Roine frowned.

"You're the Athan. What will the king do to Incendin?"

"You're asking if the king plans to resume the war?" Cobin didn't answer. "If I don't manage to reach the passes first, it might not matter. If Incendin manages to get this item first..." He shook his head. "Other places within the kingdoms will face the same fate."

"What is it? What does Incendin think to find that would let them enter the kingdoms so easily?"

Roine inhaled deeply. "There is an item, an artifact..."

Tan barely listened. Since his father's death, he'd argued with his mother about leaving Nor. She feared he would settle, never experience the world around him, never understanding that he loved the forests and mountains around his home. But now? Now there was nothing left for him. Even if he wanted to stay, he couldn't.

He could go to one of the neighboring towns. Velminth. Delth. Maybe as far to the north as Galesh. Towns similar to Nor. But they wouldn't be the same.

Tears streamed down his face and he didn't bother to wipe them away. Would his mother finally get what she wanted? Now that she was gone, would he finally have to leave?

A hand on his shoulder startled him. He looked over and saw Roine standing alongside him. "Tan—"

Tan swallowed, understanding the question in Roine's tone. What would he do?

"I'll still see you through the mountain pass."

Relief washed over Roine's face. "And then what?"

He shook his head. "I don't know. My mother…" He couldn't finish.

"She said that she wished you would go to Ethea."

Tan sighed. Ethea. The capital. The university. Going meant he'd owe the king service. Like his father. Seeing the crater that had been Nor, Tan knew he wouldn't serve, not willingly. What was he in the face of such destruction? A weak senser, nothing more. No…Ethea wasn't the answer.

Only, he didn't know what he'd do.

"When this is over, I will bring you there if you choose."

Cobin watched him. Tan didn't want to meet his eyes. What would Cobin do? He was as homeless now as Tan. And without Bal, Cobin had nothing left.

"I'll see you through the pass."

Beyond that…Cobin needed him now. Tan wouldn't commit to anything more.

# CHAPTER 14
## *Footprints and a Friend*

TAN WALKED INTO THE FOREST, wanting to look out at Nor one last time before he left. Nor was completely leveled. The earth curved downward in a slope, as if a huge boulder had been dropped onto the town. Everything around it was blackened and covered with ash. Low-lying smoke still hung like a fog over the land. Nothing moved.

Tan didn't want to go near the crater—something about it just struck him as wrong—and let his feet carry him along the once familiar woods. He paused, listening as his father had long ago taught him. Everything was silent.

He circled the remains of the town before stopping near what had once been Cobin's farm. The pens had been destroyed. Some of the wooden fencing remained, blackened and charred. There was no sign of the sheep.

Cobin stood in the center of what had been his land, looking around as if in a daze. Tan considered going over to him, but decided to give him space. He mourned just the same as Tan. Tears coursed down his cheeks and Tan turned away.

As he did, marks in the dirt caught his attention. Tan paused, staring for a long while before realizing what it was about the prints that seemed out of place. There was nothing unusual about these tracks; it wasn't the type of print or the size that caught his attention. Rather it was the direction in which the tracks traveled.

They headed away from Nor.

The ground had been dry for weeks before this recent rain, so he knew these were new tracks, but with the rain, they should be heading toward the safety and shelter of town, not away.

His heart skipped. Could there have been survivors?

He followed the footprints as they led away from Nor, away from the crater of ash and smoke and into the forest. Farther from town, he found another set of tracks.

"Tan?" Roine called.

Tan waved his hand so they knew where he was.

Roine came up behind him. "We should go. I'd like to get as far as we can before night falls."

They didn't want to be stuck in the open and Tan wanted to be as far from the crater as he could. Standing near this much destruction felt wrong. "I found tracks. Boots in the mud. Several different sets."

"Probably your townsmen moving for shelter when the rain began."

Cobin joined them and knelt in front of the nearest set of prints. "These move away from town."

"Then they're from earlier. Nothing could have survived this."

Tan turned away, intentionally not thinking of what his mother was doing when the lisincend attacked. Had she known? She was a shaper—and powerful, once, from what Roine said. Could she have done anything? Or had she simply died like the rest of the town?

"We should follow them. They're heading north, like us. If we find any survivors…"

Roine looked from Tan to Cobin. "Can we move quickly?"

"There's nothing special about these prints," Tan said. "They should be easy enough to follow." Knowing that someone—anyone—else from Nor might have survived gave him something to hold onto. Both he and Cobin knew the prints were too big for Bal's feet, but that didn't change the hope written on his friend's face.

Roine seemed to sense that. "I hope we find them, Tan. But if we don't…"

"Then we'll get you to the pass."

They started away from Nor. The tracks led up into the mountains, traveling off the known paths. This was not simply aimless wandering. The prints moved upslope quickly, forcing them to lead the horses. When the ground leveled off, they stopped for a break.

Roine grabbed something from his pack before turning into the woods. Tan caught a flash of gleaming gold before he disappeared.

Cobin frowned as he stared after him. "Tan, if we don't find any-one…"

"We have to look."

"Your ma would have fought them. Don't think she died sitting still."

Strangely, the thought lifted his spirits. "I know. And Bal…" He looked out into the woods after Roine, trailing off. He crouched in front of the ground, his back facing them. Cobin swallowed loudly. "What do you think he's searching for?"

"I don't know. But if it'll let Incendin cross the barrier, it must be something powerful."

The barrier again. "Doesn't seem the barrier does much good, does it?"

"Not sure what changed, but it's held for years. Shapers made it, back when they were powerful. Your ma once said she thought the elementals aided."

Tan didn't know much about the elementals. Didn't know much about his mother, either. "Was she part of it?" The idea that his mother helped create the barrier between Incendin seemed almost impossible to believe.

"I don't think so. She was in Nor when the barrier went up. Pregnant with you."

"I thought the barrier was older than that?"

"There were earlier attempts, but none successful."

Tan turned. Roine pushed something back into his pack before looking over at them.

"Could the Aeta have crossed the barrier through Incendin?" Tan had been wondering about that since first seeing them. He'd never seen the barrier, but his father always said it wasn't something you saw. Just felt. Tan wondered what he'd feel if he neared it.

Roine nodded. "It's not a physical thing. It's not brick or stone or anything you'd have to climb. It's meant to hold back Incendin shapers."

"How do you keep back only Incendin shapers?"

Roine didn't answer. "The barrier is the reason the lisincend shouldn't be here. It should have kept them out. If they've figured out a way past...well, then all of the kingdoms are at risk again."

They started off again. Tan led the way, following the tracks made in the soft earth taking them gradually upslope. After a while, they stopped again. Roine grabbed the item from his bag and headed into the woods like he did at the last stop.

Tan saw it this time. A golden box made with five sides cupped in his hands as he left the small clearing.

"What do you think it is?" Tan asked.

"What?"

Tan nodded toward Roine. "Some kind of box. He carries it away when we stop."

"What did it look like?"

"I didn't see it any better than that."

Cobin shrugged and took a swallow from his water skin.

Tan sat and listened to the forest, sensing it. Squirrels slipped along branches, a few deer moved at the edge of what he could sense, but nothing else. Except...something felt off.

Not hounds; that he felt as an absence. This was different.

Tan started into the woods toward where he sensed something off. He held on to his bow, wishing for something more useful like Cobin's axe or Roine's sword. He kept his focus on what he sensed, listening.

And then he heard it.

Whimpering.

Tan ran forward. Rocks piled together formed a small cave. He leaned in front of it and listened. The whimpering came from inside.

"Hello?"

A face poked out. Dirt and leaves covered it, but he recognized Bal. Her hair tangled with small branches into knots. "Tan?"

She leapt at him, wrapping her arms around his neck.

"What happened, Bal?" If she'd made it, could there be others?

She shook her head. "Nor..."

"I saw it."

"Huge storm. Lightning blasted it like it was...like it was..."

He cradled her as he carried her back up the slope toward the others. "I know. How'd you get away?"

She sobbed, her mouth and nose pressed up against his chest, huge shivers working through her. "I was stupid, Tan. I saw him leaving again, going up the slope, and thought I'd follow. I should know better."

"Who? Who did you see?"

"Lins. He started out of town when the rain started. I thought it was strange so I followed…" She sobbed again. "I wasn't far from town when the lightning hit. I saw it…saw the…the…"

When she couldn't finish, Tan didn't push, but questions filled him. Why had Lins left Nor when the storm started? Did he see something?

Did that mean he tracked Lins's prints?

Tan stumbled as he neared the horses. Cobin ran up to him and grabbed Bal from him. "Bal? Bal!" he sobbed. He looked at Tan, his eyes wide. "How? What?" He shook his head and turned away, cradling her tightly against him as he gently brushed the dirt from her face. He carried her to a fallen log and sat down with her, rocking her as if she were a babe.

Roine came up behind him. "Who's that?"

"Bal. Cobin's daughter." He pointed down the hillside. "I found her holed up. She said she followed Lins from town before the storm struck." He turned and met Roine's eyes. "She saw Nor get destroyed."

A look of sadness washed over Roine. "Lucky she escaped."

Tan wasn't sure if it was luck or just Bal being Bal. She'd followed Lins again, but what would Lins have been doing leaving Nor? "If Lins left before the storm, we should see him too."

Roine seemed to consider for a moment. "What lies in this direction?"

Tan tried to think about where they were. They'd gone mostly upslope since leaving Nor, but somewhat south too. Velminth wouldn't be too much farther.

"Probably Velminth." Tan looked back at Roine. "You think the lisincend might have attacked Velminth?"

He shook his head. "Not sure. How much farther until we reach there?"

Before answering, Tan closed his eyes and listened, trying to sense the distance, searching for the void in the forest where the town would be. Just at the edge of his abilities, he felt it. "Probably a few hours still."

Roine looked over at Cobin. "Then we'll make for Velminth. Leave them there if the town's safe."

They couldn't bring Bal through the passes, but Tan didn't like the idea of leaving Cobin and her behind. They were all he had left of Nor. Once they were gone, what did he have left? What would he do?

Cobin looked back at him. Tan didn't miss the expression of relief on his face as he clung to Bal.

# CHAPTER 15

## *A Lost Village*

R OINE THINKS YOU SHOULD STAY in Velminth."
Tan expected more of an argument with Cobin but there
was none.

"Probably best. Not sure Bal should..." He didn't finish. "Listen,
Tan. After everything that's happened, he'd have to understand if you
didn't want to go. You could stay with us. Not sure what we'll do once
we reach Velminth. Find a place to settle. Start over." He placed a hand
on Tan's shoulder. "We've got to stick together."

Tan couldn't deny the idea appealed to him. But a part of him
wanted to make sure Roine reached the pass first. Without knowing
the way, would he? What would happen if Incendin reached it before
him?

"I'm going to see this through."

Cobin opened his mouth as if to speak before shutting it and nodding. He clapped Tan on the shoulder.

A sudden sound interrupted the growing night.

Echoing through the forest came the call of an Incendin hound. They hadn't heard from the hounds since finding the destroyed Aeta caravan. Another voice, then another, answered the call. He waited, counting at least a half-dozen distinct cries.

A pack.

"Does that mean the lisincend are still out there?" Tan asked.

"If they are, we will sense them," Roine said.

Cobin clutched Bal to him. "Like Nor did? Like the Aeta?"

"Besides Zephra, would any in Nor have known what they felt?"

Cobin looked as if he readied a harsh retort, but he bit it off and looked over to Tan. "Probably not."

"I should, though."

"But you haven't," Cobin said.

"Not so far. But we should be safe still tonight. There's a limit to their power."

Cobin glanced down at Bal. "A limit? Didn't seem like it in Nor."

"That was a powerful demonstration. They won't be able to do the same again so soon."

"Velminth will be safe?" Tan asked.

Roine looked at Cobin and Bal before turning to Tan. "I don't know. I doubt we'll see anything like what happened in Nor. Beyond that..."

Tan nodded. For Cobin, they needed to check.

They continued onward. As they made their way forward, following the prints, Tan began to doubt their direction. Tan had never approached Velminth from any direction other than the road. They seemed too high in the mountains for Velminth, yet he couldn't shake the feeling that the small logging town was nearby.

They reached a small stream. Tan waded across, thinking to follow the tracks as they continued to climb, but saw no additional tracks on the other side of the stream. Tan wandered up and down the stream, searching for signs he might have missed, but saw nothing.

"They stop here," Tan said.

"You see nothing on the other side of the stream?" Roine asked.

Tan shook his head.

"Perhaps they waded through the stream itself," Cobin offered. He still cradled Bal in his arms, letting Roine lead the horse.

The painful cry of the Incendin hounds broke the silence of the forest, nearer this time. The horses whinnied and stomped their feet, made every bit as uncomfortable by the sound. Thankfully, Bal seemed to be sleeping in Cobin's arms. There was no answering call.

Tan looked at the darkening sky. The longer they traveled, the more treacherous their footing became. "We should stop for the night. There should be some old mine shafts along the way. We could be safe there."

Cobin eyed the stream and then looked to Tan, nodding in agreement. "He's right. And she needs to rest. We'll all feel better if we sleep."

Roine sighed. "Won't do us any good getting hurt tripping over a root."

They had not gone more than two hundred paces when something in the fading light stopped Tan short.

"What is it?" Roine asked.

Tan pointed to the ground at the small indentation half covered by leaves and debris. "Another print. Hound."

Roine looked at the stream then up to the sky that had continued to darken. Soon it would be too dark to see much more than the outline of the trees. "How long do you think you could track this still tonight?"

Tan considered the lighting and the tracks. "Not long."

"Then we'll go until you can't see it any longer," Roine said. He unsheathed his sword and held it ready as they followed the tracks. The fading light caught the blade, revealing symbols etched into the metal.

As the last of the daylight faded and night grew darker around them, Tan became aware of something else. Light, far in the distance, flickered faintly ahead of them. "Could that be Velminth?" he asked aloud.

Roine's face was an unreadable mask. "We need to be careful here. If there were hounds…"

They approached slowly before realizing stealth wasn't necessary.

The stream they followed flowed down a steep rocky grade and led to a large clearing. Several fires burned brightly on makeshift pyres. Velminth spread out beneath them, small wooden buildings practically abutting each other in the clearing. Though the mill could barely be seen toward the end of town, the scent of sawdust hung heavy in the air.

Tan became aware of another sensation. The air temperature had risen and a dry heat radiated up from the town. The cool wind that had chased them all the way from Nor faded. Roine grabbed them and jerked them back to the trees.

"Stupid," he said quietly.

"What?" Tan asked.

"Me." He shook his head again and his eyes darted around the small clearing around the town. "Can you feel it?"

"It is warmer. Is that what you feel?"

Cobin looked down at Bal, as if suddenly aware of what the others felt. "No…not Velminth."

Roine nodded slowly.

Tan looked between the two men, waiting for an answer. "What is it?"

"The lisincend. They are here."

# CHAPTER 16
## *A Plan*

TAN FOLLOWED ROINE as he crept toward the rocky edge overlooking the town. Cobin stayed back, holding Bal against him. As he looked into the town, Tan wasn't prepared for what he saw.

Like Nor, Velminth had once been a mining town. Over the years the iron mines in the surrounding mountains had run dry and the people of the town had turned to logging for easier profit. The wide Drestin River ran near the south edge of town, winding slowly out of the mountains, across the plains of Ter, all the way to Ethea and beyond. Loggers used the Drestin to send their bundles of logs downstream.

The haphazard mining town had disappeared when the loggers took control. Now the small sturdy buildings of the town were neatly arranged. The streets of Velminth were wide and straight, making it easy for the logging carts to roll the felled trees toward thesawmill and the river. Tan remembered from his previous visits to Velminth

the overwhelming scent of sawdust and the rough hardworking loggers. The people had always been courteous if not overtly friendly, and
though he never quite understood why, his mother had always had a
special place in her heart for the town.

Now, a few lanterns lit the wide streets, but it was enough to see the
strange shadows flickering over the town. A sudden gust of wind from
the high mountains set the lanterns shimmering, clearing the shadows
briefly. As they moved and danced, Tan saw something he struggled
to believe.

A creature stalked near the north edge of town, practically slither-
ing down the street toward the town square. There was no hair on its
head and Tan could not make out any sign of ears, either. Its dark skin
looked almost scaled and leathery.

Tan gasped. Roine jerked a hand up and covered his mouth, only
letting go of him slowly.

"What is that?"

Roine nodded, motioning with his eyes.

"That's a lisincend?" Tan asked.

Roine pushed them both down. A wave of heat radiated toward
them, hot and dry, as if the moisture had been suddenly sucked from
his skin. Tan licked his lips, trying to wet them, and painfully blinked
his now-dry eyes.

"Careful," Roine warned. He looked back at Cobin. He sat back
away from the edge, the reins of the horses in one hand, Bal propped
up on his shoulder with the other.

"What was that?"

"One of their weapons," Roine answered. "They were fire shapers
first."

The heat gradually faded, though a warmth radiated from the
town below, like a bellows fire blowing up to them. Roine crept

closer, raising his head carefully to see over the stone ledge. Tan crawled up next to him, mimicking the man's cautious movements.

As he peaked over, the lisincend was no longer visible. "Where did it go?"

Roine nodded toward the center of town. "Follow the heat haze."

A smoky haze hovered along the street and moved steadily, thickening. Another quick gust of wind fluttered the lamplight and caused the haze to clear briefly. Again he saw the frightening figure of the lisincend at the center of the haze.

"They can use their shaping to hide." Roine spoke softly, careful to keep his voice little more than the sounds of the night. "The heat becomes a veil."

Tan looked back down into Velminth and stared into the darkness. Two more areas appeared to have a haze hanging over them. How many more lisincend hid under the shadows? Between them and the Incendin hounds still roaming the forest, how would they escape? How would Cobin get Bal to safety?

Tan wished another gust of wind would blow over the haze so he might see how many lisincend were out there. A pressure built in his ears and a cold blast of northern wind whipped through the trees. The wind cleared the heat and the haze hanging over the streets of Velminth long enough for him to see two other lisincend.

"Three lisincend," he breathed softly.

Roine nodded, staring at him, a strange expression on his face. "It's rare to find lisincend working together. Three together tells me how important this artifact is to Incendin." He stared at the town, eyes narrowed as he focused. "There's something else here."

The wind gusted, lessening the heat radiating up to them from Velminth. Other shapes prowled along the streets. Like an enormous wolf, its large ears flickered at each sound and bright eyes searched the night, scanning it with an uncommon intelligence. Massive jaws twitched and then one of them howled.

Tan counted at least a dozen hounds along the streets. Some paced while others sat relaxed on their haunches. All looked aware. Waiting.

Other figures moved quickly through the town as well. Darkly dressed, they moved almost nervously through the streets, careful to avoid the hounds. They swerved away from where Tan had seen the lisincend, though the shroud of the heat haze covered them.

A large, squat structure cast long shadows near what had been the center of the town. It seemed slatted, like cage or a pen, and several hounds sat watching it. A few men paced around its perimeter.

Clouds shifted overhead, letting in a silver shaft of moonlight. There were people caged within the structure.

"Roine?" he whispered.

"I see it."

"What is it?"

"You don't want to know."

Tan turned to him, waiting. Roine looked back toward the cage and didn't answer.

A low whistle pierced the night. All the hounds suddenly stood, their stunted tails pointing straight behind them, ears perked. Each hound moved toward the square at the sound. One of the lisincend stalked over to the pen and motioned to a man standing guard, grabbing him roughly by the wrist when he didn't move fast enough.

The man swung open the gate. The people within crowded back and away from the open door and their captors. Someone shouted but he couldn't make out anything of the words, only fear and screams like nothing he had ever heard.

"You shouldn't watch," Roine cautioned.

"Is this what happened in Nor?"

Roine shook his head. "You saw Nor. What happened there was something else entirely, destroyed before there was a chance for this type of torture."

Two captors pulled a man from the cage. The lisincend seemed to watch, though with the heat veil Tan could not be entirely certain. The moonlight gleamed across his flesh and Tan saw dark tattoos twining around the man's arms. Tan's breath caught as he recognized him.

"He's Aeta!"

The man kicked and punched at his captors as they dragged him out of the pen. Voices inside screamed, their cries filling the night. Suddenly, the man was thrown toward the open part of the square. Now free, he stood, looking around with uncertainty. The terror in his eyes was plain, even from a distance.

He ran.

A rumble followed him, loud and painful, the roar of a dozen Incendin hounds all growling at once. It was the sound of thunder. Tan cringed, unable to look away.

As if one creature, the hounds throughout Velminth lunged. The Aeta never had a chance.

He cried out as they caught him. The sound died in a flurry of eager howls. Blood exploded out from him as the dozen jaws latched onto him, tearing him apart.

As Tan turned away, Roine watched him. "You were lucky to survive them," he said.

He remembered how the hounds had treed him. What would have happened had they not been scared away? Would he have suffered a similar fate?

He looked back toward the center of Velminth, unable to help himself. If the wagon driver had survived, had others of the Aeta? Amia?

And what of Nor? Could there be people he knew down in

Velminth? Other survivors?

His mother?

Emotion overwhelmed him. "We need to help them."

Roine shook his head. "There is no help for them."

"Not if we do nothing," Cobin said.

He'd crept toward the edge of the rock. Bal rested back near the horses, not moving. Anger twisted Cobin's face, an expression Tan had never seen from him.

Roine shook his head. "I've faced one of the lisincend and barely survived. There are at least three lisincend down there. Anything we tried would only lead to our capture too." He shook his head. "It would be best if we moved on. Hide for the night. Get Cobin and Bal away from here, down the mountains and to safety. Tan and I will keep going up. We need distance between us and the hounds."

Tan looked down at Velminth, staring at the barely visible shapes hidden in the cage. The sound of quiet whimpers penetrated the silence of the night. The hounds had finished their meal, leaving little of the Aeta other than a dark stain upon the ground. He couldn't see the lisincend.

Could he leave the rest of the Aeta to the same fate as the wagon driver? And if there were any survivors from Nor, could he just leave them?

The answer was easy. His father would not have risked leaving anyone he knew and neither could Tan. "I have to try something."

"Even if all three of us did this, we couldn't rescue those people from the hounds, let alone the lisincend. What you are suggesting is suicide." He fixed Tan with a hard stare. "I have to get to the upper pass before Incendin. I can't do that if I'm dead." Thunder rolled in the distance, as if in emphasis.

Tan imagined the Aeta trapped in the cage, perhaps Amia among them. Or his mother. He couldn't live with himself if he did nothing. "We need to try. I've got my bow…all we need is a distraction."

Cobin placed a hand on his shoulder. "I will help."

"Cobin, Bal needs you."

A grim look tightened his mouth. "And them? If we do nothing, how do I explain that to her?" He looked from Tan to Roine. "Look, I can be a distraction. Make enough noise that I can draw them off. Bal will be safe."

"This is foolish—"

Roine said it louder than intended and his voice carried into the quiet night. A low growl from one of the hounds answered.

When the growling died away, Roine turned to both of them. "You can't hope to rescue those people. Even with a dozen shapers, you couldn't rescue them."

"They're people," Tan said.

Roine looked at him with a pained expression. Tan could tell he wanted to help, but the desire to reach the mountain pass before Incendin—the lisincend and the hounds—weighed against him.

Another scream from the pen made them all turn. Tan waited, anxious, as he wondered whether the lisincend would feed another Aeta to the hounds. When the sound died off, Roine turned to them.

"If I agree to help, we will do this my way."

Roine looked at the town and the wind picked up again, revealing the lisincend briefly. Two stood near the edge of the town square. Another waited at the edge of town surrounded by several hounds. The rest of the hounds scattered through the town, prowling after the men not in the pen.

"This will require two diversions. I will provide one." He stopped and looked over to Cobin. "You will be the other. Take Bal. Head down the slope on horseback. Make some noise as you go, but get her to safety. You just need to distract them long enough for my diversion to be effective." Roine turned to Tan. "Your role will be to sneak into town and open the cage. Once you do this, you run."

Cobin looked at Tan and then down into the town. "Tan and I should provide the diversions," he said. "We know how to move in the forest and—"

Roine cut him off. "My way."

Cobin watched Tan. "Can you do this?"

What Roine asked was dangerous. Could he sneak into Velminth, all the way into the center of town, past the hounds and the lisincend, and release an unknown number of prisoners?

But he had to try. He couldn't simply leave these people to die as Roine suggested, not and live with himself later. Even thinking about it left him remembering his mother admonishing him.

A howl erupted, breaking the quiet of the night. The sound was nearby and followed by a harsh throaty growl. The hounds in Velminth all stood, hackles up, and sniffed the air. Ears flicked and turned and their eyes stared into the night, piercing the darkness.

"Great Mother," Roine swore under his breath. "Go!"

Cobin scooped Bal off the ground. She moaned briefly.

"Are you ready?" Roine asked.

Cobin looked down at Bal. "Just get downhill?"

"Make a little noise. I'll do the rest."

"How will I know?"

Roine smiled. "You'll know."

The hounds began baying. They had been scented.

Roine met Tan's eyes. "Wait until the hounds leave. Then do what you can to save the people down there."

With that, he ran into the darkness, disappearing.

Cobin watched him go. "Tan, if this doesn't go well—"

Tan didn't look at his friend. "I have to try."

"Your pa would be proud."

Tan swallowed the thick lump in his throat. "Go. Get Bal to safety. I'll find you when I can."

Cobin clapped him on the shoulder. "We'll see each other again. I promise you that."

Tan turned away. He didn't want Cobin to see him cry twice in one day.

# CHAPTER 17

## *Rescue*

THE ROCKY SLOPE OVERLOOKING VELMINTH was Tan's safest option. He scrambled up the slope to reach the small stream, afraid to leave a scent the hounds could follow. The water was colder than it had been earlier in the day, and though his heart was beating wildly, the cold still startled him.

Tan started down, moving carefully in the water, trying to keep his profile low. The farther he climbed, the more he realized it was unnecessary. The rocky slope quickly grew steeper and the stream moved through larger and larger boulders. Tan no longer worried about being seen but rather about being ambushed and caught unaware.

Though he moved as quietly as he could, the howling of the hounds filled the night. Tan stayed hidden along the rocks as he crept lower, slowly moving his way toward the town.

What kind of distraction should he expect from Roine? There hadn't been time to discuss. How would he know when it was safe to move?

Tan hunched behind smaller rocks. The braying sounded louder here. Tan kept himself tight against the rocks as he moved, inching his feet forward, fearing a rockslide with each step.

Peering over the nearest stone, he was high enough that he stared down into town. Nothing moved along the streets. He saw no sign of the hounds. Or, more importantly, the lisincend.

This close, the heat they radiated was a dry heat, powerful and caustic. His lungs ached as he breathed it in. What sort of distraction would be enough to draw them away?

The distant howling intensified, as if cornering its prey. Then the ground started to shake.

The rumbling started far up the slope, a slow shaking of the ground such that Tan had to steady himself on the nearest rock, and gradually intensified. A deep rumble came with it, vibrating his body. Tan had only once before experienced something like this and that was during a rockslide long ago. A few small rocks slid toward him from up the slope, but nothing larger.

The shaking knocked Tan off of his feet.

He tucked his head to his chest, trying to protect it during the fall, and rolled. When he stopped, he jumped to his feet. The baying hounds cried painfully before falling silent.

Now Tan saw the lisincend clearly, as if the shaking ground disrupted the veil.

It looked around, sniffing the air carefully. The men within Velminth cowered toward the protection of the buildings. A few looked ready to run, staring at the lisincend as if waiting for an opportunity. Finally the lisincend looked down the slope, toward the south, and slid down the road and out of sight. Toward Cobin and Bal. He prayed they would be fine.

Tan moved down the rest of the slope, trying to use the still-sliding rocks as camouflage for any noise he might make. Then he reached the soft ground at the base of the rock.

Tan followed the stream as it wound toward the Drestin. The stink of sulfur and heat filled his nose. Breathing through his mouth didn't help much. As he reached one of the town's streets, he snuck quickly along the muddy road, hurrying to a nearby building. The structure was squat and built of huge logs, and Tan pressed his back into the wood, hoping to blend into the shadows.

Already he worried that he had been discovered. His heart pounded wildly and he strained to control his breathing. Any loud sound would give him away.

But nothing moved in the night.

Down in the town, the distance to the pen at the center of town seemed so far away. He moved from building to building, pressing against each as he passed. Constant fear of hounds and lisincend worked through him.

It seemed to take an eternity as he moved through the town. Buildings that had seemed small now loomed large and imposing. Streets that had looked like straight conduits through town were no longer as certain.

And then he saw the square. It was small, more of a grassy opening, a place for the weekly market and somewhere for the townsfolk to gather and conduct meetings, yet on this night and with the strange shadows over everything, it appeared immense.

The cage stood at the center of the square. There was nothing exotic about it; it was constructed of simple stripped lumber and did not look as large as it had from above. People cowered toward the middle of the cage, fearful of getting too close to the open slats. The door opened on this side.

The challenge now was getting to the cage.

Two men made their way around the square, pacing with muted steps. Occasionally, they cast glances at the other or at the cage and the prisoners within. What would it take for someone to work with the lisincend? Fear would drive someone, he knew. But could there really be any sort of reward?

Tan needed his own diversion. Any distraction would do, something to take the men out of the square. Roine couldn't have planned for this, which meant he'd have to do it on his own.

A sudden crack of lightning sizzled through the air so close it could have been over his shoulder. A clap of thunder followed, a deep rumbling that shook the building where he hid. The men standing within the square looked at each other nervously a moment, then the man closest to Tan walked across the square to the other.

"It could be them," one said. It was the man who had been closest to Tan. He was shorter than the other and his voice was pitched low.

The other shook his head. "They left to check on the hounds."

"Not them."

"You think more?" His voice rose in a moment of fear.

The shorter man shrugged. "Let's pray it's not. Perhaps they simply return."

"Great Mother!" He looked up the street in the direction of the last lightning strike. "We probably should check."

The men took off at a jog up the street. Tan waited until he couldn't hear them before peeling away from the building to peer around the square, looking around and searching for signs of men, hounds, or worse—the lisincend.

Nothing moved in town. More importantly, no heat radiated toward him. So he ran.

Sprinting across the square, he looked around him, keeping his head low. Clouds had shifted, covering the moon and leaving everything in strange, twisting shadows. The run felt like it went on forever, but it couldn't have been more than a few seconds until he reached the cage.

Someone inside cried out and was quickly shushed. Tan looked between the slats at the people within and saw no more than ten, each wearing the bright colors of the Aeta. Their clothing was stained and covered with ash and mud, yet still unmistakable.

He felt an overwhelming sense of sadness and disappointment. No survivors from Nor.

"I'm here to help," he whispered.

"Who are you?"

The voice carried more strength than Tan would have been able to muster under the same circumstances. "I'm from Nor. I'm Tan Minden."

"Son of Ephra?"

He recognized the voice and the authority it carried. The Mother still lived. Could Amia as well? "Is this all of you?"

"All that are left," the Mother answered.

Tan shivered with the connotation, remembering the caravan of Aeta that had ridden into Nor only a few nights before. So many now lost. Fewer than lost in Nor, but lost just the same.

A heavy iron lock hung on the door, but the rest of the cage and the door were wooden. If he could cut through the wood, he could free the captives. If only he had Cobin's axe.

The only thing he could find was a large rock laying half buried. He struck at the wood around the lock. He dented it, but the door suffered little other damage.

There were cries within the cage and someone urged him to hurry. He struck harder upon the wood to no avail.

Another crackle of lightning split the sky, briefly blinding him. Clouds seemed to have thickened. Rain would come next. Pressure began building in his ears again, as it had several times throughout the day. Tan ignored it, focusing on the door. Yet the pressure built to a painful level, getting worse with each strike on the wood.

Still he did not stop. He could not stop.

With a sudden explosion, the wood around the door shattered. Lightning burst in the distance and the pressure in his head was gone. Tan pulled the broken door open, leaving the lock in place. The Aeta stumbled out.

"Six?" he asked, counting the Aeta as they left the cage. Amia was among them. She stared at him as she came through the door. "That is all who remain? Where are the rest of your people?"

The Mother shook her head, a pained expression upon her face that quickly passed, replaced with a steely resolve. "Gone. As we should be."

There was no time to waste. If they made their way back toward the stream and up, they might hide their departure as long as possible. As they reached the edge of the square, a voice in the shadows stopped him.

"I can't let you do that."

Tan skidded to a stop. His heart beat rapidly.

A dark shadow stepped forward from the street and Tan felt his stomach drop. His hand went for his hunting knife. He paused, the knife forgotten, as he recognized the person blocking his way.

Lins Alles stood before him. Rain and muck slicked his black hair from his head. A heavy cloak hung over his shoulders. He held an unsheathed sword casually in his hand. In spite of that, a nervous twitch pulled at his eyes and they flicked around him, searching the darkness.

"Lins," Tan said, completely surprised. After seeing only the Aeta within the cage and no signs of anyone from Nor, he had not expected to see anyone he knew, least of all Lins Alles. Yet here he stood, blocking his way. "What are you doing here?"

Lins sneered at him. "I would ask you the same." He flickered a glance at the Aeta and a half-smile turned his mouth. "I'd tell you to leave the food alone, but the hounds will only capture them again anyway."

The Aeta cowered away from him. "What are you doing?" Tan asked, confused. "You're working *with* them?"

Lins shrugged. "Incendin will come one way or another," he answered, his eyes growing distant. "My father didn't understand. I brought it to him first but he didn't believe me. Said Incendin's time had passed. Now…now I'll rule much more than a manor house."

Tan didn't think Lins would live long enough to see that time. "What happened in Nor?"

Lins shook his head and his eyes snapped back into focus. "Does it matter?"

Tan shook his head, unable to wrap his head around what he heard. Lins had betrayed the people of Nor. His friends. His mother. Everyone he had ever known.

"Are you the reason the lisincend crossed the barrier? The reason they destroyed Nor?"

Lins just blinked.

Rage worked through him. The arm holding the knife shook. "Are you, Lins?"

Lins's face went blank. "Back in the cage. All of you." He waved his sword.

Amia stepped between them. The rage within Tan simply vanished. Tan looked at Lins and saw an expression of sadness and regret, mixed with fear.

"Go. Now." She spoke with power and authority. Energy seemed to sizzle in the air.

"The lisincend," Lins stammered. "I didn't know. It was only to be Incendin shapers. No hounds. No lisincend. No one was to be hurt."

He shook his head and his eyes bulged, as if surprised by his admission. "I didn't know."

Amia frowned, tilting her head as she considered him a moment longer. "No," she said, agreeing. "I sense that you did not." She sighed and fixed him with a firm gaze. "Go. You will not forget what you did." The words rang with command.

Lins started whimpering. Tears streamed down his face. Looking to Tan with terror, he dropped his sword before running from the square. Tan watched him leave, uncertain of what had just happened.

"What was that?" he asked Amia.

She shook her head. "We should go."

He led them through Velminth toward the stream at the northern edge of town, hugging the shadows of the buildings as much as they could. The muddy streets slowed them. Tan had them step carefully, praying for silence each time the mud sucked his foot into the ground. Finally, the stream was visible.

As they neared the rocks, a terrible sound, like that of hot coals exploding in a fire, came from behind them. Heat rolled over him, enveloping him.

A surge of fear stole through him.

He did not turn, knowing without looking what he'd find.

The lisincend had returned.

# CHAPTER 18
## *An Impossible Request*

HEAT BLASTED THEM. Tan ducked, but it made no difference. "Hurry!"

When they were about halfway to the stream leading out of Velminth, the temperature of the air doubled. A dizzying sense of movement spun around him, and the pressure of heat forced him to stop.

"Hand me the girl." The words were like a crackling fire.

Tan turned. One of the lisincend stood behind them, blocking the
road. A shimmer of heat surrounded him, creating a hazy veil.

"I will not." The Mother stepped forward, straightening her back as
she faced the lisincend.

It laughed, the sound like steam hissing. "You have no choice in
this."

The Mother pushed Amia behind Tan, stepping backward as she
did. Her eyes darted to the side and fixed briefly on the small stream.
"Why do you do this?"

She tried to buy time. There was nothing they could do against the lisincend other than buy time. But for what? No one was coming to help them.

"You are not to question why, Aeta."

"My people have been nothing but peaceful with Incendin," the Mother answered.

Another laugh. "Peace is no longer enough. The lost are nothing, will be nothing. Give me the girl."

The Mother shook her head. "You know I cannot. Why not let us go? You can report that you never found us." She pressed back a step as she spoke. The rest of the Aeta all moved with her, taking the slow and cautious step deeper into the shadows.

"Report?" the lisincend growled.

There was a sudden flare of heat, scorching. Tan's throat went dry. His skin felt like it blistered, as if standing in an open flame. He wished for nothing more than the rain to return.

The Mother smiled. "I mean no offense." She took a slow step to her left. "I assumed Fur commanded the lisincend. If that has changed—"

The creature only laughed again with the strange hissing way that it did. "You cannot play me like you seduce these villagers, Mother of the Lost."

There was a strange click in its throat.

The Aeta closest to the lisincend burst into flames. Fire engulfed her quickly, burning as if from inside, ripping through her flesh and clothes. Everyone took a step back. Someone cried.

The woman's scream, a horrible cry splitting the night, ended abruptly as she crumpled to the ground in a pile of char and ash.

Tan struggled not to vomit. How was such a thing even possible?

Pushing Amia before him, he tried to move away, but there was nowhere for them to go.

One of the hounds sat not far from them, blocking escape to the stream. Bright eyes stared at him. Tan almost imagined a hungry smile across its lips. He stopped, turning to see another hound watching them near the edge of town. As if waiting for him to run.

"I'm sorry," he whispered to Amia.

She looked up at him, her wide eyes softening. "You've nothing to apologize for, Tan. You did what you could."

In any other time, he would have melted at the way she said his name. Worse than being unable to do anything, he'd probably hastened her death. He looked away in shame, unable to meet her gaze. "This is my fault."

She reached a hand up to his face and forced him to meet her eyes. She laughed softly. The sound surprised him, so out of place with the terror he felt. "The fault lies with Incendin. You give us the hope of freedom."

A knot formed in his throat. Tan couldn't look away from her.

"Where is the girl?" the lisincend asked again.

The Mother breathed heavily as she looked deliberately at the fallen Aeta. "There is no girl such as you seek." She took another careful step toward the stream.

The lisincend flared heat again. It was angry. Was that part of the Mother's plan?

There was another *click*, followed by a slow hiss. Another Aeta burst into flames.

They screamed and the rest took a quick step back, trying to move across the dark jumble of weeds at the edge of Velminth toward the stream.

The unnatural fire of the immolated Aeta briefly illuminated the night. She writhed in pain until stopping, moving no more.

"How many more of your people will you sacrifice for her?"

"How much longer will you defy the Accords?" One foot touched the stream, barely sinking into the water.

The lisincend laughed again. "How much longer will you cling to them? The day soon comes when the world will see the last of the Lost." It clicked again. Another of the Aeta shrieked as flames engulfed him.

The lisincend let the fire linger, reveling in his torture of the Aeta, slowly burning the man to a char. The heat around it faded, clearing the haze and the veil. A smile could almost be imagined tugging its lips.

Only three Aeta remained.

"You will leave this town."

Amia spoke behind him, startling him with the intensity and command in her words. A beautiful anger hung about her. She blazed with energy.

"You will leave these lands."

Power from her words thrummed through him, past him, and directed at the horrible creature. The lisincend did not answer.

"You will honor the Accords."

Amia hammered each word in such a way that Tan felt them tear through him. He could not imagine defying her request.

"Get out of my *head*!" The lisincend flared heat and disappeared behind the shimmering veil.

Another Aeta vanished in a flash of flame and smoke, dying without a word, leaving only the Mother and Amia. Amia flinched behind him and he felt her stagger, nearly falling. He turned to help keep her on her feet.

She stared past him, toward the lisincend. Her eyes flashed fury at the creature. Her forehead was reddened, almost as if slapped, and her hair smelled like it had been singed, as well. Amia took his hand. Tan held it, too afraid to run.

The lisincend turned its rage on the Mother. Heat rose around her. The veil around the lisincend parted, splitting like a curtain in the shimmering haze, and the creature stepped forward, grabbing the Mother and lifting her chin. Her face sizzled and smoked as it touched her. Somehow, she did not flinch. The scent of burnt flesh hung pungent in the air.

"You still deny that she exists?" He stroked a long nail along her cheek, leaving a blistering streak where it touched.

The Mother kept her expression blank and did not meet the lisincend's gaze. Her mouth mumbled something silently and she stared down at the stream she had barely touched. Amia pressed into his back, her soft hand reaching up to his shoulder and squeezing. Tan felt her shaking.

The lisincend's lips parted and a long red tongue darted out. "She will help Incendin find great power," it growled. The lisincend continued the stroking motion along the Mother's cheek, searing her flesh with each flicker of its nail, leaving blistered and burned skin behind.

"You know nothing of power," the Mother whispered. "Only fear. Report that to Fur when you grovel at his feet." She tilted her head back defiantly.

A low rumbling came from deep within the creature. Smoke started at the Mother's feet. The fire spread gradually, a controlled crawl. Tan couldn't imagine the agony the Mother felt. Yet she said nothing to the lisincend.

Then she turned. Her eyes met his, growing wide. Her breathing quickened. "Protect her," she whispered to him.

He felt compelled to answer. The look on her face begged his help, but what could he do? "I can't do anything."

The Mother smiled then and a wave of compassion flowed over him, through him, as it surrounded Amia. "You can do more than you know," she said. Her eyes widened as the fire spread up past her waist. "For the sake of your people and mine, protect her, son of Zephra."

The last was said so quietly that Tan found himself leaning to hear over the crackling flames rising up her body, enveloping her clothing and spreading to her hair. Heat and smoke and ash filled the air. Tan coughed and leaned away, pressing Amia back with him as he did.

Finally, the Mother screamed. The lisincend's mouth twisted in a horrible smile.

The Mother fell in a pile of burning ash and bones as the flames consuming her leapt brighter, fed by some invisible fuel. Amia pulled on his shoulder and he turned to look at her.

Her face was a mixture of emotions. Rage. Sadness. And disappointment.

"Give her to me," the lisincend commanded. "I am no longer amused."

Tan stepped back, shaking his head. One of the hounds growled, a low threatening rumble. The lisincend laughed, a horrible raspy sound that tore into his ears. The heat around him increased as his feet began to burn. Knowing what would come next terrified him. But he refused to move away from Amia.

"Release us now," Amia said.

Her words carried an energy to them, a command, and Tan could not imagine the lisincend doing anything but releasing them.

The creature only laughed again. "I know your trick now. You can sacrifice this boy, but he cannot protect you much longer."

Tan cried out as the heat flared. Fear coursed through him, pounding, paralyzing him. He smelled the leather of his boots burning yet he could do nothing to move.

Amia looked at him. Her eyes pierced his fear. "Protect me."

Her voice was a soft command in his mind. He could no more

ignore her request than the day could ignore the rising sun.

Pressure suddenly flared in his ears, building so quickly that he didn't know what he could do to release it. It felt as if his eardrums would burst. Tan screamed from the burning at his feet and the pounding pressure building in his head.

*Protect me.*

The lisincend smiled again.

That was the last thing Tan saw clearly.

As the pressure in his head increased, he felt the growing compulsion from Amia's words.

The wind whipped into town in a torrent, sending dirt and mud and leaves flying, nearly knocking Tan off his feet. The heat the lisincend radiated was blown away. The creature stared in the direction of the oncoming gusts of wind before turning its fiery gaze upon Tan. Sheets of rain poured down from the sky. Thunder rolled continuously overhead, beating like a drum, almost in time with Tan's heart.

The pressure behind his ears built even more.

*Protect me.*

Another gust of wind threw Tan and Amia forward. He had no sense of direction. He couldn't see streets or buildings through the whipping wind. Mud and flying leaves blasted past his face.

*Protect me.*

Entwining his fingers into hers, he pulled her along with him. The force of the wind pushed them, sending them practically flying. The hounds howled against the raging wind, growing stronger, and then another powerful gust blew in, drowning out the hounds' horrible sounds. It nearly lifted Tan and Amia off their feet as it threw them from the town. Tan clung on to Amia.

*Protect me.*

Another gust sent them airborne. They flew over a small cart. Tan pedaled his legs frantically as he flew, squeezing Amia's hand so he wouldn't lose her.

Then they landed in a tumble.

The wind knocked from his lungs and he lay there, only for a moment, before leaping to his feet. Amia came with him and they ran, letting the wind push them.

Then they were within the trees. The wind still whipped and blasted him forward but the intensity had died. They ran blindly, moving as quickly as they could, afraid to rest and with no clear path in mind. Behind them lay death.

Over the noise of the wind and rain came another sound, something unlike Tan had ever heard. An earsplitting roar raged through the night, flaring hot and wild, before dying quickly, drowned by the wind and rain.

The lisincend screamed in rage. And it was targeted at Tan.

He shivered, running hard, clenching Amia's hand tightly in his own as he ran into the night on exhausted legs. The horrible scream echoed again before it too was put down by the wind and rain. Tan dared not stop.

# CHAPTER 19
## *A Chance to Relax*

THEY RACED THROUGH THE THICK PINES of the forest. Harsh wind whipped around them and a cold from the upper mountains seeped into his bones. Rain came down in icy needles upon his skin. He dared not slow.

Amia clenched his hand tightly. Any other time he would enjoy the sensation of her soft fingers resting on his, but for now, he thought only of taking another step. They ran blindly, moving along the slope. Tan chose not to run them uphill or down, uncertain where he was and not wanting to disorient himself further. They ran from Velminth, and for now it was enough.

Each step grew harder as a growing exhaustion from the day began to settle into him. From Amia's slowing steps, he realized she felt the same. Still, Tan dared not slow. The words Amia had spoken to him in Velminth still echoed in his head.

*Protect me.*

The wind gradually lightened as they moved through the forest. Over the sound of the wind he heard the now familiar howl, the ringing call of the hounds. He cringed without thinking about it. Amia squeezed his hand, saying nothing. The gesture provided reassurance.

As he listened, sensing the forest, he realized the hounds were far in the distance. Other voices answered the first, each farther than the next. There seemed an angry edge to their baying.

The wind began to shift, growing colder with the crisp bite of the northern wind, blowing down from the upper slopes and through the tight passes. After the dry radiating heat of the lisincend, the cool northern air was a welcome return and provided a reassurance that they had put distance between themselves and the lisincend.

Amia must have felt the same way. She released his hand as they slowed from running to a fast walk. The downpour changed to a gentle cleansing rain. Tan glanced at Amia. She wore a tight expression and he knew she did not allow herself time to grieve. Yet.

"Do you know where we are?" she asked quietly, breaking the silence that had fallen between them.

Tan glanced up at the sky, wishing for a sight of the near full moon. It remained hidden behind the dark and low-lying clouds. "I'm not sure. Probably north of Velminth, but..." He trailed off. The strange wind that had blown them from Velminth left him unable to tell where they were. As far as he knew, they could be anywhere. "I don't know how we escaped. I don't think the lisincend are near. Or the hounds."

A question hung upon her lips left unasked. "Nor I," she finally said, looking behind her as if wondering whether the hounds and the lisincend were truly gone. "But I'm thankful we did."

They walked for a while, silent. Fatigue pressed on him, threatening to collapse him under the weight of everything he had experienced. An elevated tree root seemed to reach up and grab his ankle, and he stumbled, righting himself as Amia grabbed his shoulder. She had been lagging behind, each step slowing slightly, and caught up to him in time to prevent him from falling into the detritus along the forest floor.

"We need to stop. Rest for the night."

Amia nodded. Her eyes drooped, though her head turned at any small sound in the night. "Do you think it safe?"

He felt the pull of the words she had spoken to him earlier in the night. *Protect me.* "I think so."

She brushed a hand through her golden hair, pushing it away from her face, and looked around the forest. Even the hounds could not be heard any longer. Finally, she nodded.

Trees thinned in places as the ground became increasingly rocky. Dark, low-hanging clouds had been replaced by gray wisps and the moon occasionally lit the forest with muted light, enough for them to move more safely. Rain finally stopped; only occasional light drops still fell on them.

A large cluster of rocks loomed in the distance. Tan pointed, directing them toward it. The rocks could provide a natural defense for the night. As they climbed toward the rocks, Amia struggled to stay on her feet. She was dressed lightly and not at all for the growing cold. Tan worried how she would tolerate the rest of the night.

"We need to get you warm." He pulled off his cloak. As he draped it around her, she shook her head as if to push him off, but he persisted. "I'm sorry I didn't notice earlier."

"I should be apologizing to you."

He ignored the comment and led her underneath an overhang of rock where the ground was dry. It formed a small ring of rocks, nearly a cave. They sat and she leaned into him for warmth. Both slipped in and out of sleep in the comfort of the other.

A howl woke them both, splitting the night with its cry. Amia looked at him fearfully, renewed terror on her face. This sound was close. Tan raised a finger to his lips, silencing her, and waited for the call to come again. When it did, it was farther away, and he relaxed again.

"A wolf." The huge wolves that called these mountains their home were nothing to take lightly, but also were not nearly as terrifying as the hounds. The wolves, he knew, would be scared away by a volley of arrows.

Amia pulled away from him, wrapping her arms around her chest. A distant look came to her eyes. Tan understood her loss; he'd experienced the same today. "I wish I could tell you it will be all right, but there's nothing I can say that will make it better."

As she looked at him, a strange sensation fluttered through him. Then she smiled. "I know. I'm sorry."

Tan shook his head. "The lisincend took my mother from me. Destroyed my town." He tried to block the memory of the crater that had been Nor.

"I'm sorry," Amia repeated.

Tan frowned and looked at her. "Not you," he said. "Incendin. The lisincend."

She looked away from him. "Only because they followed us," she began, closing her eyes and shivering. When she reopened them, tears had welled up. "We were making our way across Incendin," she said, starting slowly. "It'd been years since we traveled their lands, but always we had been welcome, and several of my folk remembered the roads well."

Letting go of her knees, she leaned back against the cool rock and stared into the darkness. "Mother knew Incendin wares would entice trade, so she pushed us. We traveled deeper into Incendin than even the oldest of our folk were comfortable." She paused, turning briefly to meet Tan's gaze before turning away again. "We had gone into unknown areas of Incendin when we first came across them."

She paused and Tan was uncertain whether she would even continue. "The lisincend?"

Amia shook her head. "Not at first. Hounds." She shivered again with the memory, as if hearing their harsh and painful cry again. "We have come across the hounds before and know how to avoid them. This time was different."

"How?"

She shook her head. "Always before we have encountered only a single hound at a time. This time they ran as a pack and chased us."

She fell silent and Tan let it linger for a moment. "Is that why you left Incendin?"

Amia turned to him and there was a look of fear in her eyes, a haunting he'd not seen before. "No. We were able to evade the hounds. It was as we neared the border to your kingdoms that we began to notice signs of the lisincend. The air drier and hotter. The way the wind died. Mother pushed us hard then, hoping to cross before we came in contact with them."

"How did you cross the barrier?"

She looked at him strangely. "It's not meant to keep out Aeta," she said, as if that answered it.

She fell silent again and Tan didn't press. When she didn't speak again, he let the silence settle between them until a question came to him. "The Mother spoke to the lisincend about some Accords."

"She did," Amia agreed.

"What Accords?"

Amia tilted her head slightly, considering Tan before answering. "How much do you know of the People?"

Tan thought about the question and realized he knew very little. "The Aeta have visited Nor only a few times during my life. I have nothing but happy memories of the visits, the festivities that accompanied the visits, and the Aeta." He paused, remembering something his mother had said after meeting with the Mother outside Nor. "My mother once said the Aeta were wanderers with a history filled with sadness."

Amia nodded slowly and took a deep breath, reaching a hand up and pressing back a strand of stray hair. "We are wanderers," she agreed. "But it was not always so. Once, our story goes, the People lived in a peaceful land, a place of beauty unlike any other. Then we lived as you do, in cities, off the land, and not out of a wagon." She closed her eyes, as if imagining. When she opened them, there was a relaxed expression upon her face.

"Something happened. Some great event that forced us from our homeland so long ago that its telling is lost, or protected. The Mothers keep the records, and I have not yet been privy to them." Her eyes grew moist. "And will not now," she whispered. Amia fell silent for a moment before continuing. "Since we left our lands, we've wandered, always peacefully and carrying no weapon save what we need to hunt."

"What of the Accords?" Tan asked.

"The Accords grant the People a certain protection," she answered, turning to meet his gaze. "Written and agreed upon long ago by the men and kings of the earliest nations, places like Ter and Vatten and Galen before these lands were all bound under a single throne, they are a promise of peace and fair trade. They have been honored by all lands since."

"Even Incendin?"

She nodded. "Always Incendin. Even during the war."

"Then why would they violate the Accords now?"

Amia shook her head, and started to answer when Tan sensed something nearby. He raised a finger to his lips to silence Amia. She frowned at him and the relaxed expression she'd worn left her eyes, replaced by a wild fear.

The compulsion suddenly flared within his mind, the request Amia had made back in Velminth. *Protect me.*

Signaling her to wait, he crept quietly from the rocks, moving stealthily. As he moved, he let his focus wander and stretched out with his senses, reaching his awareness out toward the trees whispering soft susurrus from the wind, the quiet hoot of the owl, the steady chirp of the cricket, using any disturbance he could sense to help guide his feet.

The wind picked up, cold and biting. A slow pressure built in his head, the same that he'd felt the last few days. Muscles tensed with sub-conscious fear, worry about Incendin hounds and the lisincend threatening to break his concentration. He forced away those fears. The hounds never moved quietly and the cool night air made the lisincend unlikely. Ahead he sensed something amiss, a void in what should be the noise of the night. Tan froze.

Moving as quietly as he could muster, he crept toward the nearest tree, hugging its rough trunk, before ducking from tree to tree toward what he sensed.

Then a dark shape was visible. Tan scrambled quietly into the nearest tree and climbed onto the lowest limbs. He held his body away and tight so he wouldn't be outlined in the night's shadows.

*Protect me.*

The thought suddenly surged to the front of his mind and he reached to quietly unsheathe his knife, holding it tightly in his free hand. As the shape passed beneath him, he dropped, shouting a warning while mindless of the harm he placed himself into, only aware of the need to protect Amia.

The figure below turned with amazing speed and blocked his knife, throwing Tan to the ground. He dropped with a hard *thud*. The wind knocked from his lungs.

Tan's vision grew hazy. A dark shape loomed over him, holding a sword pointed down at his chest. The figure reached up a free hand and pulled back a hood, holding the sword leveled at Tan's chest.

Relief flooded through him. Roine had found them.

The only question Tan had was: *How?*

# CHAPTER 20
## *Another Shaper*

"DID COBIN MAKE IT?" Tan whispered.

Roine shook his head, his dark eyes darting around him, scanning the forest for movement. Tan stretched out his senses yet felt nothing unusual. Roine looked at him quickly, a strange questioning expression to his eyes, but said nothing.

"Did you see him?" Tan asked again.

"No," Roine answered quickly.

"Do you think the hounds got him?"

Roine shook his head without pausing to consider the question. "I doubt it. I drew them off." His voice was barely more than the sound of the breeze yet Tan heard it clearly.

Tan stared at the dark stranger for a long moment, thankful that at least Cobin and Bal would reach safety. "The lisincend—" he began, but was cut off.

"Not here," Roine whispered, motioning for Tan to lead.

Tan nodded, questions crawling through his tired mind, yet he left them unasked and led Roine toward the rock cluster, sensing his way back to the shelter in the fading darkness. Roine said nothing, leading the horses forward. A slight limp slowed him.

Roine nodded upon reaching the rocks, as if giving approval for their shelter. Tan walked him into the crevasse where Amia waited. She sat up quickly as he entered and her gaze flickered nervously to Roine before turning to Tan. A question burned in her dark eyes.

Roine turned upon entering and looked at Tan. "This is it? She was the only captive?"

"There were others."

Roine exhaled slowly. "What happened?"

"I crept into the town after you and Cobin had ridden off. Only a few men remained. Something happened to the south and even they ran off. The cage held six Aeta—"

"Six?" Roine interrupted, looking over to Amia and considering her for a moment.

Tan nodded.

"None from Nor?"

Tan closed his eyes and shook his head, trying to suppress the surge of emotion that threatened him again. "There was one from Nor," Tan answered. "Lins Alles, the lord's son who attacked me.He said he worked with the Incendin." Tan paused, pushing away the brief anger rising in him at the thought by taking a deep breath. "There were no others from Nor, though."

Roine watched Tan and reached toward him, as if thinking to re-assure him, but Amia was there first and placed a soft hand on his shoulder.

"That's how they came across, then. They needed someone on this side of the barrier to help. I should have expected that."

"He said they promised him power."

Roine shook his head. "He'll never see it. That's not the Incendin way." He paused, cupping his chin as he thought. "You said there were others? How did only you two escape?"

"After I opened the pen, Lins ran and we headed toward the stream. I thought we could follow it out of Velminth and use the water as a way of masking our scent from the hounds."

Roine nodded. "That might have worked."

"We never made it to the stream. One of the lisincend caught us."

Roine frowned. "You were attacked by a lisincend? And you survived?"

"The Mother helped," Tan answered, then shivered as the memory of the burning Aeta flashed through his mind. "She distracted the lisincend."

"The Mother?" Roine asked as he nodded thoughtfully. "I suppose she would try. What did she say?"

"She mentioned someone named Fur. The lisincend seemed to fear or respect Fur. That didn't stop it from killing the other Aeta. It was only because of a sudden storm that we escaped." Tan looked at Amia, whose expression looked withdrawn as she relived the experience. "Otherwise we would have suffered the same fate."

Roine looked at Amia for a long moment, staring at her with calculating eyes. The pressure in the air slowly built and Tan felt his ears pop as it quickly disappeared. "Fur?" Roine finally said, and Tan nodded. Roine let out a long sigh. "That…is unfortunate."

"Who's Fur?"

Roine motioned Tan to sit. They were cramped now, the small space that had been cozy with just he and Amia was now crowded with another person and two horses. Tan was forced to press close to Amia, and he did so willingly.

"Fur leads the lisincend," Roine said as they settled. "As much as any can truly lead them. Some think he was the first."

"First what?" Tan asked.

"Lisincend. So little is truly known about the lisincend. Some think they are immortal, others are not as sure. One thing we know is that Fur has always led the lisincend. And Fur serves the Incendin throne in his own way."

"What do you mean?"

"The lisincend don't always serve the king as he would wish. From what I know, they've long been felt to have their own agenda, but Fur manages to lead them, to bend them to his will, and it is *his* will to serve the throne. That makes their chasing of the Aeta especially worrisome."

Amia stared at Roine and said nothing, but now her eyes widened as an understanding passed through them. Tan looked from her to Roine.

"You think the Incendin king sent the lisincend after the Aeta."

Roine nodded slowly. "I don't know." He hesitated. "I know Incendin wants the same artifact, but the Aeta…that means they know something." He roughly scrubbed a hand through his hair, fatigue and agitation plain upon his face. "This artifact…it is powerful. Powerful enough to destroy the barrier. Enough to defeat our shapers."

"What is it?"

Roine sighed. "Well, that's just it. Only Althem knows for sure. His archivists discovered its existence, and he sent me for it. I know little other than that it's an ancient item, infused with power by some of the earliest warrior shapers. I don't even know what it's called."

Tan frowned. "How has it never been found?"

"There's the question, isn't it? Finding it is more complicated than that." He reached into his bag and set a golden box in front of Tan, the same box Tan had seen before. "This was also shaped by the ancient warriors, infused with all the elements." He looked at Amia. She turned away, unwilling to meet his gaze. "From what the archivists have learned, it serves as a compass, guiding the bearer toward the artifact."

Tan looked at the box. It was shaped with five sides as he had seen before and seemed made of solid gold. There were carvings in the surface and along the sides—he saw leaves and trees and moon and stars—made with incredible detail. Small etchings of vaguely familiar figures were made in each corner. At the center was a raised circle with a five-pointed star, each point of the star pointing toward one of the corners of the box.

"What is it?"

"The box is simply a vessel." He ran his fingers along its carved surface. "Though a vessel of its own type of power. This power is directed to finding the artifact. Was," he corrected.

"'Was?'"

"The archivists think the artifact was intentionally lost and the box was made to help find it." He paused, considering his words. "They were designed as a set, like a lock and key, but the shaping is imperfect. I can no longer make it work."

Had Roine just admitted that he was a shaper? If that was the case, why hadn't he attacked the lisincend? "I don't understand."

"The shapers who made this had power unequaled in centuries. They were trained as no shaper has been trained in nearly four centuries, working with the elementals to craft their shapings. Those shapers could call upon power unlike anything seen since." Roine looked down at the box. "So I must believe the shaping was correct and that I'm not using it correctly. And sometime during the run from Velminth, it took damage."

"How do you know?"

"This is what guided me toward Galen. Toward Velminth. Always pointing into the mountains. Only…now it no longer points toward anything."

"Can you fix it?" Tan asked.

Roine eyed the box for long moments. "I wouldn't know how to begin."

Tan frowned. "What kind of shaper are you, Roine?"

Roine only smiled in answer, saying nothing as he took the golden box from Tan's hands and placed it back with his saddlebags. Then he turned and stared openly at Amia. She looked away. The small voice again sang out in his head, like a quiet whisper, yet a command nonetheless.

*Protect me.*

"How will you find the artifact now? If this device, your key, is broken, how do you expect to find it?"

"When I discovered the device was no longer working, I thought the search would be over. Now I'm no longer certain."

"Why?"

Roine turned to Amia. "I think she can help."

Amia looked up, a defiance burning in her eyes. Her hands clenched tightly at her sides, gripping the brightly colored pants she wore. "You're mistaken," she answered softly. A hint of strength had returned to her words.

"Am I?" Roine asked.

Amia nodded once, relaxing a hand and bringing it to her still damp hair, smoothing it as she pulled it back from her face before crossing her arms over her chest. "You are."

"What is this?" Tan demanded, sliding a step closer to Amia. What-ever was happening between them, Tan was not about to let Roine threaten Amia. After everything she'd experienced, he couldn't shake her request to keep her safe, even if it meant keeping her from Roine.

Roine flicked his gaze to Tan and there was a sense of pressure, almost a weight, which came with it. Tan felt a slow buildup of pressure, could almost hear it, before it whispered away and Roine took a small step back.

"What do you know of the Aeta, Tan?" Roine asked.

Tan turned to look at Amia. The question was nearly the same as the one posed by her earlier, but this time the tone was darker. He decided to answer Roine much the same as he'd answered Amia. "Memories from my childhood. Warnings from my mother to be courteous to them and welcome their arrival. Why?"

Roine chuckled. "She would have warned that. The Aeta are a wandering people. Traders whose visits are welcomed into towns throughout the kingdoms and beyond."

Tan understood more since speaking with Amia. "The Accords."

Roine turned to Amia. "She shared that?" Tan nodded, not understanding the significance. "Yes. The Accords grant the Aeta free travel and have long been honored. Did she tell you *why* the Accords were needed?"

Amia wouldn't meet his gaze. Tan shook his head. "She did not."

"I'm not surprised," Roine continued. "The Aeta aren't proud of the reasons behind the Accords."

"Why?"

"The Aeta are sensers."

"So?" Tan was a senser. And his father before him. "The kingdoms have many sensers. Many shapers, even." He thought of his mother and how little he knew of her before she'd come to Nor. Now he would never know more about her.

Roine looked at Amia. "They aren't sensers like we have in the kingdoms. They can't sense earth, wind, fire, or water."

Tan frowned again. "Aren't those the only elements we can sense?"

"You've known the Aeta as skilled traders. I'm sure you've seen some who feared them for that very reason."

Tan thought back to Lord Lind's reaction to the Aeta. "Some."

"Have you ever wondered why?"

Tan looked at Amia. She didn't meet his gaze but didn't turn away. "Why?"

Roine took a deep breath and waited for Amia to answer. When she didn't, he shook his head. "The Aeta are sensers of spirit."

"Spirit? How is that possible?"

Roine laughed. "Most scholars think the ancient elementals endowed the earliest shapers with aspects of their abilities. Back then, we had shapers of fire, of earth, of wind, and of water. But also of spirit. For some reason, spirit has been lost." His eyes lingered on Amia. "But not the Aeta. Many are born sensers of spirit. When the Aeta first left their lands, they were initially welcomed. The Aeta lived peacefully yet apart from their new neighbors. Still, some were allowed to travel among the Aeta and came to know them, noticing that they always had the upper hand in trading. Over time, suspicion grew. Rumors. Some who didn't understand named the Aeta evil."

Amia's face had tightened. "So we left our new settlement," she continued quietly, "and have wandered since."

Roine nodded. "The Accords have provided a sort of protection since then. Protection from the Aeta and protection for the Aeta."

"What does this have to do with why you think Amia can help?"

Roine looked to the Aeta for long moments without speaking. Amia said nothing as well, biting her lip and clenching her fists. "There have long been rumors that some among the Aeta are more than sensers. Rumors of shapers."

Tan frowned again and looked from Roine to Amia. As he did, a realization came to him of the words that had been imprinted into his mind, a quiet call for help that had stayed with him.

*Protect me.*

With the command, he knew what Roine said was true.

Amia was a shaper.

# CHAPTER 21
## *The Journey Explained*

AMIA FINALLY MET HIS GAZE. Her dark eyes gave away nothing. Tan felt his heart race when she looked at him. Could she have used him? Had she shaped him from the very beginning, from their first meeting? Was that why he had reacted to her the way that he had?

Did she still use him?

Would it have mattered anyway? He'd gone willingly into Velminth. What did it matter if she shaped a command for him to get her to safety?

They shared a look and she nodded, an acknowledgement to him only. At least Tan now understood more of what had happened in Velminth and why Lins Alles had left so quickly. Amia must have worked a shaping on him.

Had she tried it on the lisincend? Is that why it became so angry?

"I must know," Roine began quietly, breaking the heavy silence that had grown among them. "Can you shape spirit?"

Amia was silent for a long time, long enough that Tan didn't think she'd answer at all, but finally she turned to them and looked from Tan, meeting his eyes and holding the gaze, to Roine. "The Aeta have many feelers," she started. "What you would call a senser. This fact has never been hidden. All of the Mothers have been and still remain skilled feelers."

Roine blinked, taken aback by Amia's honesty. "Are there feelers among the men of the Aeta as well?"

"Some," she said with a nod, "though they aren't as common as women."

"That's why your women lead."

Amia laughed softly. "That's only a part of it. But true enough." She paused again, considering her words carefully as if deciding how much to tell. "There are others, born rarely, once or twice to a generation. They are powerful feelers, able to not only sense the emotions of others, but influence them as well, direct them. We say they're blessed by the Great Mother, infused with her spirit, able to use it to help her people. Once found, these women—they are always women—are raised to lead the Aeta."

"These are the shapers?" Roine asked.

Amia nodded.

He leaned forward. "And were you blessed by the Great Mother?"

A cloud seemed to pass over her face before she nodded. "I am."

"They exist," he said to himself. "All this time we thought we'd lost spirit shaping." He looked at Amia. "How have the Aeta kept this secret?"

Amia frowned. "It's not a secret to the Aeta."

"No? How have you maintained secrecy outside the Aeta?"

"Some things can only be taught to one of the Aeta," she answered.

"There is one truth I have seen on our travels. Every culture has secrets."

"Some are larger than others," Roine said.

Amia met Roine's eyes. "Already I've shared more than is right. I would not if not for the son of Zephra. The Mother had great respect for her." She turned to Tan. "Your mother was well known to the Aeta, though we knew her as Zephra. She stayed with my people for a time. All who knew her had great respect for her."

"Before recently, I'd never heard my mother called by that name." Tan looked at Roine. "The first was when she named you Theondar."

"And you recognized the name Theondar?" Roine asked.

Tan nodded. "Many would, I think."

"I think you'd be surprised."

Tan frowned, remembering how his father always used to speak of Theondar. "But he's one of the greatest warriors!"

"Perhaps he is," Roine agreed. "Or was."

"So why would my mother call you by his name?"

"Because it was mine, once."

The comment came like a jolt of lightning.

Tan shouldn't have been surprised. Athan to the king, speaking with his voice. More than that, he came to Galen—alone—on a mission for the king. And only one of the warriors could face both hounds and the lisincend without becoming incapacitated by fear.

"You're a Cloud Warrior?" Tan asked. How much could have gone better had Roine admitted that to them? How much could they have done differently? "Why do you need me to reach the mountain pass?"

"There have been no known warriors in the kingdoms for decades," he answered. "Those who had remained became targets, hunted by the Incendin and other enemies of the kingdoms until only a few were left. Theondar the warrior is no more. And Roine is no warrior."

Tan frowned. "But you still serve the king?"

Roine nodded. "As Athan. Not as a warrior."

Tan leaned back. Roine was Theondar. His mother was Zephra, a powerful wind shaper. And Amia the Aeta could shape spirit. More than ever, he felt lost, worse than he ever felt after learning of his father.

"What do I have to do with your search?" Amia asked. She watched Tan as she spoke, probably sensing the struggle raging through him.

"At first I wasn't certain. I hadn't considered the Aeta. It wasn't until I met Tan and he told me about the Aeta chased from Incendin that I considered the possibility. Then I heard of the hounds and I feared I wasn't the first to think of it." He looked from Tan to Amia. "I think a senser of such strength could find the artifact. Such strength would doubtlessly make her a shaper. That's why they pursued you."

"It don't think it'll work."

Roine tilted his head. "I'm not certain it will, either. But this device," he said, pointing toward his saddlebags, "was shaped by those who wield the elementals. *All* of them."

Amia shook her head. "I don't understand."

"Let me try explaining it differently. A shaping carries a certain signature," he began, "something that can be felt and detected by those who know how and where to look. If you are skilled enough—or strong enough—you can trace the shaping, follow it, either along its course or back to the shaper."

Amia began to nod a little. "I think I understand."

Roine smiled. "I hoped you would," he answered. He turned and went back to his saddlebag and retrieved the golden box once more. "This device amplifies that shaping so that one who is skilled enough can use it to follow its course."

"You said all the elementals were used in its shaping?" Tan asked.

Roine nodded. "Recent warriors are thought to be able to use all the elementals," he began, "but there hasn't been a warrior who can shape spirit in a thousand years." He shook his head. "It was these warriors who made this box and the reason it has never fully worked for me."

"Then why do you think I can help?" Amia asked.

"I'm unable to even sense spirit. I could follow the others. Some of the shapings were stronger than others. Wind particularly. Water. I have some strength with earth, not like some, but this device never had much strength with earth." He swallowed. "And fire had been quite strong—possibly the strongest of them. That's why Fur thinks he can track the shaping, I suspect. Now none of them work. When the device was damaged, it was no longer safe for me to use."

"Then why Amia?"

"I don't know if the spirit thread has been damaged. That's why she's needed."

"What you ask requires a skill I don't think I have."

"You have to try."

"Why must this artifact be found?"

Roine inhaled deeply. "If Incendin reaches it first...not just the barrier will fall. This artifact, if it's half of what scholars think it might be, can't reach Incendin. I'd rather see it destroyed than that."

Amia shook her head. "You haven't answered the question."

There was a surge of energy with the words, a directive, and Roine smiled. "You don't need to shape me."

Tan *felt* whatever it was Amia had done. He'd felt it before.

"Many scholars have searched for it. None have succeeded."

"Why now? Why you?" Tan asked.

Roine sighed. "Shaping is changing." He shook his head. "I can't explain it more than that—I'm no archivist—but our shapers have grown weaker. Even sensing is weaker. But this," he said, tapping the golden box, "if the archivists are right, this could change that." He sighed. "As to why now? It's not just now. I've been searching for nearly a decade. Even more time before that, trying to understand the damn compass. I don't know why Incendin suddenly makes a push when I'm finally getting close."

They sat in silence for a moment. "How is shaping changing?" Tan asked.

"Questions for those who study such things, not me. In the kingdoms, they're known as archivists, and they have access to records dating back over a thousand years. But what they tell me is that with each generation, our connection to the elementals grows weaker. Once, creatures like the lisincend would not have challenged even a strong shaper. Now full warriors struggle against them. Given enough time, it could be that we will not see another warrior again."

Roine turned to Amia. "Please. You must try. Focus upon the box, upon the symbol for spirit. Push your focus outward, as if you were performing a shaping, and listen, as if sensing. All I need to know is whether spirit still responds."

"And if I'm not strong enough?"

Tan touched her arm. She didn't pull away. "I've seen what you can do. I didn't know what it was I was seeing, but you shaped Lins. And I felt you shaping the lisincend. It was working, if only for a moment."

"You tried shaping the lisincend?" Roine asked.

Amia nodded.

"It should not work," Roine said.

She shook her head. "It didn't."

"I think it could have," Tan said. "Whatever you did made it angry. That must mean you're strong enough to do this."

Amia stared at the box for long moments before finally nodding. "I'll try." She didn't sound as if she expected it to work.

Roine nodded. "Thank you."

Amia sat upon the nearest rock with the gold box resting on her lap. She rotated it until one of the points of the star was directed at her. Her face slackened and her eyes lost focus until they closed completely. Tan felt the slow sizzling of energy, a gradual building of pressure in his ears.

As the energy rose to the point where Tan's hair felt like it would stand on end and the pressure in his ears had grown to a sharp stabbing pain, there was a whooshing release as it shot away from the rocky cavern and up into the mountains.

Tan wondered why he could almost see it.

"It's done," Amia said. She sounded more fatigued than she had been at any point since leaving Velminth.

"What happened?" Roine asked.

Roine sensed nothing. How was it that Tan sensed what Amia had done? Was it tied to the shaping she had done on him, the command urging him to protect her? Had she bound him to her somehow?

She shook her head. "This device directed my shaping," she answered, fumbling with the last word. "Pulling it from me and sending its energy out and up the mountain."

Roine looked around. "Can you follow it?"

If Tan closed his eyes, *he* could follow it.

Amia nodded. "Yes."

"Then we need to go."

"Let her rest, Roine." The voice in his mind whispered to him. *Protect me.* He recognized the shaping now and did not mind the silent reminder; he would have done what he could to protect her anyway. "She's tired. After everything she's been through, she deserves that."

A moment of compassion lingered on Roine's face. "Can you feel it?" he asked Tan.

Tan listened, thinking Roine asked him to use his earth sense. The night was lightening and the first slivers of daylight had begun to creep through the sky, an orange hue to the clouds. The wind had died at some point and the air that had been so cool earlier in the night had grown warmer. Too warm for the early morn. Then Tan knew what Roine had sensed.

The lisincend were coming.

# CHAPTER 22
## *The Lisincend Attack*

ROINE HURRIED THEM TOWARD THE HORSES and he climbed atop his mount, motioning to Tan and Amia to do the same. He started away from the shelter, riding his horse in the direction Amia had indicated.

"Are you going to let me ride with you?" she asked. She seemed genuinely uncertain how he'd answer.

"Can't you sense my answer?" He tried to sound playful, but came off more abruptly than intended.

"I'd understand if you said no. After what I did…" She sighed. "That's why we have the Accords. The earliest of my people didn't hesitate to…shape…others to do what they wanted. That's not what I wanted with you."

"I wouldn't leave you to the lisincend." Just thinking about it bothered him. And there was still that echo in the back of his mind, the quiet command.

*Protect me.*

"Only because of what I did."

Tan held her dark gaze with his eyes and shook his head. "I would have done what I could to rescue you regardless of the shaping. It just serves as a reminder."

She bit her lip and narrowed her eyes. "It is still with you, the shaping?"

Tan nodded. Like a voice in his head, he could hear it whisper if he closed his eyes, felt its pull and knew he would struggle if he tried to refuse its call. "I can hear it if I try."

She shook her head. "That should not be. It should disappear and you certainly should not *hear* anything."

Tan shrugged. "I do."

She looked at him a moment before nodding. "If I haven't said so before, thanks for saving me, Tan, son of Zephra."

He pulled Amia into the saddle behind him and she placed her arms around his waist, pulling herself into him. She was warm and soft and, in spite of everything she had been through, the destruction of her caravan and imprisonment by the lisincend, she smelled of lavender and lilacs. He was all too aware how Amia clung tightly to him.

She chuckled then. The sound was soft and a hot whisper in his ear.

She sensed him. How much would she know without needing to ask?

He felt exposed...but didn't mind. At least she couldn't see him flush.

Roine waited for them as they emerged from the rocky shelter. His eyes were closed and his face locked in concentration. His hands were slack at his side, fingers spread wide, and he breathed deeply. The horse beneath him was completely still.

Tan felt a stirring in the air, like the sizzle of energy he had sensed as Amia had done her shaping, and felt the pressure building in his ears. This was a slow buildup, different than what Amia had done, and there was neither the force nor the pain he had sensed during her shaping. Then Roine inhaled deeply, suddenly exhaling, and the energy was released in a wave outward. Tan had never known anything like it before.

Roine looked at Amia. "Which way?"

Amia removed one hand from his waist and pointed up the slope. "Up."

Roine looked up the slope and Tan followed his gaze. A trail meandered up the rock, cutting between some of the towering pines and ash trees. He didn't recognize these lands.

How far had they come running from Velminth?

"We should hurry," Roine said.

"Did your shaping tell you how far they were?"

Roine looked at him with a strange and curious expression upon his face. His mouth pursed as if he had a question he wanted to ask but did not. Instead, he nodded. "Not a definite distance. More like a vague sense." He looked down the slope. "Several lisincend."

"How many hounds?"

Roine looked back to him and smiled. "You've faced one of the lisincend and survived, but ask about the hounds?"

"I think we can outrun the lisincend. I'm not as certain about the hounds."

Amia shivered behind him. "I don't wish to see either."

Roine watched them for a moment. "I don't know how many hounds," he said, and then turned his horse and spurred it forward. Tan and Amia followed, hurrying the horse up the slope after Roine. The climb was steep, though manageable, and led quickly upward. The sky began to lighten even more. The wind picked back up, sending hot gusts blowing through the trees.

The harsh baying of the hounds startled them when it started. It came as a sudden chorus of calls, howls, and snarls.

"They found where we stopped last night," he called to Roine.

He'd been riding ahead of them, silent as he rode up the slope. With Tan's comment, he turned and nodded. "They've never really lost us."

"How'd they find us so easily?" Tan asked.

"The hounds are relentless," Amia answered. Her voice was soft in his ears yet filled his mind. The words carried to Roine's ears as well, for the man nodded. "Once they have your scent, they never forget it and rarely give up."

"So they follow you?" Tan asked.

He felt Amia shake her head behind him. "There were too many of us for them to have a clear scent of me."

Tan turned to look at her. Amia's face was pleasantly close to his. "Me?" he asked. Was he the reason Nor had been destroyed? Had *he* led the hounds to it?

"That's what I fear," she answered. "You said they attacked when you tracked them, that you were treed. Something scared them off, but they didn't forget the scent."

"You should go with Roine. I won't be the reason you are captured. Or the reason his mission fails." Doing so meant certain death, but if he had led the hounds to Nor, didn't he deserve it?

Roine slowed and looked over to Tan. "Though noble, Tan, it wouldn't matter. I fear these hounds have my scent, as well."

"How?"

"The distraction in Velminth," Roine said. "So it seems it doesn't matter. We'll continue forward."

"You aren't concerned about the hounds?"

"Hounds I can manage. Their lisincend masters present a different challenge altogether."

Tan shivered each time he heard the braying of the hounds. The day was fully light, though the clouds threatened rain again. The wind blew, alternating warm and cool. He suspected they managed to stay just ahead of the lisincend.

What would happen when they had to rest? Did the hounds or the lisincend have the same needs?

They stopped at a stream to rest the horses and let them drink. Roine pulled some stale bread from his saddle and passed it around. They each ate in relative silence. The hounds howling behind them were a constant reminder that they were being hunted. The air grew ever warmer as well. They did not stop for long.

"Do you still sense it?" Roine asked.

Amia nodded, closing her eyes and pointing. "Still up."

Tan felt the energy Amia created during her shaping on the box— could almost see it if he tried. Like a straight line up the mountain face, disappearing from view over the peak. If that was where they traveled, then they had a long climb left before them.

"I don't know that I'll be able to find the pass from here," Tan said.

Roine looked over.

"When we ran from Velminth, I…I lost my bearings," he admitted.

Roine smiled. "If we follow Amia's shaping, it shouldn't matter."

"If it does?"

"Stick to the trail. It's faster," Roine said.

They continued the slow switchback up the mountain. Roine began to look around more frequently, his eyes darting from side to side along the trail.

Not far from the stream, there was a subtle flurry of brown movement, streaking so quickly that Tan wasn't sure what he saw. Roine raised his hand and the ground trembled. At first just a tremor, but soon the ground on the slope below them started to slip and peel away, tumbling into a rockslide. A howl erupted, a harsh and pained sound, which was silenced as the rockslide moved farther downhill.

"Was that—"

Roine shushed him with a gesture.

Tan had felt a tingling, like a sizzling across his skin, with the shaping.

Roine closed his eyes and Tan again felt the steady buildup of energy quickly released, spreading out from them in a wave. Roine listened for long moment.

"There are several others near," Roine started, and then closed his eyes again. A low and steady rumbling began again, building like rolling thunder, far down the hill from them. A few pained cries followed. Roine's mouth turned in a satisfied smile. "That should buy us a little more time."

As they continued, Tan suspected each shaping taxed Roine more and more. He'd seen how weakened Amia had been with just a single shaping. Roine did several, each enough to trigger a landslide. What would happen if they encountered one of the lisincend? Would Roine still have strength to face it?

"I don't think we can continue much farther like this," Amia whispered in his ear.

Was there a sag to Roine's shoulders that wasn't there before? Tan wasn't certain. They paused several more times and each time Tan felt the building pressure before it was released, followed by the low rumble of another rockslide. Roine was slowly eliminating the hounds chasing them, but each time he grew weaker.

Did Roine spend himself too soon? Even if he did, what other choice did they have?

By midday, the clouds thickened and darkened. Thunder started from the north, rolling toward them. With it came a heavy wind. Roine looked up to the sky, staring at it as if expecting something more than rain that never came, before shaking his head.

Not long after, lightning struck. It repeated, loud crackles that fried the air followed by sharp claps of thunder. Roine closed his eyes and Tan felt the building pressure, more quickly this time and not as strong as earlier in the day. When it was released, it was directed up the mountain face, pressing out before fading.

Roine listened for long moments before snapping his eyes open. "Off the path! Now!"

Tan didn't argue. They hurried into the light underbrush of the forest. Their horses had to move slower to avoid the tangles and roots, but were able to pick up speed across the level ground.

As he wondered what Roine feared, a wave of heat answered his question. His eyes and mouth went dry. His skin felt boiled and tight.

Roine kicked his horse forward, moving in front of Tan. He held his hand out before him. A gust of wind pressed forward, sweeping through the forest.

One of the lisincend stood before them. The creature was horrible and immense, and radiated heat like a raging fire. A smile pulled at its lipless mouth and what Tan saw of the thick and scaled hide seemed as if it was peeling away. Its tongue lashed out quickly as it smiled at them. The creature wore dark black leather. No…that wasn't quite right. Rather, the leather was so red that it appeared black, the shirt and pants pulled tight across the creature's muscular frame.

"Theondar," it hissed. "The girl. That is all. Then you may live."

Roine eyed the creature for a moment. "That's all you want? Then you will leave my kingdoms?"

Tan's heart raced at Roine's words. Would he give Amia to the lisincend? Tan wouldn't allow it, realizing it a moment before hearing the echoing command in his head.

*Protect me.*

Amia clung tightly to him, trying to hide within the folds of his cloak.

"Your kingdoms? You are king now?" The lisincend laughed, a dry crackle. "You have always wanted to rule Theondar."

Roine shook his head. "You have no idea what I desire, Fur. I would like to know how you penetrated the kingdoms."

The lisincend appeared to smile again. "You would."

Roine frowned and the lisincend crackled again with the strange sound that could only be laughter. "I can't hand over the girl."

The lisincend hissed again. "Give me the girl. Now."

"Leave. Now." Energy sizzled with the words, though nothing like Amia's commands.

"Then you will die. And I will still have her."

It raised its arm and a torrent of flame shot from its arm. Roine was ready and brought his own arm up. A surge of water shot as if from his palm. Roine raised his other fist, bringing it down, and the ground rumbled, nearly splitting at the feet of the lisincend. The creature started to stumble, righted itself, and then laughed again.

"Weak, Theondar," the lisincend hissed. "You spent too much on my hounds. And you have barely injured them." A chorus of howls cried out in answer.

Tan felt power building moments before he felt the heat that came with it. Roine's eyes grew wide as he realized what the lisincend prepared.

He had been played.

He thrust one hand in front of him and another toward Tan and Amia. There was a surge of energy, much stronger than any Tan had felt before, building to a near ear-splitting level of pain. It stabbed into his skull like a knife.

The pressure built until he could no longer take the pressure and pain.

He felt it behind his eyes, through his head, and under his skin. It built so quickly that he trembled with the energy, more afraid than ever.

He prayed for some kind of release.

Roine looked over to him. "Hold on to Amia!"

Tan spun, grabbing onto Amia and hugging her. Her body shook and he felt her fear in his mind with the silent command to protect her.

He did not see the explosion.

Tan felt the release of pressure and pain within him like a dam bursting, then heard something loud, a horrible roar, followed by screaming. It was only later he realized it had been him screaming, yelling as he was thrown in the air, caught in a torrent of wind up and over trees and forest, holding Amia as they flew across the sky, propelled by the immense blast.

There was another surge of energy, something foreign and powerful, that caught him, leaving his skin tingling and his ears pulsing with its thunderous energy. It pulled upon them, streaking them higher and farther across the forest, and they sped like a loosed arrow. The wind howled around them. Droplets of glistening water formed on his arms and eyes and he blinked to clear his vision as they streaked through the air.

Then they were coming down. The ground flew up to meet them. Amia met his eyes, a mixture of fear and acceptance written upon her face. Both knew that there was no way they could survive the landing.

Then they crashed through trees and brush. The ground came up quickly and they landed with a splash.

# CHAPTER 23
## *Place of Convergence*

TAN AWOKE SLOWLY. He rested against the trunk of a tree and his back ached from the position. His head throbbed, a slow pulsing, and he closed his eyes again, hoping it would help. Pain stretched everywhere in his body and he worked his legs and arms, slowly realizing that nothing was broken.

Opening his eyes, he saw the lake where they had landed. A green film covered the water and his prints led from the water's edge toward the tree. When had he crawled out of the water? Massive trees, huge roots curling up out of the water, lined most of the lake. Farther down the shore it turned rocky. Stretches of sandy beach interrupted the rocks. A small mountain peak rose up at the far end of the lake.

Amia lay next to him, still breathing but not awake. Tan let her rest and stood carefully to investigate, feeling a wobbling dizziness as he did. At least he still had his bow, though water had seeped through and it would need time to dry. And he still had his hunting knife. Better than nothing.

Near the lake, a small feeder stream flowed slowly enough that the water was still clear. He drank thirstily. The encounter with the lisincend had dried his mouth, and he worked his tongue over his lips to moisten them. Tan sighed as he finished drinking, standing again. Still lightheaded, at least he was a little better and able to stand without holding his hands out for balance.

The lake was set into a small valley in the mountain. Tan didn't recognize anything around him. How far had they been thrown?

Or pulled? The vague memory of another energy pulling on them echoed in his mind.

What he should do now? Wait for Amia to awaken, but then what? Roine had convinced him of the need to find the artifact. If nothing else, Incendin couldn't be granted the power Roine thought it possessed.

But how could he do that? Follow Amia's shaping? Without Roine's compass, would it even work?

Or did they wait for Roine? If anyone could survive the blast of energy from the lisincend, one of the warriors could.

As he walked along the shore of the lake, he stopped. They couldn't wait for Roine. This task was his now. Somehow, in spite of everything, he still had to serve the king.

But the alternative—letting Incendin pass easily into the kingdoms—was not acceptable. War would return. Other towns might end up like Nor or Velminth. How many would die?

He closed his eyes and let his focus wander, sensing the forest around him. There was no unusual sound in the forest. There was the underlying buzz and hum of the late summer insects. He heard the quiet burbling of the stream and smelled the pungent algae growing within the lake. Somewhere far in the distance, a lone wolf howled plaintively, a reassuring sound, though Tan sensed that it was very far away. A circling hawk cried overhead before it fell silent. There was a rustle of the wind through the leaves of the trees, cool and steady across his face as well, and the air smelled of crisp pine.

All of this felt reassuring.

Over everything, he felt the shaping Amia had made. It was clear and bright within his mind, like a streamer of light pointing up the nearest peak. He wondered again how it was that he saw it.

He made his way back to Amia. She had sat up and looked around, eyes touching on the lake and the mountain in the distance.

"What happened?" she asked.

Tan shook his head. "I'm not entirely sure. Roine did something and then we were here." He motioned around him. "Wherever this is."

"I remember an explosion."

"There was that," Tan agreed, laughing softly. "And something else. Do you remember landing?"

She looked at him with her dark eyes and frowned. "No. Why?"

Tan laughed quietly again. "Your body will remember for you."

"That's why I am so sore?" Amia looked at him. Pressure built behind his ears, the sign of a sensing or a shaping. "You're uncertain." Amia placed a hand on his arm. "But that's not all. You blame yourself. You think the hounds followed you to Nor."

"No secrets from you?" he asked and Amia smiled. "They followed my scent. I know I couldn't help it, but if I hadn't tracked them into the forest, would they have come after Nor?"

"You lost everyone."

"So did you."

A pained look pulled at her face. "We've been chased away before. As Aeta, we come to expect that. But what Incendin did…what the lisincend did to my people…the Mother…"

"I'm sorry."

"Why? If not for you, I'd be dead too. What you did gave me a chance."

"If we don't find this…artifact, it won't be much of a chance."

"You'll go on without Roine?" Amia asked.

"What choice do we have? If we do nothing, everyone suffers. If we try—"

"Then we might suffer."

Tan laughed. Considering everything they'd been through, it seemed they'd already suffered enough. "Better that then watching when we could've helped."

"That's not your real reason. Not all of it."

Tan sighed. How could he put words to why he wanted to make sure Roine's task was completed? Amia touched his arm and a wave of relief washed over him. Tan wondered if he'd been shaped, but didn't really care. "Since my father died, my mother has wanted me to go to Ethea."

"The university?"

Tan nodded. "You know of it?"

Amia breathed out softly. "Mother always tried to avoid Ethea. She was afraid one of the shapers there would recognize my…gift. You have to understand, not visiting Ethea creates challenges for my people. The trading is always good at the heart of your kingdoms, the prices better than we can get anywhere else, and there are things we just can't trade for anyplace else. Not visiting Ethea was a sacrifice made for me."

"Did your people resent you for it?"

Amia smiled. "They understood the reasons. And we followed the Mother where she led. I can't say I wouldn't like to visit Ethea some day.

I've heard the palace is breathtaking. Shaped by your earth shapers in such a way that can't be replicated by masons."

Tan shook his head. "I wouldn't know."

"You don't want to visit?"

Tan hesitated before answering. "My place isn't in Ethea. My place is…was…in Nor." He looked around. "I'm an earth senser like my father. It's not a skill with much use anywhere else." He didn't say anything about not wanting to serve the king. Not as his father had served. Still, he suspected Amia knew anyway.

"Then why do this?"

Tan looked over at the distant mountain. "It's the last thing my mother asked of me."

Amia squeezed his hand and they sat there for a long while. "It's out there," she said. "I feel it, trailing into the mountain. Closer than before."

Tan could practically see the shaping, it pulled so strongly on him. "Will you help?"

"What else can I do? At least this way I can do something to stop Fur."

Tan felt relief that she would help and pulled her to her feet. "Are you ready or do you need to rest longer?"

She forced a smile. "Resting will only let the pain set in more. Better to move."

They circled around the lake, following the shore, and moved through soft leaves and detritus. All the recent rain had made the ground soggy and Tan led them away from the shore, toward the trees. Though they didn't gain any speed, he no longer felt as if the ground was trying to suck him under with each step. The lake was much longer than it was wide, filling much of this part of the valley, and fed by several small streams running down from the mountains.

"There's a lot of water around here," he said as they stepped through another small stream.

"Do you know where we are?"

"South and east of Velminth," he said. That much he'd determined. "Other than that, I can't say. I'm not certain we're still in Galen."

Tan kept expecting to see the edge of the lake as they continued forward but did not. Amia pointed them down the lake. The white-tipped mountains never seemed nearer. The clouds managed to block the sun and they traveled by an overcast light. After everything they'd seen, the dour day fit his mood.

After a time, a distant howl rang out from the forest. He froze, tensing with the sound. It was the unmistakable cry of one of the Incendin hounds.

"If they reach the valley…we won't be able to outrun them," Tan said.

"And if there are hounds…" Amia began.

They ran.

Had the air grown warmer? A breeze blew through the valley and across the lake, but had it not been a cool wind? The sky was darkening and the cloud cover made it difficult for him to gauge the time, but he suspected night was coming.

There was another howl, nearer now, and they froze, looking in the direction of the sound, before starting forward at a run. The wet ground slowed them.

"We have to move into the trees," Amia said.

"Stay near the water," Tan said. "Lisincend. Fire shapers." He knew little of shaping, but he knew how sensing was paired. "Fire is tempered by water. Earth by wind." He struggled for a few more steps to catch his breath. "Safest by water."

Thick mud and muck clung to their legs as they slogged forward. The harsh cry of the hounds continued to echo through the forest, growing strangely muted as the sound passed across the valley. With each howl, the hounds closed on them.

"We aren't going to outrun them," Tan said.

He reached for his knife before thinking better of it and placing it back in its sheath. Instead, he unslung his bow and pulled a few arrows from his quiver. Though wet, he hoped the fletching had dried enough for the arrows to fly true.

Tan looked at Amia. Her face was blank but her eyes flashed with her determination. "We need to slow—" he began. A loud sound almost directly in front of them cut him off.

A dark shape stood outlined against the trees one hundred paces in front of them. The large creature stalked forward, hackles raised, and it growled again.

Tan didn't think. He raised his bow, sighted, and released. The arrow flew true, striking the hound under its chin. It took a step, cried out weakly, and fell. Tan readied another arrow as Amia grabbed his arm and pulled him forward.

A chorus of howling sounded off to their left, loud and growing louder. Tan listened and counted at least three distinct cries. His grip upon his bow tensed. Amia pulled him along toward a large rock cluster that loomed in the distance.

"If we're to make a stand," he said, pointing to the rocks. It would be as good as any and still near the water.

As they reached the rocks, Tan spun, sensing something close. One of the hounds leapt from the shadows, directly at Amia. Tan released his nocked arrow and it caught the hound between the eyes. The creature fell limp nearly at Amia's feet. Without thinking, Tan grabbed it and slung it out into the lake. It sank with a strange hissing sound.

Two more creatures slid forward from under the cover of the trees, low growls in their throats. They moved more cautiously than the others. A light haziness surrounded them, much like with the lisincend. It reminded him of when he'd been treed after tracking them. A steady heat radiated from them as well.

He fired an arrow toward the nearest creature and heard a low cry, but was not certain that his arrow had struck true. The haze was difficult to see through. Tan reached into his quiver and pulled out his remaining arrows. His stomach dropped as he realized only three remained.

A streak of movement shot toward them. He drew and fired. A satisfying *thump* came as the arrow struck home. The hound howled and went down thrashing, kicking mud and dirt at them as it fell.

Tan turned away, blocking Amia from its death throes. He barely saw the other hound as it leapt toward them.

With no time to nock an arrow, he grabbed his knife and swung it at the hound, slicing it beneath its throat. Warm blood sprayed down his arm. The hound fell to the ground and crawled away. When it touched water, steam rose from it.

Amia shivered near him. "Two arrows left."

The air temperature had risen sharply. No wind blew. Through the trees, Tan heard another low rumbling growl, followed by another. It was not the hounds prowling the forest that he feared.

He feared the lisincend that had arrived with them.

"Lisincend," he whispered.

There came a low, dry laugh, starting like the rustling of leaves, and rising to a loud hiss. "Yes," a strange voice said. "You are right to feel fear. Now. Where is the girl?"

"There's no girl here," Tan answered.

The lisincend laughed again. "I smell her. And her fear. Give her to me."

Tan shook his head as he answered. "No."

The lisincend laughed again. "You have been surprising, boy, but you cannot hope to defy me any longer."

Amia gripped his arm. Tan glanced over. "Run," he mouthed.

She released his sleeve and he stepped forward, hoping to block the lisincend from seeing her. "You're Fur?"

The lisincend hissed. "I am Fur."

"Where is Theondar?" Tan demanded.

"Theondar?" it asked, its dry voice cracking over the name. "Theondar troubles me no longer. And neither will you."

Tan felt the energy building around the lisincend and knew he should be more afraid than he was, knew that he had only moments remaining. Yet instead of fear, he felt anger. The lisincend had attacked his home. Had killed his friends. And had taken his mother from him.

And under all of that, he heard the soft command, Amia's shaping from the night, which now seemed so long ago.

*Protect me.*

Tan could do nothing else except try.

He raised his bow, letting his senses stretch out, sensing the forest around him and listening. He knew where the lisincend stood and fired quickly, grabbing his remaining arrow and loosing it as well. The arrows whistled and hissed through the air before striking.

Tan felt the lisincend begin its shaping, felt the enormous power it used. Time seemed to slow. The hairs on his arm stood on end and sweat dripped from his face as the heat in the air surged. The lisincend began to glow with a reddish light. Whatever it was shaping was more powerful than anything he had seen before.

Had he given Amia enough time? He dared not turn to look, watching the lisincend with morbid fascination, knowing he would soon die. Pressure built like he'd felt with shapings before, but this was different.

His head started pounding and a whistling sound whooshed behind his ears. All of this he sensed with a curious detachment.

Streamers of flame burst all around him, leaping from the ground and stretching high into the sky, slowly encircling him. Tan saw this and stepped back, raising his hands instinctively. The wind whipped around him, a cool blast from out over the lake, making the flames flicker and dance though not disappear. Fire pushed back, surging more powerfully, and he took another halting step backward.

The whooshing in his ears increased and it was all he heard, drowning the crackle of the flames and the low, dry laugh of the lisincend, covering even the deep, rumbling growl he felt from the nearby hounds.

Tan wanted to scream. Everything they had been through, everything they had seen, and now he would lose. Amia still wouldn't be safe.

There came another surge of wind, blowing spray off the lake toward the lisincend. As it mixed with the flames, steam and smoke sizzled away. Still the flames pressed Tan backward. His foot touched water and he sunk, losing his balance, and faltered. Now daring to glance over at the rocks, he looked for Amia and saw her staring at him, her eyes wide and fearful. She had not run as he had asked.

"Stop!" she commanded.

Her words hummed with energy, and Tan froze, unable to do anything except obey her. The flames in front of Tan flickered and faded and the glow around the lisincend went from bright orange to reddish to a dark glow.

"Leave us!" Amia yelled.

Her words were a thunderclap and not to be ignored. The energy behind them rivaled what the lisincend channeled.

One of the hounds hiding within the forest whined. Another

ceased growling and simply howled. The lisincend looked from Tan over to Amia. And then laughed.

"Impressive. Though I cannot be so easily swayed." It started toward Amia. "You will be useful," it hissed. Raising an arm, it sent a blast of heat toward Tan.

Tan was not prepared for it, could not have prepared for it.

The heat hit him like a hammer, throwing him up and into the air, tossing him roughly into the water. Pain burned across his chest and through him, eating through his flesh. He smelled himself burning as he struck the water. The air had been sucked from his lungs and he couldn't cry out.

As he sank, he saw a last glimmer of Amia, saw sadness written upon her face, then he faded into the darkness of the water.

# CHAPTER 24
## *A Lesser Elemental*

TAN DIDN'T AWAKEN, NOT TRULY.

Water flowed around him yet he had the sensation he was sinking. Something told him not to take a breath and he obeyed, though not really sure why. The water was cool and strangely comforting. He drifted, slowly lowering to the soft bed of the lake, before sinking into the sand. It swirled around his arms and legs, holding him gently.

Distantly, he was aware of movement around him. At first it was a simple fluttering, a soft ripple in the water around his face, but it increased in strength and urgency.

Tan opened his eyes and looked around. Somehow he breathed, yet did not. He couldn't explain it, knowing only that he did not feel the urge to take a breath. Still his chest moved slowly as if he did. The water was murky, dark, and shimmered with a faint light only visible along the floor of the lake, like stars in the night sky.

He was dreaming. Or dying. Tan didn't know and was no longer sure that he cared.

The rippling water around him ceased and he turned his head, looking for whatever had caused it. Slowly, he became aware of a soft pressure in his ears, now familiar, and wondered who was shaping nearby. This was different, though, a more gentle shaping, a slow build-up, and without the threat of pain like he'd felt so often before.

Something swam past his face, translucent and moving quick-ly. Tan couldn't see what it was, having only a sense of great size. He struggled to move but his arms were stuck in the sand and his legs didn't move. Only his head and neck were his own. The movement came again, flitting past him, more slowly this time, and a trail of glow-ing pale green slid past.

A fish? An eel? Tan didn't know what creatures called these deep mountain lakes home, and this one was larger than most, fed by count-less springs. What else could swim past him, taunting him as he died?

He should feel fear, should be concerned about this strange crea-ture swimming around him and the fact that he couldn't move, but all he felt was a sense of peace and serenity.

And then a face appeared in front of him.

Not that of a man or any other animal he had ever seen. Rather, this face seemed formed of the water itself, soft, undulating, and nearly translucent as it shimmered with a faint green. The face flowed with a light energy, hovering in front of him. There was no sign of body, only the face. Only then did he feel the beginnings of nervousness.

The face smiled. *What are you?*

No lips moved, yet the voice was plainly heard, as if spoken in his head. The voice was foreign and gentle yet there was an underlying command to the question. He sensed a shaping similar to what Amia had used upon him.

Tan tried to open his mouth to answer but found he could not. His lips, like nearly every other part of his body, didn't respond to his direction. How, then, could he answer?

*I am Tan*, he thought.

He heard the words clearly. Somehow he knew they carried through the water to the strange creature.

The pressure in his ears piqued gently before easing. It didn't completely disappear.

*What is a Tan?*

*That's my name*, Tan thought, and again the words carried. *How is this possible?*

He hadn't meant to ask the question, only thinking the words, but his thoughts carried like words.

*A name?* It seemed to smile. *Then you are human.*

Tan nodded. *Of course.* It came out quickly, unintentionally, and Tan shook his head. *What are you?*

The creature appeared to smile. *I? Not I. Nymid.*

*Nymid? That is your name?*

The creature seemed to smile again. *Not my name.*

Suddenly dozens of faces surrounded Tan, each similar to the first, yet with enough differences that he realized they were distinct creatures. The soft pressure increased painlessly. He realized these creatures were shaping.

How was this happening? Was he dreaming? If he dreamt, how did he breathe?

The first nymid smiled again. *Breathe?*

*Humans require air*, another of the creatures answered.

Tan looked but could not tell which spoke, though wondered if it mattered. The nymid communicated with thought and what one thought, they all heard.

*What are nymid?*

Tan felt a sense almost like a smile and then there came the sense of fluttering all around.

*Nymid are water.*

Water. Did that mean they were elementals?

Most knew so little about the elementals, only that they existed. How else to explain sensing and shaping? Yet he'd never known anyone to actually speak to them. How could he do it now?

He tried moving his arms but, stuck as he was in the sand, he could not. *Why can't I move?*

*You were injured*, one of the nymid said.

Tan looked down but could see nothing of the rest of his body, only the soft sand that covered him. He remembered the blast, the force of the heat that hit him like a physical weapon, and the brief excruciating pain as his flesh burned from him.

He should not have survived.

The soft pressure in his ears told him the nymid had saved him. Were still saving him.

*Why help me?*

The nymid's face lost the smile and for the first time, Tan felt something other than peace from the creature. A subtle agitation came from the creature, from all of them. The softly glowing light surrounding the creatures flickered quickly and Tan sensed that they communicated in other ways.

*I'm sorry*, he thought quickly, feeling a surge of fear. *But I don't understand why you would help me.*

The flickering lights around the creatures slowed and the first nymid smiled slightly. *Twisted Fire. You oppose Twisted Fire and help the Daughter.*

Tan didn't fully understand. *Twisted Fire?* he asked as realization came to him. *The lisincend.* He pictured the creature with the thought. There was a slight shimmering in the water near Tan and the image of the lisincend appeared, hazy but there.

The nymid turned to the picture and a long-fingered arm appeared and wiped the image away, leaving nothing but ripples and a glowing trail in the water. *Twisted Fire,* it agreed. *Fire is natural, is part of the world, exists with it, like water,* it said, waving its arm through the water as it spoke. *Twisted Fire is unnatural and should not be.*

*And the hounds?* They seemed to share some of the same traits as the lisincend, able to hide themselves in a smoky haze much like the lisincend. Were they born of fire as well?

The water rippled into the shape of one of the hounds before slowly disappearing. *Like Twisted Fire, they are unnatural.* The other nymid faded then, gradually growing more and more translucent until they were but a trail of faint glowing green.

The first nymid remained, staring at him as if waiting, though Tan had no idea what it would be waiting for.

*And the Daughter?*

The nymid did not respond but did not need to. Tan suddenly understood.

*Amia?*

*The Great Mother's hand rests upon her.*

The nymid waved a thin arm through the water again, soft glowing ripples following it, and another image formed, this time of Amia held bound and gagged, with a ring of fire around her like a cage. Trapped and captured by the lisincend. One of the hounds rested nearby, watching her.

*You must help the Daughter. Twisted Fire must be cleansed from the land.*

*They are too powerful for me. This happened,* he started, thinking of

186

his injuries, *the last time I faced them.*

He could barely sense his arms and legs trapped beneath the sand. Even if he were able to move, there was nothing he could do against one of the lisincend. The creatures were powerful. He had nothing like their ability.

The nymid stretched its long glowing arm toward Tan and touched him on the forehead with a thin, faintly glowing finger. A warmth seeped into his head, just under the skin, and worked its way around his neck and down, through his chest and into his buried arms and legs. A surge of energy flooded through him. He would have gasped had he been able to open his mouth to do so.

There was something familiar about their presence, their energy. Tan could not quite place what it was, but recognized it.

Unbidden, the memory of Roine's blast and their flight over the trees came to mind. He recalled the energy that had seemed to pull at them, guiding them.

*You?*

The nymid did not answer. There was only a flittering of movement, more imagined than real. Instead, the nymid turned to him. *You must help the Daughter.*

The sand of the lakebed eased and relaxed and his arms were freed. Something squeezed him from below and he was pushed free, oozing forward. As he was released, he looked down at his chest. A large burn had torn his shirt, leaving much of the cloth singed. The skin underneath that should have been burned was instead unmarked.

The water began to buoy him forward, lifting him out of the water. Tan turned to the nymid that had started to fade.

*Thank you.*

The nymid smiled. *There is no need for thanks. The Mother smiles upon you, as well.* There was only a trace of the nymid remaining, a faint glow. *You will see*, it whispered.

Then Tan broke the surface of the water. The night was dark and the clouds hung low and thick, illuminated by a faint glowing across the water. At first he felt nothing, then a sharp burning began in his chest, tearing through him with a pain unlike anything he had known. Had the healing the nymid worked upon him failed? Had it all only been a dream?

Yet when he looked down, he saw his skin unmarked. He heard a soft voice, like a whisper, come up from beneath him, and he strained against the pain in his chest to hear.

*Breathe.*

And he understood. After his time under the water, he had forgotten to breathe.

Tan opened his mouth and took a deep and painful breath, like a newborn baby taking its first gasp of air. Cool air entered his lungs. Slowly the pain subsided, fading until it was gone. Tan scissored his legs as he reacquainted himself with the concept of breathing, and his body relaxed.

Tan was able to take stock of where he was. Somehow, he had been thrown far into the lake, practically into the middle. He swam, careful not to make too much noise. He needed to reach Amia, the force of her shaping still compelling him.

Tan scanned the shoreline, searching for what the nymid had shown. Across the faintly glowing water, he saw a nearly identical scene. At the edge of the forest, as far away from the lake that it could be, streamers of flame stretched from the ground nearly twenty feet into the air, staggered only a hand's width apart and forming a fiery cage. Within the cage Amia hunched, hugging her legs, her head down. Tan did not need to see her hands to know they were tied, nor her mouth to know she was gagged.

Outside the cage of fire sat one of the hounds, larger than any Tan had seen before. The beast sat watching Amia. Even from his distance, the hound's eyes carried a dark intelligence. There was no sign of the lisincend, but Tan knew it must be near.

*Protect me.*

The words rang needlessly through his head. Amia looked up suddenly, her dark eyes staring out toward the water. Was it his imagination, or did they widen?

She shook her head slowly, as if warning him away, then looked back down toward her feet.

The hound near her growled softly. The sound carried across the water, a throaty rumble. It stood and sniffed the air and Tan ducked under the cover of the lake, fearful the hound could smell him.

He stayed underwater, swimming slowly toward the shore, carefully coming up only long enough to catch a quick breath before diving down again. He was able to hold his breath longer than he remembered, though wasn't sure whether that was real or imagined. The light from the cage of fire was visible even underwater as Tan made his way toward the flames, toward Amia, still unsure how he would rescue her alone.

The water gradually became shallower. Now he could touch the bottom of the lake. The ground was different than the sand that held him under. Strands of thick green vines grew from the bottom, sending soft fingers toward the surface. The faint green glowing of the water he'd seen was no longer visible.

Tan peeked over the surface of the water, barely enough to get his eyes and his nose above the surface, and took a deep, slow breath. The air was much warmer here. Somewhere nearby the lisincend waited.

The bright light from the flames making up Amia's prison made it hard for him to see anything else. He closed his eyes and took a deep

189

breath, stretching his awareness, sensing the forest as his father had taught him long ago. The warm air smelled of char and soot. There was no real movement in the night, no animals or wind or even insects; yet Tan did feel something where nothing had been seen before. A void, an emptiness that should not be.

*They are unnatural.*

He heard the words echoed in his mind, like a whisper, or a memory of a whisper. Tan shivered, knowing the truth to the nymid's words. Opening his eyes, he focused on the spot where he had sensed the void, peering through the darkness and the distracting bright light of the fire. There he saw a dark smudge different than the surrounding darkness.

Tan squinted in an attempt to block the firelight. Pressure built in his ears. A cool breeze blew in from the lake, and Tan took a deep breath, savoring the change. Where the air hit the dark haze hiding the lisincend, the veil shimmered and lifted, if only briefly. Three lisincend stood near the cage of fire. Two spoke to each other while the third stared toward the ring of fire and Amia, as if holding her prison in place. Fur stood larger than the others, taller and wider.

Fur suddenly stopped, twisting and looking out over the water, and sniffed. "He is here." His words were dry, like tearing parchment.

Tan froze and slipped back under the water, fearful that he'd been discovered. Holding his breath, he peered through the water and out toward the lisincend. He could do nothing for Amia if he was captured.

"Where?"

The question was muffled as the word carried out over the water and down toward him. Tan heard a rumble of thunder and could almost feel it as it echoed through the valley.

"Out there," Fur answered. "I can smell his shaping."

Shaping? Not him then, but worse. Someone else.

What else would the lisincend be sensing? What shaper did they expect?

Tan tilted his head back, barely enough to get his mouth out of the water to take a breath. A loud crack of lightning came and was quickly followed by a long peal of thunder. Light split the sky, and Tan looked at the lisincend. Their attention remained on the clouds.

"He will be displeased," one of the lisincend hissed.

Fur laughed. "He is always displeased."

Another blast of lightning followed his words, nearer this time.

"At least we have the girl."

Fur laughed again and it was a frightening sound. "She lives," he agreed. "For now."

The first raindrops hit the surface of the water softly but growing harder, sharper, and building to a downpour. The pressure in his ears had built again and held steady, piercing painfully through his head. A powerful shaping was taking place.

One of the lisincend snarled. "He knows not to come with the rain."

Fur grunted, then stopped, peering into the dark sky and watching as the rain came toward them, growing more violent as it did. The air around the lisincend hissed and sizzled, and steam rose from the creatures where the water struck their skin. The strange fiery cage still burned, and Amia remained trapped inside her hot prison.

"He would not," Fur said. Heat surged from the lisincend and the air around it popped, turning the rain into a hot blanket of steam.

"He has before."

Fur turned to the other. His angry eyes seemed like candles flickering. "Only when there was no other way."

"What then?"

Fur hissed. The sound carried his anger and rage and the night surged again with heat as he did. Tan sensed it clearly from the protection of the water, and felt a swell of its fear.

"Theondar."

# CHAPTER 25
## *Twisted Fire*

TAN LOOKED UP TO THE DARKENING SKY. Though he saw nothing but the sheeting rain and darkness above him, his heart leapt in his chest with sudden hope.

The lisincend had said Theondar.

How could Roine have survived the lisincend attack?

Thunder rumbled through the valley in response.

He held his head low and walked along the lake, inching slowly toward where Amia was imprisoned. The hound guarding her paced around the flames, looking from Amia to the night, sniffing the air as it did and growling low in its throat. The streamers of flame stretching from the ground sizzled with the downpour, not weakening even as the rain came harder.

Another crackle of lightning split the sky, followed by the loudest peal of thunder yet. Rain sluiced down and Tan ducked under the water for protection. As he did, a blast of lightning streaked toward the lisincend. It struck the ground in an explosion of earth and water.

Tan pushed his head out of the water and rubbed his eyes. A painful scream, like the splintering of a falling tree, tore through the night as another explosion spewed rocks and spray toward the lisincend.

Theondar?

Was this a warrior in his fury?

Tan needed to reach Amia. Whatever was happening would provide enough of a distraction. If he could slip past the hound, he might reach her.

Another explosion crashed through the night. The lisincend sent blasts of flame and waves of heat at something unseen. The night grew bright with the fury of their attack. Smoke rose from the flames to cover everything in twisting shadows, like the veil of the lisincend.

With his focus on the lisincend attack, Tan almost didn't see the hound.

It had prowled close to the water, spying him. It sat back on its haunches to stay clear of the water and swiped a long paw at Tan's face. Wickedly sharp claws whistled too close, almost shaving the surface of his cheek.

He dropped below the surface of the water and grabbed his hunting knife. Determination rolled through him. He had to get rid of the hound to reach Amia.

Tan broke the surface of the water and launched himself forward, the knife held outstretched in his hand. The hound pranced back and Tan landed awkwardly on the ground, nearly at its feet. It surged forward, teeth bared, lunging for his throat.

Tan rolled wildly, struggling to keep his knife in front of him. He came to his feet just as the hound pounced.

Dropping low, Tan hoped to have the hound leap over him, but the hound had timed its jump well. Sharp claws dug painfully into his back as it passed over him, roaring in his ears as it jumped past his head. The hound's breath smelled of a fetid rot, hot upon his face. Tan stabbed with his knife, frantic. He had less chance of survival the longer the hound attacked.

A pained cry erupted from the hound. The burning on Tan's back eased.

He spun, clutching tightly to his knife, now slippery with hot blood. The hound backed from him a few steps, the hackles upon its back raised. A long gash along its side oozed blood that steamed as it struck the ground.

The short tail twitched once. Then the hound growled and jumped.

This time, it was not as well timed. Tan turned, thrusting his knife into the hound's belly as it jumped. He pushed it out and over him, toward the water of the lake.

The hound cried as it struck the water, which bubbled as the hound sank slowly, thrashing and howling wildly.

Tan watched until the beast was no longer visible, fearful that it would spring forward once more. It never did.

He turned to Amia. Pain tore through his back where the hound had gashed his flesh. Warmth and wetness different from the rain ran down his back. Tan ignored the injury. He'd taken too long with the hound. How much longer would the lisincend be distracted?

Amia hunched inside the fiery cage. The rain didn't seem able to penetrate the cage and she remained dry. Heat unlike anything Tan had ever experienced radiated from the flames and he struggled to near but was pressed back. If he couldn't pass through the cage, there would be no way he could save her.

"Amia!"

She looked up, a lost and sad expression upon her face. Her eyes were distant, slowly focusing on him. Shaking her head, she spit out the gag. "Tan? How...?"

"There isn't time. Roine attacked the lisincend. I need to get you out of here."

She looked over toward the lisincend, knowing immediately where they were. "You can't," she said. "This can only be brought down by one of the lisincend. I think Fur himself holds the cage."

"I need to try!"

Amia shook her head and turned away from him. Her head dropped and she didn't move.

Taking a careful step forward, he couldn't do more than that. The heat from the flames pressed him away from the bars of flame, away from Amia.

How could she tolerate the heat, sitting within the center of it all?

Tan paced to the water's edge, looking for something—anything—to extinguish the flames of the cage. He needed to act quickly.

As he kneeled at the edge of the lake, a faint glowing ran along the shore. He had seen the same glowing earlier, near the nymid. Desperation made him wonder if they could help.

Letting his mind grow blank, he stretched out his senses, not knowing what he would need to reach the water creatures, but he had to try. Tan tried to ignore everything around him: the chaos of the explosions, the crackle of the nearby flames, the pulsating heat threatening to overwhelm him. All of it he pushed out of his mind.

Slowly, hesitantly, he pressed out with his thoughts, remembering like a dream what it had felt like when he had communicated with the nymid. A soft pressure built in his ears and remained.

*Nymid.* He sent the thought out as a request, focusing a pleading note to the thought. *I need your help to save the Daughter.*

Tan kept his eyes closed, listening intently, afraid that the noise around him would make him miss any communication from the nymid.

196

Nothing came. There was only silence within his head.

He opened his eyes and looked out over the water. In spite of the down-pouring rain disturbing the surface, there remained a soft glow toward the middle of the lake, faint and pale and almost imagined. Had Tan not had the memory of his time underwater surrounded by the nymid, he would think nothing of the glowing light. As he stared, the light moved slowly, swimming and undulating almost purposefully through the water.

Tan fixed his focus upon the glowing water, praying quickly to the Great Mother that the nymid would hear him. He had no other idea how to save Amia.

He stretched out his focus toward the light, listening and sensing as his father had taught him, sending his awareness far across the water. Vaguely, he had a distant sense of vertigo. Tan pressed that away, as well.

*Nymid! I need your help!*

Tan staggered back, exhausted from everything he had been through. The night around him swam and he slumped to the muddy ground, sinking into the muck.

*He Who is Tan.*

Tan heard the words distantly, an echo in the back of his mind. He looked up, bringing his eyes into focus as he tried to stare at the surface of the water.

The soft glowing light swam toward him, slipping through the water as if unaffected by the pouring rain. Slowly, the light neared, and Tan felt his strength gradually returning as it did, able to regain his footing and pull himself from the mud as he stood.

*Nymid,* Tan thought again.

They were nearer and it was not as difficult to send the thought as it had been before. Tan felt only a momentary wave of dizziness that passed quickly.

*You called us, He Who is Tan.*

There was a hint of surprise that Tan felt as much as heard in his thoughts. He tried to structure his thoughts in a way the nymid would understand. *I called. I cannot save the Daughter. Twisted Fire has her trapped in such a way I can't rescue her.*

*Twisted Fire*, the nymid repeated. The water around the faint light rippled and formed the figure of the lisincend before smoothing.

Suddenly, the water surged up, forming a figure as if standing atop the water. Tan recognized the figure as one of the nymid, a physical manifestation of the creature. The nymid glowed more brightly than before and eyes formed on the watery face, peering around at the destruction littering the shore where the lisincend still battled Roine before turning to Amia's fiery prison.

*You must save the Daughter.*

Tan looked from Amia to the nymid. *I can't get past the fire.*

The nymid sank back into the water. The pale light swimming slowly in the lake moved closer together, clumping. *We will help.*

An image formed in his mind then and Tan knew what the nymid would do to help, though not how it would help. As he reached toward the water, the light coated his hand in a soft film. Tan took this and rubbed it across his arms and legs, his chest, everywhere on his body, as the nymid directed him.

*What now?*

*Save the Daughter.*

*How?*

*You must trust. The Mother smiles upon you.*

The last seemed more distant. The remainder of the light atop the lake slowly swam away from the shore as the nymid returned to the depths of the lake.

*Save the Daughter*, the nymid whispered again.

The soft light of the nymid on his skin felt like a cool kiss, soft and comfortable. He stepped toward the cage. The flames didn't feel as hot as they had and he was able to move closer than before seeking the nymid.

But how, he wondered, was he to rescue Amia?

Tan took another step closer to the flame, expecting the heat to overwhelm him and push him back. Instead, he was able to move easily, as if the soft nymid light was some sort of armor.

*Trust.*

He stepped forward again, almost to the edge of the fire. He still could tolerate the heat, if only barely.

*Trust.*

Then he stepped through the fire.

Tan expected to be burned, or worse—blown back and away from the prison—yet he moved through the flames unharmed, like a curtain parting.

Amia lay unmoving at the center of the circle of fire. Tan worried he was too late. The air within the circle was hot and dry and burned the inside of his mouth and his throat with each breath he took. Still, the nymid armor held.

Holding his breath, he ran to Amia and picked her up. She did not look up or open her eyes as he hefted her. Tan cradled her carefully in his arms, enveloping her as much as possible to shield her with the nymid armor as he stepped back across the flames. Though Tan felt nothing other than a surge of heat as he crossed, Amia moaned softly under his arms.

He needed to get her away from the lisincend but a feeling, an instinct, made him run toward the lake. A slight residual film of the glowing light remained on the surface. He lowered Amia carefully into the water, keeping her mouth above the surface.

She gasped as her body hit the cool water. Her eyes fluttered open.
*Protect me.*

The thought rang through his mind again, like a tolling bell, and Tan knew he'd done what needed to be done. He lifted her from the water, her clothing dripping and glowing faintly, and ran with her toward the edge of the forest to escape the lisincend.

Once they reached the trees, he paused. A loud explosion rocked the night. Tan held Amia carefully in his arms and looked to see what had caused the explosion.

Not far from him, near where the line of trees thinned and became lakeshore, two of the lisincend lay motionless upon the ground. One was twisted awkwardly; one of the creature's legs had bent underneath it. Or was simply missing. Tan couldn't tell, nor did he care.

That left only Fur standing.

Roine stood before Fur, his face alight and nearly glowing. His hair stood on end. Roine was dressed in the same dark green Tan had first seen him in when meeting in the forest what felt like ages ago, yet something about the clothing seemed different, mystical, and exuded a sense of power.

Roine reached his hands toward the dark sky and clenched them tightly into fists and thrust his closed fists toward Fur. The sky overhead darkened before a huge blast of lightning erupted, shooting straight down toward the ground and striking Fur, throwing him toward the water's edge.

Roine slumped, his shoulders worn and tired. This battle took nearly everything out him.

Fur pulled himself back to his feet, appearing unharmed. He laughed as he stepped toward Roine. "You think to use fire against one of the lisincend?"

Roine smiled then, and though tired, there was a dark malice to the expression. "Only to move you back." Raising his hand again, this time toward the lake, he made a motion, pulling toward him, and the water in the lake surged forward in a wave.

Fur looked over his shoulder, almost casually, and flicked a finger at the water. The water that had surged toward the lisincend turned to hot steam and the rest of the lake withdrew.

Fur laughed again, a hot and dry sound, and looked back to Roine. "Not all of the lisincend fear water, Theondar."

Tan felt the building pressure of the shaping Fur readied, the rising heat the lisincend prepared to blast at Roine. Roine looked tired, nearly too tired to fight back.

Roine closed his eyes, almost as if awaiting his fate, motioning again at the water.

A wave, larger than the first, surged toward Fur. The center of the wave started to glow, flickering brightly, and the wave surged higher and stronger. Fur turned to see the approaching wall of water.

Fur made a sharp movement with his wrist, sending a shaping toward the water, but the power of his blast glanced off the wave and shot into the sky.

The wave struck Fur, washing over him in a loud hiss. Swept from his feet, he went sliding across the muddy ground toward Roine.

Tan heard a satisfied sound deep in the back of his head. *Twisted Fire*, it seemed to say as the water receded.

Roine stood overtop Fur. The lisincend hissed as Roine lifted a booted foot and brought it down quickly, stomping upon the ground. Earth split under his feet. Fur slid into the crack in the earth, screaming a horrible sound. Roine made another quick motion with his hand and the ground closed, sealing overtop the lisincend.

Roine stared at the ground blankly, a mixture of surprise and exhaustion plain on his face. Then he turned and looked at where Tan stood hidden and limped toward him. Roine's face was bloodied and there were a few small tears in the flesh of his cheeks. His peppered hair, though soaked and sodden, stood nearly straight up.

He fell, landing near Tan. "Surprised to see me?"

Tan laughed softly and shook his head. "Surprised…yes. And relieved. But you need rest," Tan told him. After Roine's shapings, he would have to be exhausted.

Roine shook his head and pulled himself to a stand. "We need to keep moving. I was not strong enough to destroy him. That will not hold Fur for long."

Tan dared not argue. Lifting Amia, he carried her as they walked along the edge of the trees, keeping the lake to one side and the forest to their other. She breathed slowly, but regularly. Tan felt relief that she appeared otherwise unharmed.

After a while, the rain eased as they made their way around the edge of the lake. Tan felt Amia's shaping, and followed its pull. When the clouds finally parted, the moon hung fat and bright overhead. When it seemed that neither he nor Roine could continue on, he stopped next to a fallen log to rest.

He struggled against his fatigue to keep his eyes open. As tired as he felt, Roine looked ten times worse. The warrior was barely able to stand, keeping upright by the sheer force of his will. When they stopped, he fell forward to his knees. Tan carefully set Amia down and positioned Roine against the log for protection. They could go no further until they had rested.

Tan sat as well and moved Amia so that her head was atop his lap and gently touched her golden hair. It was soft and in spite of all that she had been through today, still smelled of lavender. The tension in his body began to ease. He would not be able to stay awake much longer.

*Watch over us.* Tan sent his message out and over the lake. He doubted that the nymid would even hear him.

As he drifted to sleep, though, he distantly heard a thought circling in his mind that he should not have been able to hear.

*We will.*

# CHAPTER 26
## *At the Edge of the Lake*

TAN OPENED HIS EYES SLOWLY, squinting against the light of the sun. Roine crouched nearby, tending to a small, crackling fire, roasting something over the flames. Tan's mouth salivated at the thought of fresh meat. He couldn't remember how long it had been since he'd last eaten.

"Good," Roine said. "You're awake."

"How long have you been up?"

Roine shrugged. "Long enough." He frowned at Tan before turning back to tend the fire. "You know, I'm surprised that you're alive."

Tan shrugged, not quite ready to explain the nymid. "I would say the same to you."

Roine laughed. "I'm not killed as easily as Fur would believe."

"And you think Fur survived?"

Roine frowned, setting his hands upon his legs and working his fingers for a moment before answering. "Fur is the oldest, and most powerful, of the lisincend. Perhaps once I could have destroyed him. Perhaps. Now I'm no longer strong enough."

"Why not?"

Roine laughed softly. "There are many answers, probably. The simplest is likely the truest. Strength takes confidence—some would say arrogance—and I'm not the same man."

Tan watched Roine while he rotated the meat over the fire. "Who are you, then?"

Roine looked up and there was a playful smile about his face and reaching his eyes. "I am Roine."

"You mean *roinay*," Tan said, repeating the word as his mother had said it.

Roine smiled again and shrugged, not offering an explanation.

Tan looked out over the lake. The pull of Amia's shaping still drew on him. "What of Theondar?"

"Theondar?" Roine said the name comfortably and with a wistful tone. "He is gone, lost to the world almost two decades ago."

"But *you're* Theondar."

"No," Roine said, his tone firm. "No longer. Once I claimed that name. Once I thought I could shape the world." He shook his head. "Years grant wisdom, I think. Now I'm no longer him. Just Roine. That is enough."

Tan didn't push, though wished he knew more. "The lisincend feared another shaper," Tan said instead, changing topics. "When you came, they thought you were someone else."

Roine turned to him, eyes growing more alert. "How'd you hear this?"

"I was in the water then," he answered. "Moving to try and save Amia. When the wind came in, the lisincend said they smelled someone, smelled the shaping. Then the rain came and they were surprised."

Roine looked to the sky and his eyes went blank. He sat motionless like that for a long moment before opening his eyes again and staring at Tan. The sudden tension that had surged through Roine seemed to ease.

"What did they mean?" Tan asked.

Roine shook his head slowly before answering. "I hadn't expected this. You're certain?"

Tan nodded.

"There have been rumors," Roine began. "A warrior, though not of the kingdoms. One who's never made his alliances known. I've long wondered if he could have sided with Incendin."

A warrior. What was the name he'd read in his mother's book? "You think it's Lacertin?"

Roine's eyes widened. "How is it that you know this name?"

Tan hesitated before answering. "My father," he said. "There were letters he sent my mother. I…I don't think he meant for me to see them."

Roine tilted his head and his face wrinkled. "He mentioned Lacertin in the letters?" he said, speaking the name distastefully.

Tan nodded. He didn't want to say what else the letters said.

Roine fell silent for a moment. And then he sighed. "Once," he began, straightening his back and looking out across the water with a distant expression, "there were twelve of us. Twelve Cloud Warriors. We served the kingdoms as the king commanded. There had not always been this twelve. There had been more, many more, long ago, but something changed. A connection lost. The scholars have never been able to learn why."

He took a deep breath and looked over at Tan. "Lacertin may have been the most powerful. He was certainly the most ambitious. We served the kingdoms, always at the direction of the king. Yet Lacertin did things his own way, defying the king in subtle ways." Roine shook his head. "I suppose we all did to a certain extent. Probably why we overlooked his faults. For they *were* faults.

"And then Genan died. The first of the twelve lost. Lacertin and Genan had been fighting off an invasion of the Talin riders to the south when Genan was lost. Lacertin was never able to fully explain what happened. There were many who wondered, even then. It was only later we realized we should have pressed Lacertin further."

Roine fell silent, his eyes unfocused, as he worked the meat over the flame. After a while, he motioned to Tan and handed him a chunk of steaming meat. Tan took it wordlessly and chewed it slowly, savoring the taste as his stomach rolled with hunger. They ate in silence. Roine saved meat for Amia, who still slept, her breathing slow and easy.

Tan decided to ask the question then, uncertain how Roine would react. But knowing that he was Theondar, he needed to know. "What happened to Ilianna?"

Roine looked away, but there was a pained expression to his eyes, still fresh and raw after all these years. "I had everything to do with her death," he answered softly.

Tan felt shocked. He'd thought Theondar innocent. "Then why did Lacertin leave the city?"

"Lacertin," Roine spat. "We should have exiled him long before." He turned back to face Tan, his eyes welling with restrained tears. "I couldn't protect her. I should have suspected him. I knew he had ambitions, and I should have protected her." He stopped and took a deep breath.

"I'm sorry," Tan said.

Roine looked at him and sighed. "We've all lost much, Tan. Some wounds never fade." He turned to the fire and Tan thought that would be the end of it. "Ilianna didn't have to die. That's the worst part for me. All he wanted was the heirloom."

"What was it?"

Roine shook his head. "Only the women of her family knew. It was passed down through the years. I still don't know why Lacertin wanted it. I've never been able to learn."

"I'm sorry," Tan said again.

Roine offered him a weak smile. "How could you have known? So many years ago, yet I feel it and see it like it was only yesterday. If only I'd been there when he attacked, it might have been different."

"Could you have stopped him?"

Roine shrugged. "Lacertin was always a powerful shaper, perhaps more than Theondar."

"Now?"

Roine shook his head. "I'm no longer that man."

Tan didn't say anything more.

Slowly, Amia started to awaken. She looked up at Tan and met his eyes. "How?"

Tan wasn't sure whether she spoke or whether he heard her question in the same manner he heard the nymid speak. "You're awake."

Amia pushed herself up, propping against the log as she huddled near Tan. She pressed one hand up to her face, brushing the hair away before looking at Tan and seeing his badly damaged shirt hanging in tatters from his chest. "How?" she asked again.

Roine watched them both. He handed the remaining meat to Amia and she took it carefully, smelling it for a long moment before taking a tentative bite.

Roine walked over and sat facing Tan and Amia, staring at him as if suddenly seeing him for the first time. "How did I not notice?" he asked, reaching out and fingering Tan's shirt. A calloused hand brushed the tattered remnants of his shirt away and he looked at Tan's slightly pink chest. "What happened here?"

Amia looked from Tan to Roine, chewing slowly as she did. "I saw the blast Fur aimed at you. You should not have survived."

Roine's eyes widened. "Fur did this?" He leaned and smelled the edges of the shirt. "That should have killed you."

Tan hesitated. For some reason, he was reluctant to speak of the nymid, uncertain they wanted their secret revealed. He suspected that they were water elementals, and powerful enough to heal him. More than that, they had been nothing but helpful, saving his life and providing a means of saving Amia's life, as well.

"Tan? How is it you survived what should have killed you?"

Tan looked from Roine to Amia. She watched with a question in her eyes. He felt a soft pressure and Amia frowned briefly and closed her eyes. When she opened them, she nodded.

Tan looked out toward the water. The soft reflection of the sun almost made it seem to glow. Would the nymid care if he shared their secret? They wanted Amia saved, likely helping him only so that he could rescue her. But how would they feel about Roine knowing about them? Or Theondar?

"I shouldn't have survived," Tan finally said. "I was thrown out into the lake, and sank, and was rescued by creatures of the water."

Roine's face tensed. "What kind of creatures?"

Tan paused, feeling another moment of hesitation. Would the nymid care? If only he could speak to them, could hear how they felt about him sharing their secret. Tan didn't have the energy to try and communicate with them and wasn't sure whether they would answer this far on shore.

But they wouldn't care if Amia knew of them. He would just have to trust Roine. "They called themselves the nymid."

Amia stared at Tan, a strange curiosity and a hint of recognition upon her face, but she said nothing. Her eyes flickered out to the lake, looking from the water and then back to Tan, all while wearing a strange expression.

Roine had a different reaction. "Nymid? How do you know that name?"

"They told me."

"You *spoke* to them?"

"I didn't really speak to them. I think they communicate with thought." Tan worried for a moment that Roine did not believe him.

Then Roine stood, pacing to the edge of the water. He knelt there and touched the water, swirling a finger through it. "None have seen the nymid in centuries."

Tan felt surprised. "You know of them?"

"They are water elementals. They are old, thought to be nearly as old as the great elementals, and powerful. I understand now how you survived." He stared out into the water, a wistful expression upon his face. "I still don't know how you spoke to them."

Elementals. At least that much confirmed what Tan suspected. "Why?"

Roine stared out into the lake. "Few have the ability," he began. "Once, when others knew the nymid, the ability to speak to them was a gift seen only in the most powerful—"

He cut himself off, not finishing his thought. He turned from the peaceful water of the lake and looked carefully at Tan, watching him intently. "No matter," Roine decided. "What matters is that they healed you. I wish I knew why."

"They wanted me to save Amia."

She smiled at him with a hint of amusement though did not appear surprised. "I wish I could thank them."

"I can try," Tan offered.

"It won't work outside the water," Roine said.

Tan frowned, remembering the attack. Had he been in the water when he called to the nymid, asking for help? He didn't think he had, and wondered whether that was important.

"How were you able to penetrate the barrier?" Amia asked.

Tan remembered the cage of fire and the strange armor the nymid had given him. He could think of no other word for it. "The nymid helped."

"The nymid healed you and they helped save Amia?" Roine asked, obviously surprised.

"They healed me *to* save the Daughter," he answered.

Amia's smile deepened.

"You were attacking when I reached the shore. After I killed the hound, I couldn't get near enough to Amia and called to the nymid. They shaped me some sort of armor," he said, wondering if he still wore it. "It let me to tolerate the heat to save Amia."

"You called to them. And they answered." Roine looked as if he did not believe.

Tan nodded. "They helped another time, as well."

Roine waited.

"When you were fighting Fur. During the second wave. The nymid helped."

Roine looked out to the water again. "That makes sense," he admitted. "I was nearly spent and would not have been strong enough to finish Fur. But why would they help?"

Tan shrugged. "They called the lisincend 'Twisted Fire,'" he said.

Roine snorted. "Twisted Fire?" A strange smile came to his face. "Fitting. It suits them."

Tan looked over the lake before turning his attention to the mountain rising overhead. They were nowhere near the mountain pass—the reason he'd left Nor with Roine to begin with—and now he was even more tightly tied to what the king wanted. After everything he'd been through, that should bother him.

Amia sat with her hands holding her head, chewing the strip of meat. She'd lost as much as him. Possibly more. And for no reason other than Incendin wanted more power.

And then there was Roine. How much had he gone through over the years? Whatever happened with Ilianna still troubled him, even years later. Yet he still served the king. Just like his mother even after losing his father.

He sighed. "What now?"

Roine looked at him and seemed to understand the emotions working though him. "We still need to reach the artifact. Fur was slowed, but he'll come again."

"Even if we reach it before him, what makes you think we can escape with whatever we find?" Tan asked.

Roine's eye twitched. "We just have to get to it first."

Amia pointed down the valley, along the trail of her shaping. How much farther before they reached it? If Fur escaped and followed them, how much longer would they be able to outrun the lisincend? The hounds?

Roine cleared the remains of the fire, carefully burying it. Then they all stood and started down the shore of the lake. The sun overhead was warm and comfortable and a softly blowing breeze drifted across the water and down through the valley.

Tan watched Amia as they walked. She showed no emotion, but Tan didn't know how she could feel anything other than loss, the same emotion he struggled to suppress. Maybe once they found the artifact they'd be able to mourn.

They stopped a few times, once to eat and another simply for rest and drink. They drank freely from the water of the lake and found it cold and invigorating, and were able to continue onward with faster steps after each stop.

When the sun dipped below the horizon and the moon began to peak above the trees, Roine readied them to stop. Tan was thankful for the break and ready for rest. From what he sensed, they were barely halfway along the length of the beach and probably another day's walk until they reached the end.

An explosion thundered through the valley far behind them followed by a roaring cry.

Roine sighed. "We shouldn't rest yet."

"What was that?" Amia asked.

"That was Fur. He is free." The fatigue in his voice was clear. The effort of the search drained him more than he admitted.

Tan shivered, wondering what would happen the next time Fur reached them.

# CHAPTER 27
### *Tracking a Shaping*

THEY WALKED THROUGH MUCH of the night, crashing late, with the nearly full moon that had been lighting their way now slowly dipping out of view in the night sky. The air was crisp, cool, and each breath was visible. The lake lapped quietly upon the shore, soft murmurs that almost seemed to speak. A faint glowing slid across the middle of the lake could be reflected starlight, but Tan chose to believe the nymid still watched.

Tan caught Roine looking at the lake, his features slack, before shaking his head. Tan suspected he reached out to the nymid, trying to sense them, to speak to the elementals. And they didn't answer.

He wondered how it was that he could speak to them. Why had the Great Mother gifted him with that ability?

Another thunderous roar split the night, echoing around them. The sound came as they crossed a small stream. There had been dozens of similar streams, some wider than others, that fed into the lake, and they were forced to wade through this stream rather than jump over it. A plume of flame shot high into the sky, briefly lighting the night like the lightning had the night before. A call for help, he suspected, though wondered if that were true.

It was not much later when he heard the harsh, painful call of the hounds. At least half a dozen different cries echoed through the valley. He listened for them, sensing the trees around them, but couldn't tell how many hounds prowled the forests.

When they couldn't walk any further, Roine motioned toward a natural shelter where the trees pressed against the waterline, leaving branches exposed, arching up and over the ground, forming a shelter. Inside, the ground was dry and firm, almost as if the rain from last night had missed this spot of land.

Tan plopped down next to Amia. She looked at him and smiled and he stared into her dark eyes, unable to look away. She held his gaze and then slid herself back, resting her head on her arm and staring at Tan before finally closing her eyes. Her breathing slowed almost immediately.

"You should sleep, as well," Roine said. "I will take watch."

Tan looked up at the warrior standing under the woody arch, staring into the night. "You need it as well. You well rested is more important than me."

Roine looked back at him and slowly smiled. "You think so?" He turned to stare at the night again. "I can get by on little sleep. I suspect that you can't. Not yet. Rest while you can."

Tan didn't have the strength to argue. Lying next to Amia, he drifted quickly to sleep. He dreamt of faintly colored creatures swimming around him. He felt safe, watched, and when he awoke, there was the memory of distant conversation in the back of his head.

It was dark when he awoke and Roine still stood in the same spot, staring into the night. Tan moved quietly, careful not to disturb Amia, and stood next to Roine. His eyes were closed though he opened them as he approached.

"Good. You're up." He didn't turn but tossed a dark bundle to Tan. "Try this."

Tan grabbed the bundle from mid-air and shook it out. It was a shirt, dark green like Roine wore, and the fabric was soft, supple. Tan touched the large hole in his shirt from the blast that should have killed him, running his finger along the singed edge fibers, and decided to pull the shirt Roine gave him overtop the one he wore. Luck, perhaps. Or something else.

"Thanks." Tan rubbed the sleep from his eyes. He still felt tired, though felt better for the small amount of sleep he had managed. "You should rest now."

Roine shook his head. "They near."

Tan didn't need him to explain who he meant. Instead, he closed his eyes as Roine had done and let his focus wander as his father had taught him years ago when first learning to hunt. He felt along the water's edge to the trees, listening for any disturbance. Down the shore, within the trees, and closer than he would have expected, Tan sensed the void. Lisincend.

Opening his eyes, he nodded. "We should go then," he agreed.

Roine frowned at him. "Your mother thought you just a senser."

"An earth senser." Tan shrugged. "Not very strong. And usually not very useful. Helps with hunting, but not much else."

Roine chuckled. "Weak? Great Mother, if you think that's weak, then I'd hate to think what you consider strong. I have to focus most of my energy to learn what you gathered in moments."

Tan frowned. "My father was a strong earth senser."

Roine frowned again. "Is that what he told you when he taught you to sense?" Tan nodded. "I understand now how you were able to follow the hounds in the first place. Or how you discovered the lisincend trail by the Aeta caravan. I'm not a particularly strong earth shaper, but I've at least tracked lisincend before." He patted Tan on the arm. "Nothing weak about your sensing, Tan." He laughed. "I think your mother knew. Probably why she wanted you to go to Ethea."

"What do you mean?"

"That's how it begins, at least for me. First a strong senser. If strong enough, you can learn to shape."

"A shaper? I don't think I'd ever be strong enough for that."

Roine laughed again and looked out to the lake. "You spoke to the nymid. Not many shapers can claim the same. I think with training, you could be a powerful shaper."

Tan looked out at the lake, at the swirling green floating across it. "Like my mother?" He wished there had been time for him to learn more about her shaping. Now that he knew, he had so many questions.

Roine nodded. "The gift is handed down through generations, some stronger than others."

"But my mother was a wind shaper."

"And your father was an earth senser. If you choose to go to Ethea, you could learn much about your ability. In time…" He shrugged. "It's possible you could learn to shape."

Ethea again. This time the suggestion was different. Could he really learn to become a shaper? Could he pass up the opportunity to try? But doing so meant paying the price with service, and Tan still didn't know if that's what he wanted.

"Why the nymid?" he asked. "If I'm an earth senser, why can I speak to the nymid?"

Roine took a deep breath. "You're asking the wrong person. None remain with the ability to speak to the elementals, but from what I know, it should be paired with your ability. Not always; the archivists claim some speak to the elementals and never shape."

More reasons for him to go to Ethea. Tan wondered if his mother told Roine how he didn't want to go. Could Roine answer his questions but chose not to do so?

Roine closed his eyes. Pressure built with his shaping, releasing as a wave washing away from them.

Tan did the same, sensing the forest, and felt it closer this time.

"We should leave," Roine said.

Tan crawled back under the branches and moved to Amia, shaking her gently. Her eyes fluttered open and she jerked back quickly.

"Time to go," he whispered.

She looked down the shore with a flash of fear. "Are they—"

Tan nodded once.

Amia looked at Tan a moment and nodded. She pulled herself to her feet a little stiffly and once back outside the shelter she stretched, working her legs and arms quickly. She frowned, looking at the lake.

Roine stood with a nervous energy. "Can you still follow it?"

Roine led them along the edge of the lake, always a dozen or more paces ahead of them, pushing them at a faster and faster pace. After a while of walking in silence, Tan turned to Amia. "Roine thinks I could become a shaper."

She looked over to him and tilted her head, pressing her hair out of her soft face as she watched him. "And you don't want to?"

He thought of his father answering the summons from the king without question. Of his mother, and how much she'd changed after his father died. "I don't want to owe my life to anything."

Amia looked at him and frowned. "I was five when I was discovered. My people inspect each newborn, always searching for one blessed by the Great Mother. As I said, most are feelers, and they thought me the same. This would have been enough for me to follow my Mother."

Roine slowed to listen. "You know with the newborns?" Amia nodded. "Is this something your feelers can detect?"

Amia nodded again. "What we have is different than you. You work on the outside, on the world around you. We work on the inside. This is our gift from the Great Mother."

"When did you know?" Tan asked Roine. "When did you know you were a warrior?"

Roine laughed softly. "I was wind senser first. That is how it works. First a senser. Then a shaper. It was only later I learned I was a warrior."

"Is that how you knew my mother?"

Roine nodded. "We studied together. Zephra was always so powerful. She had a command of the wind none matched, even the Masters."

Tan wished he would have known that part of his mother. "And you knew when you were five?" he asked Amia.

"My Mother always suspected something was different. When I was five, we met another family and with them was another blessed by the Great Mother. She was able to see what my Mother could not. She taught me the earliest of my skills." She looked to Roine. "We don't have a place like your university. We must learn to understand our gifts on our own. It's not always easy."

"Learning shaping with a guide is difficult. Without…" he shook his head. "You've done well to learn what you have."

Amia looked around. "I've wondered why the Great Mother blessed me. Maybe had some other been chosen, my people would still be safe."

"Or not. Perhaps the Mother knew what she gifted," Roine suggested.

They walked in silence for a few moments. "Why don't the kingdoms have spirit shapers?" Tan asked.

Roine looked at Amia before answering. "The answer requires a greater understanding of shaping in general," he said. "The kingdoms have known shapers as long as we've existed, long before the separate nations united. Shaping was part of the reason they came together. The university has long studied the origin of shaping, though for a different reason."

He turned to Tan. "I told you our shapers were once much more potent, more powerful, than they are today?" Tan nodded. "The scholars have searched for the reason it changed. The simplest explanation is that the abilities were simply watered down over time." He paused, running a hand through his hair. His eyes were drawn and though he had refused sleep, his sagging shoulders and slowly returning limp revealed his need. "We know little about the earliest shapers other than that their shapings were strong and crude. Not until we started seeing warriors did shapings become more complex. Incredibly so. Most of those early warrior shapings can't be replicated."

"Where did the first shapers come from, then?" Tan asked.

Roine shrugged. "Some think the earliest shapers were simply born to it as they are today. Others wonder whether shaping was a gift from some of the older elementals."

"Like the nymid?"

Roine nodded. "Like the nymid, but older."

"But why do only the Aeta have spirit sensers and shapers?" Tan asked.

"They haven't always. The ancient warriors, those who created the artifact and the compass, could shape spirit too. But what changed?" He looked out over the lake. "I can't answer that. Probably the same reason few still speak to the elementals. But none know that answer, either."

They fell into silence as they walked, following the lakeshore. They crossed several small streams, each flowing down from the mountain as it joined the massive lake. In the distance Tan became aware of two things. The first was that the end of the valley grew gradually closer. The base of the huge mountain shadowing their path loomed finally near. The other was that a large river ran down from the nearby slopes, wider than any of the other streams, and cascaded noisily as it flowed into the lake. They would have to cross the river to continue along their path.

A harsh cry behind them made him jump. Another of the hounds answered the cry, baying in response. Tan closed his eyes, stretching out his senses and listening, sensing the lisincend presence in the forest, following closer than the last time.

Roine quickened their pace.

The river loomed before them, blocking their way. The river looked to feed much of the lake by itself. He looked up the river, searching for a good place to cross, but there was none. They would either have to swim or hike upriver a long distance to find an easy place to ford.

Roine looked back, his face slack as he sensed. "We don't have time for this."

"Can you do anything?" he asked.

Roine shook his head. "I'm too weak from before. This is too much for me even when rested."

"You could blow us across," Tan said.

Roine shook his head. "Too inexact. I may send us out into the lake. There's only one way I can travel with precision and you would not be safe."

"What is it?"

Roine flickered his eyes up to the heavy clouds in the far north as an answer.

Tan followed his eyes. A Cloud Warrior, shapers who could walk the sky. Of course Tan wouldn't be safe. "Then we have to swim."

Roine shook his head. "Fur is closing in quickly and the hounds have our scent. We need to buy ourselves some time. We can't do that swimming this river."

Roine paced up the river a ways, quickly disappearing from view. Amia looked at Tan and then out to the lake. He knew what she asked.

The nymid.

"I don't know," he began. Tan looked out into the lake, not sure with the growing light where the nymid would be, and simply let his mind go blank. He gathered himself, drawing in as much concentration as he could muster, and sent a thought out toward the water.

*Nymid. We need your help.*

Tan staggered, dizziness and fatigue hitting him. Amia placed a reassuring hand upon his arm to steady him. He tried to keep his mind calm as he waited, uncertain his request would even be heard. Would he need to get into the water? Would it have been easier?

*He Who is Tan.*

The thought tickled at the back of his mind, making a soft connection, but Tan heard the words clearly.

*Nymid. Can you help? Twisted Fire follows, and we cannot cross the river.*

Tan was aware of conflicting thought. Nymid anger and repulsion of the lisincend was mixed with curiosity.

*Twisted Fire must not have the Daughter. Or He Who is Tan.* There was a pause, as if the nymid considered. *What can we do?*

Tan pictured the river as it entered the lake in his mind, sending that forward as a thought. *We must cross. And we must slow Twisted Fire.*

*The Source,* the nymid said.

There was a long pause and Tan thought they had broken off communication. Finally a response came.

222

*We will help.*

Tan opened his eyes. The water near the river began to glow with the distinct light of the nymid. Could Amia see it as well? She watched Tan with a curious expression, not turning or following his gaze. The water began to part, peeling back, slowly receding to reveal a sandy path.

*You may cross.*

"Roine!" he shouted, but needn't have.

Roine appeared behind Tan, looking at the water with a mixture of surprise and awe.

"We should hurry," Tan said. "I don't know how long this will last."

Roine only nodded as he started across, staring at the watery edges that rippled to each side of the pathway. "The nymid?"

"Yes."

"You were able to call them from shore?"

"Yes."

Roine looked back then, pausing as he passed through the strange path and stared at Tan for a moment before shaking his head and hurrying through. The water was wide, over five hundred paces here, and when they reached where the other shore had been, the water simply slid back into place as if it had never been disturbed.

*Move forward now,* the nymid said.

After they had moved a little away from where the river met the lake, the river surged, growing wider, deeper.

*Thank you.*

*Do not thank. Purge Twisted Fire.*

Tan nodded. *When the Daughter is safe.*

The nymid seemed to smile but said nothing more. Their answer was in the widely flowing river now flowing rapidly into the lake, turbulent and frothy.

Roine stared at the water, his face unreadable, before turning to Tan. "It looks like you bought us some time."

Amia smiled at him, her mouth and eyes tight. She turned to the water and spoke aloud. "Thank you."

*Do not thank.*

Tan was sure he was the only one to hear the nymid's response.

# CHAPTER 28
## *A Greater Elemental*

THE ANGRY ROAR LET THEM KNOW when Fur reached the river, now far behind them. A loud and angry hiss followed the cry of frustration. The lisincend tried to heat the water, to blast its way through the barrier.

"Do you think it will work?" Tan asked.

Roine shook his head. "Too much water in that river, especially after what the nymid did."

"How far do you think Fur will have to go to cross?"

Roine shrugged. His shoulders sagged, though somewhat less since they had passed through the nymid path, and his limp was barely noticeable. "Not sure. Depends on how wide the river is farther upstream. We probably bought half a day."

Tan and Amia shared a glance, neither speaking much. They walked quickly, mostly silently, along the lake, coming across several smaller streams but each passable. The lake was a spider web of the small streams, all coming out of the upper mountains and all leading to the huge lake in the valley.

"What is this place?" Tan asked as they crossed another of the small waterways.

"I've been trying to understand that since finding you. With the nymid's presence and control of the river, I think I understand. Truthfully, I never expected to see a place like this in person." He looked at Tan. "The scholars would call this a place of convergence. I've known they exist...just never thought to see one. They're rare. Focused energy, natural strength, and rich in the elementals." Roine looked at the water as he spoke. "It's also why I struggled finding you. These natural convergences mask themselves, protecting the power they store, protecting their guardians. That makes the nymid's help all the more surprising. It also tells me that these nymid are more powerful than I'd thought."

"And there are other places like this?"

"There are, though they can't be mapped. Any attempt to try always fails. No one has ever understood why."

Amia smiled. "Perhaps the elementals that guard them are even stronger than you think."

"Perhaps," Roine agreed.

"And this...convergence...is tied to your artifact?" Tan asked.

"It would explain why the artifact can't be found without the compass. Why it's so difficult to trace. And provide protection for the artifact, as well."

Amia closed her eyes and tracked her shaping. "Still along the lakeshore," she said. "Beyond the lake...I can't tell clearly."

Roine continued forward, saying little as the day progressed. They stopped briefly to eat a lunch of fruits gathered from some of the nearby trees before continuing. They passed many more small streams. The water grew colder with each one they passed.

The far edge of the lake loomed nearby when Tan saw the first evidence of ice upon the lake. The water was calmer here, and had grown much colder, but even then he hadn't expected to see ice forming on the surface. When crossing the streams, Tan started to hope they could jump them, no longer wanting to wade through icy water. Some of the smaller feeder streams were completely frozen over.

"This shouldn't be," Tan finally said. "We're too low for this much cold. Even the mountain doesn't have snow until much higher on the peak."

Roine took a hesitant step out on the ice of the lake. It groaned and creaked under his weight, but held. He backed off the ice, stepping back upon the cool shore, and looked down the lakeshore. "Not much further."

With each step, the ice thickened. They no longer had to wade through even the widest of streams, able to simply walk across. Ice stretched across the lake all the way to the far shore, faintly visible in the distance. Ahead, the rocky mountain jutted up, pointing toward the sky like a finger as it framed the lake. A few trees dotted the slope, but for the most part it was too steep to support their growth.

As night neared, they would be forced into a decision. Would they camp along the edge of the lake, hoping they had enough distance between them and the lisincend, or did they press on, into the night, exhausted?

Amia suddenly veered out onto the ice.

At first Tan simply watched her go, figuring curiosity drove her forward, but she continued out onto the ice, venturing farther and farther from shore. She didn't look back to see if anyone followed.

"Amia?" he called after her.

She did not answer, did not look back.

Tan started after her, his first steps hesitant. The ice groaned with his weight at first and he froze, listening for any sound that it was not tolerating him. Nothing came.

"Amia!" he called again, taking another hesitant step forward.

Finally she looked over at him. Her eyes were drawn and her brow furrowed in an expression of concern. She turned and continued onto the ice, heading toward the center of the lake.

With as warm as the rest of the lake had been, how stable could the ice be that far out in the lake? He ran toward her.

Tan was perhaps twenty paces from shore when he heard Roine yell. "We don't have time for diversions!"

Tan shook his head. "Amia—"

Roine followed them onto the ice and paused.

"What is it, Roine?"

Roine looked up, though pointed down at his feet, toward the ice. "This ice is *shaped*," he said, puzzled. He strode forward, quickly catching Tan.

"What do you mean it's shaped? Recently?"

Roine shook his head. "I have never seen anything quite like this," he said. "This is subtle and powerful. Not until I had stepped out onto the ice could I feel the difference." He looked at Tan. "And it's immense. Old."

"How can you tell how old it is?"

"Shapings carry certain qualities, textures, that reveal much about the shaping itself. If skilled, you can learn the identity of the shaper, how many shapers were involved, the age of the shaping, or more. Sometimes much more. Something like this has so many layers I can't sense them all." He shook his head. "This is amazing."

They hurried to Amia. She had stopped near the center of the frozen part of the lake and stared down, looking toward the ice, as if trying to peer through its thick surface. Her eyes closed and her face relaxed. Tan felt the building pressure behind his ears of a shaping. Long moments passed before the pressure finally eased.

"There's something beneath the ice," she said. Her voice shook slightly and her eyes still had a bit of a faraway look to them.

Roine frowned, looking down at the ice and closing his eyes. He opened them moments later and shook his head. "I sense nothing."

"You could not," Amia agreed.

"Then what is it?" Roine asked.

"Some being. I don't know."

"Nymid?" Roine asked.

She shook her head. "I don't know what the nymid feel like," she answered, casting a quick glance at Tan, "but this is too large to be nymid."

"Large? How can you tell?" Roine asked.

"Whatever is down there is immense. Intelligent. They overpower any other sensing I try to do."

Roine froze. "They?"

She nodded. "At least three."

"And you can no longer sense the artifact?"

She closed her eyes and shook her head. "I've been feeling distracted for a while. At first I didn't know why." She looked down at the ice. "Then I began feeling them." She shook her head. "I can't feel the trail of my shaping anymore. Not while they're here."

"What are they?" Tan asked.

Amia looked at him. "I can't tell." Anguish crossed her face. "There are some of my people skilled at speaking without words, but that's not my gift. They're in pain. And they suffer." She looked from Tan to Roine. "We must release them."

"There's no time to release them now," Roine said. "The lisincend near. Much longer and they might reach the artifact first. After we find it, we can return. Then we can see what we can do to free them."

Amia shook her head. "You said convergences are difficult to find. You think we'll find this place again?"

"Amia—" Roine begged.

Her eyes went wide and her breathing quickened. "I can't feel anything else now. Whatever is down there keeps me from feeling anything else." She looked at Tan. "Not even you."

Roine took a step back and ran his hand through his hair. "We don't even know what these creatures are," Roine said, trying to placate her. "And I can't begin to imagine what would be required to release them from this ice."

"They suffer," Amia said. "And they know they suffer."

While Amia and Roine continued to argue, Tan closed his eyes, setting his feet apart, and straightened his back. He gathered up an effort of will, focusing his attention and clearing his mind as much as possible.

*Nymid!* He sent the thought as loudly as he could.

They were far from where they had last seen the nymid, far from the warm waters, and he wasn't sure this would even work. Tan staggered slightly under the energy of sending the thought, but ignored it as he strained for their answer.

Instead of the soft voice of the nymid, something else entered his mind, immense and looming, and carried with it a sense of pain.

Tan bit back a cry as he gained awareness of this other. In a panic, he tried pushing it away from him.

*Who disturbs?*

The thought was loud and grating and felt as if it tore open parts of his mind as he strained to listen. Nothing like the gentle nymid presence.

Tan frowned. *Who is this?*

*You called the nymid.*

*You are not the nymid.* Of that, he was certain.

*Do you speak for the nymid?*

*I do not. I seek the nymid to learn of the creatures frozen under the surface of their lake.*

There came a grating, almost a clawing, at his mind, as this other presence settled into Tan's thoughts, digging in and holding firm.

*What do you know of the capture?*

*I know nothing.*

Tan opened himself up enough so that the creature could sense his honesty. This had not been necessary with the nymid. They had projected only peace and there was no threat to them, but with this creature, Tan felt his mind in danger if he didn't communicate correctly.

*What are you?*

*I am draasin. We must be freed.*

"Draasin?" Tan said aloud, startled. The word rolled off his tongue strangely. The presence in his mind receded a little but was still there. Tan tried to create a barrier, a wall of sorts, to protect his mind, and was uncertain whether he was successful.

Roine turned to him sharply, biting off whatever he had been about to say to Amia, and stared at Tan. "Where did you hear that word?"

"What?"

"You spoke of the draasin. Few know of them." He watched Tan for a moment. "They were ancient elemental creatures and lived long ago. The last was hunted and killed well over a thousand years ago."

Tan looked down at the ice. He was certain the creature called itself a draasin. "They were killed?"

"The draasin were wild, savage, and intelligent. Hunters, unafraid of anything. From what is known, there was nothing quite as fearsome as a draasin." Roine stared at Tan with a deep intensity. "The university keeps the archive referencing draasin restricted. Only a few today even know of them." He looked at Tan. "Your mother wouldn't have known of them, and if she had, she certainly wouldn't have said anything to you. So where did you hear it?"

The hard presence lingered in his mind. Pain stabbed behind his eyes. The creature was aware of his thoughts and through the agony it let Tan feel from it, he sensed a cruel amusement as well. "These creatures are draasin." He pressed a finger between his eyes to reduce the pain.

"They suffer," Amia repeated. Tan nodded, able to feel only a fragment of the draasin's agony. "They must be freed."

"How do you know?"

He hesitated answering. "I...I can speak to them. I tried reaching the nymid. They should know what lies imprisoned in their waters. The draasin answered."

"The ability to speak to even one of the elementals is a rare trait," he began slowly. "The draasin are elementals, as well—fire elementals. And unlike the nymid, they are one of the four great elementals. Powerful. Dangerous. And thought lost. And you can speak to them."

# CHAPTER 29
## *End to a Shaping*

INSIDE TAN'S HEAD came a sudden hard laughter.

*Free us!*

He felt a flexing within his head. Pressure built and was followed by a sharp pain in his mind, like that of claws raking his brain. Tan grabbed his head and closed his eyes.

*I will try. But you must...release...my...mind!*

Tan sent a surge of pressure toward the sensation in his head and the draasin released its grip with sudden surprise. The pain in his head eased.

There came the sense of laughter, not nearly as hard and tinged with the agony the draasin endured.

*Small. Yet you are fierce.* A note of respect entered the thought as well. *You must free us.*

There was less of a demand this time and the draasin allowed Tan to feel more of its pain, near-eternities of suffering, waiting, frozen in the lake, trapped.

Tan dropped his hands from his head and opened his eyes, knowing what must be done. Their suffering must end. "We must release them."

Roine shook his head, rubbing his hand through his hair in annoyance. "You know we don't have the time. And I don't have the strength. Anything we do now lets the lisincend get closer."

"I can't help if they continue to suffer. All I feel is their pain."

The draasin waited, hurting, yearning to be free once more. Tan didn't know what would happen to him if they were unable to help them. Would they release his mind or destroy it?

"Roine," Tan said, turning to him. Honesty would be the only way to sway Roine. "This creature, the draasin, has a hold of my mind. If we do nothing..."

"Tan," Roine whispered. "You don't understand what you ask." His face had taken on a pained expression, nervous. There was a hint of fear to his eyes, as well. "The records we have about the draasin are terrifying, even within the university. It is well they've been lost to time. Even one draasin would be fearsome. You tell me there are three?"

Roine turned his back on them and took a step away.

Amia looked at Tan, anxious, before staring into the ice again. Tan felt building pressure and knew Amia was preparing a shaping, though could not fathom what she would shape. The pressure built to a nearly unbearable level, sending pain through Tan's skull, piercing through his ears until he felt they would burst.

Then there was another voice in his head.

Amia spoke, a command, and he heard her though she directed the words at the draasin. He suspected the link he shared with the draasin enabled him to hear her, to feel the power of her shaping—for it was a shaping.

"You will bring harm to no human," she commanded.

The words, echoing in Tan's mind, hummed with her energy. Tan didn't know if the shaping would hold the draasin or not, but he felt the effort she used in the compulsion. There was great power being spent on this one shaping.

"You will hunt no human. You will find your food elsewhere."

Then Amia staggered, falling forward, barely staying upright long enough for Tan to lunge under her and scoop her up before she fell upon the ice.

She looked up at him weakly. "Will it work?"

Tan stared, afraid to probe the connection he shared with the draasin, afraid to simply ask whether the shaping would hold, uncertain how to even phrase the question.

*I hear the question regardless*, the draasin said.

Tan would have jumped had he not been carrying Amia. He strained to keep a barrier, a wall of sorts, up in his mind, separating his thoughts from those of the draasin, and he failed. The draasin was both powerful and skilled at communicating with thought. Tan was neither.

There was almost a chuckle in his mind. *Perhaps you should see what I see, little warrior*, the draasin said. *Free us.*

*There is one among us who fears what you would do if freed.*

*As well he should*, the draasin rumbled.

Tan let the weak barrier in his mind drop and sent a probing thought toward the draasin, searching its intent. He found a creature that longed for the hunt, for the warmth of the sun upon its skin, and for the taste of hot flesh. There was no malice, yet no regard for where the meal came from. Still, Tan sensed something there, new and puzzling to the draasin, and he recognized it for what it was.

Amia's shaping.

It had settled in and around the draasin's mind, holding tight, and the draasin eyed it curiously, uncertain what the shaping was and how the shaping would affect it. Still there was no fear. Only curiosity.

*If released, you may not hunt man,* Tan informed the draasin.

*We hunt what pleases us.*

As the draasin sent the thought, Tan sensed it running into Amia's shaping. There was a sensation of pressure, as if the creature tried to force its way through the shaping, and it struggled wildly for a moment. Finally, a grudging acceptance of the shaping, not pleased or angry. There remained a promise to overcome the shaping hidden deep in the draasin's mind.

*You may not hunt man.*

The draasin laughed then, and there was true amusement. *You surprise me, little warrior. We will agree. For now.*

Tan sent an acknowledgement and turned to Amia to answer her. "I think it worked," he said. "Though I suspect they'll struggle against it. They'll probably find a way around your shaping."

Roine turned, eyeing Tan with curiosity as he carried Amia. "What has she done?"

"She has forbidden the draasin from hunting man."

Roine laughed bitterly. "You think that will work? How many spirit shapings have held against the lisincend? And the draasin are more powerful by far!"

Tan shrugged. "I don't know why the lisincend can resist her shapings, but I can tell you the draasin are compelled by this shaping. They will bring no harm to any human."

Roine closed his eyes and inhaled deeply before opening. "Tan…" He sighed. "You can be as stubborn as your mother."

Tan smiled. "I will say thanks to that."

Roine motioned to Tan to follow and he did, trailing Roine as he walked across the ice, back to the shore. Roine signaled him to set

Amia down and Tan laid her along a dry patch of land to keep her as warm as possible. She still wore his cloak and he wrapped it around her. Amia smiled at him.

"Be careful," she warned.

Tan didn't need the warning. He felt the threat of the draasin in his mind. The creature didn't mean him harm personally, but Tan would be attacked in an instant if the draasin thought it could. Yet they needed to be freed. He could not fully explain why. Such a creature shouldn't be simply trapped like this, especially not one of the elementals.

"I don't think this is wise," Roine admitted. "Had the nymid not helped, and had we not needed Amia to sense her shaping, I'm not certain I would have agreed. As it is, I do this for you. Not the draasin. Not the artifact. You, Tan."

He stared with intent eyes and Tan could not look away. "Thank you, Roine."

He snorted. "I make no guarantees about this shaping."

Tan turned and faced the aging warrior and saw wrinkles of fatigue lining his eyes. "You will do what you can."

"Those who shaped this lake were much more powerful than I," Roine said. "And I am tired." His shoulders sagged as he spoke and he lowered his head. "Tannen," he continued, using his full name, "I am no longer Theondar. What we must do, our task—finding the arti-fact—is more important than freeing the draasin."

"Roine, you will always be Theondar."

The warrior smiled a sad smile. "There is more to Theondar than you know."

Tan looked over at his shoulder at Amia. She only shook her head, knowing the question needed to be asked. "If the draasin are elemen-tals, they can't be trapped like this. There is something *wrong* about it. They are not like the lisincend, they are not twisted." He said the word, thinking of the nymid. "The draasin are elementals, a natural part of the world. And they suffer, Roine. Amia feels it. I feel it." He met Roine's hard eyes. "If you could feel what I feel, could feel the...enormity...of what's settled into my mind, you'd understand."

"I'm not sure Theondar could have even done this, Tan," he said softly. "But I'll try." Roine unsheathed his sword and set its point into the ice. "The only advantage we have is that we try to destroy this shaping, not replicate. This is easier." He grunted. "Slightly."

Roine reached a hand to the sky and closed his eyes. A slow pressure of a shaping built. Tan's ears popped as he watched Roine. Roine's face was peaceful, his mouth slack, and his hair fluttered in wind that only he felt. His left hand held tightly to the hilt of his sword.

Tan had never truly seen Roine's sword. Carvings upon the blade curled up the flat edge of the sword and continued along the guard and up into the hilt. He recognized a few of the symbols from the golden box Roine had carried, though he did not know their meaning. Strange swirls linked with geometric shapes. Among it all were figures twisting into a flowing shape.

The pressure in Tan's head pulsed unbearably. His eyes lifted from Roine's sword and looked at the old warrior. His face had a tight and pained expression now. Roine's raised right hand formed a fist and energy coursed through him that Tan could almost see.

The pain became unbearable.

Then Roine stumbled. Tan started forward, reaching for him, and put an arm around his waist to prop him up while falling forward himself. Tan put his free hand out and grabbed on to the pommel of Roine's sword, and was able to stop the fall and push himself upright again.

Sound and color exploded in his head. Tan's vision blurred, swimming. Nausea incapacitated him. The wind whipped around him, a sudden blast of cold northern air, and the ice beneath his feet heaved. Still the pressure built.

Tan screamed, no longer able to hold it back. A huge crack of lightning streaked from the sky and slammed into the ice at the center of the lake.

Roine slipped again and Tan followed him down. Roine turned his head and looked at Tan, his expression unreadable. "That's all I can do." His set his head back and closed his eyes. "Now we must wait."

The frigid ice beneath them started to melt, turning his backside wet and cold. He felt exhausted, drained inexplicably, but still pushed up and stood, dragging Roine off the ice to lay over by Amia.

Roine mouthed something wordlessly without opening his eyes.

Tan dropped heavily next to Amia. She rolled onto her side and met his gaze. "Something has changed."

Tan let his focus wander, searching the draasin. A sense of excitement exuded from the creature. A sense of something enormous within his mind stretching, as if no longer confined. He broke the connection and opened his eyes, nodding to Amia.

They waited.

Long moments passed with only the steady cracking of ice. The sun shifted in the sky, dipping toward the horizon as it set, coloring the sky orange and blood red. Wind fluttered from the upper mountains. Roine didn't move next to them, completely exhausted as he recovered from the energy of his shaping.

Then the ice groaned loudly and split with a thunderous *crack*.

A dark gash ran across the surface of the lake, splitting wide into an icy cavern. Slowly, steadily, Tan felt something crawling its way to the surface.

He was unsure if he sensed the movement in his mind or if he felt it rumbling through the earth.

The rumbling echoed louder, finally splitting the ice again. The surface exploded outward as an impossibly long, serpent-shaped creature crawled up from the water. Massive spikes steamed from his back. The creature turned and stared at Tan with eyes dancing with fire, before looking away, sliding over the ice and toward the far shore.

Another, weaker *crack* came as the ice split again. Two smaller creatures crawled forth and followed the first, neither looking at Tan. They disappeared into the growing night onto the far shore. Tan thought that would be the last he would see of the creatures, but moments later they erupted over the treetops, huge wings beating the air, and circled the lake a moment before soaring up and over the nearest mountain and disappearing.

Tan sighed, feeling a sense of peace for the first time since making contact with the draasin, and prayed the connection in his mind had been broken. Amia sighed as she watched the draasin disappear.

*Time to hunt, little warrior.*

The thought exploded into Tan's mind, forcing him to cover his ears as if he could actually hear the words. Tan had thought the connection had been broken, yet it had not.

*Hunt well.*

The creature laughed and his awareness of the creature grew fainter. It did not disappear altogether.

"I don't know the consequences of what we just did," Roine said. He had propped himself up and stared after the draasin as well, his face drawn and his eyes wrinkled with concern. "And I am afraid."

# CHAPTER 30
## *Away from the Water*

ROINE PUSHED HIMSELF to standing and wobbled a moment, leaning on the sword clutched tightly in his fist before steadying enough to sheath it. His eyes watched the horizon, looking up and over the mountain peak the draasin disappeared behind while shaking his head.

"Nothing more we can do." He blinked quickly to shake whatever thought had been running through his head. "Can you follow it now?"

Amia closed her eyes and focused. A shaping built slowly, released as a soft wave rolling toward the mountain. "There," she pointed.

Tan followed the direction up along the mountain face. The rock itself was steep and there didn't appear to be any possible passage or any way to reach the area where she pointed. "How will we get there?"

Roine waved his hands together in front of his eyes, murmuring under his breath. There was a surge of wind and a spray of cold water.

He stared for a moment and then turned back to them. "There's a path about halfway up."

"How can you tell?" Tan asked.

Roine smiled. "Perhaps my old eyes are stronger than you think, Tan."

The relaxed comment gave Tan a sense of relief. Each shaping Roine performed obviously exhausted him. Tan didn't know what would be required once they found the artifact, but suspected additional shaping would be necessary. Then they had to return. The lisincend were still out there. The hounds still hunted.

"Are you ready?" Roine asked, more gently than he had in the past.

Tan offered Amia his hand. She took it and they stood together. She wrapped his cloak around her waist, pulling it tight for warmth. Tan stared, admiring her figure as she did. Amia saw him watching and Tan flushed, turning away. She took his hand, turning him, forcing him to meet her gaze. When she smiled at him, her face glowed. Tan couldn't help but smile as well.

She pulled him by his hand, holding it tightly. Roine led them forward, his gait slower than it had been and the limp that had been present ever since finding them again noticeable. They tracked along the shoreline and Tan noticed that the ice slowly melted, liquid water returning to the lake once more. Whatever they'd done with the shaping to release the draasin had also given the lake back to the nymid.

Near the end of the lake, the ground turned from soft soil to hard rock. Small boulders littered the shore, forcing them to walk around, and occasionally overtop, the rock. Soon they reached the rocky slope that Roine indicated, reaching nearly straight up from the ground and stretching high into the sky overhead. The rock itself was nearly smooth; it had no cracks or handholds by which they could climb up its steep surface.

"Up?" Roine asked Amia.

Amia released Tan's hand and he let her go with reluctance. She closed her eyes briefly and when they reopened, she nodded. "I can't tell any other direction from here," she said. "I know we're below it."

Roine sighed. He turned to the rock and opened his hands, palms facing the rock. With a quick shaping, the rock in front of Roine began to crumble. It cracked first then small pieces fell, tumbling to the ground in a small rockslide. Another section of rock cracked and followed the first, higher, and the trail moved its way down toward the ground. One after another there came small cascades of pebbles and rock fragments, each preceded by a tiny *snap*. As he watched, divots formed in the rock wall appeared, small and regularly spaced.

Handholds.

Roine expected them to climb the rock.

The snapping and trail of rubble continued for long moments until Roine could either do no more or he was too tired to continue. Either way, he slumped down and sat looking dazedly at the rock. Amia's mouth was fixed in a tight line of worry.

"I fear that freeing the draasin may have been too much for him," she said quietly, pitching her words for Tan alone.

Roine looked up slowly, having heard what she said, and shook his head. "Perhaps it was necessary," he said. "Perhaps too much. Either way, it's done." He pushed himself back up, standing again. "And I'll be fine. That's not a difficult shaping, just a repetitive one. That by itself is draining."

Tan looked from Roine to the rock wall. "You want us to climb?"

Roine smiled a half smile. "You can't fly. I don't have the strength to call the wind to lift us. So we climb."

Roine started first, leveraging his weight up the slope. He moved slowly, carefully, and there was a fluidity to his movements. This wasn't the first time Roine had climbed this way.

He made it about halfway up the face of the rock when he paused. "You coming?"

Tan looked at Amia. "You should go next."

She craned her neck to stare up the wall of the rock and then turned back to look at Tan. A smile quirked her lips. "You just want to watch me climb." She turned away before seeing Tan blush again.

She moved at a steady pace, her body hugging the rock tightly and her arms and legs moving steadily. Roine had disappeared from view and Amia was soon high enough that Tan felt compelled to follow. He had to admit that he did enjoy watching her climb. She was graceful and lithe and moved in such a way that he couldn't help but stare.

Tan wasn't particularly scared of heights, but the sheer drop made him nervous. There wasn't anything below him except for rock. He found the handholds to be solid and could move steadily up the face of the rock. He forced himself not to turn or look down, focusing on each handgrip, reaching and pulling himself up as he climbed.

A soft spray of rock sputtered down toward him from higher up and he waited until it passed. Tan heard grunting, then a cry. He looked up to see Amia dangling. Only one hand held the rock.

He heard the shaped command ring loudly in his head. *Protect me!*

Tan moved quickly, afraid of what would happen were Amia to slip any further. She was too far over for him to have any chance of catching her and high enough up that she wouldn't survive the fall. He looked for Roine, praying he saw Amia falling and could do something to help her, but he was nowhere.

Tan practically jumped from handhold to handhold. Amia called out. He heard it equally loud in his mind. Through their shaped connection, he felt her panic. Another spray of rock followed.

"No! Roine!"

Time seemed to slow as he saw her fall.

She spun, flailing her arms wildly, reaching for purchase in the rock, and slipping down. Panic struck him. With it came a surge of pressure and pain unlike anything he had ever known.

Pressure exploded in his head. His vision spotted for a moment. The wind gusted up from below, whipping at his clothes and stinging his face, forcing Tan to cling to the rock so that he did not get blown off of it.

And then Amia slowed.

She practically hovered next to him, floating. Another explosion burst behind his ears and he was forced to close his eyes, squeezing tightly to the rock as he did. When he opened them, Amia was gone.

Panicked, he looked down, fearful that she had completed her fall. He saw no sign of her body.

He scrambled up the rock. The rock split and then opened into the path Roine had seen. Amia lay upon the path, panting. Roine stood over her, a worried look to his face.

Tan hurried off the rock and collapsed next to Amia. She thanked him silently, though she still shook. He took her face in his hands and touched the top of her head. "Are you..." He couldn't finish.

She allowed herself to be soothed and nodded. "A gust of wind saved me."

Tan looked up to Roine. He shook his head. "She was saved, but I don't think I was the one to do it," he said. "I had wandered down the trail and by the time I saw her, the fall had been slowed." Roine shook his head again. "I lifted her. That was all."

"How, then?" Tan asked.

Roine looked at Tan with a strange frown. "I don't know."

Tan looked away, turning back to Amia, thankful that she was still alive. He put his arm around her and held her while she shivered.

Roine moved up the path, crouching down and leaning his head against the rock and closing his eyes.

One face of the mountain opened to a small path leading up and around the mountain, circling the huge stone peak. A steep drop led off the other side. Tan was thankful the path was at least wide enough for them to walk side by side comfortably.

"Where does this go?"

"I followed it for only a hundred paces or so. Once it twisted around the side of the mountain, I stopped following."

Amia finally sat up, holding tightly onto Tan's arm with her free hand. She stared at Tan, watching his face with her dark eyes. After a while, she turned from Tan and looked at Roine.

"There are wind elementals?" she asked.

Roine looked up, his eyes glazed with his fatigue and he shook his head to clear them.

Amia looked toward the mountain edge and shivered roughly before turning back to Roine. "We have met nymid and draasin on this journey. Water and fire." She tilted her head as she looked at Roine and inhaled deeply. "There are wind and earth elementals?"

He nodded slowly as if finally understanding the line of her questioning. "There are," he said. "But the fact that you've now seen two elementals is itself incredibly rare. Probably tied to the power of the lake, the place of convergence. And, I suspect, tied to the artifact."

"What are the others?"

"The great elementals? They are udilm, ara, and golud. Water, wind, and earth. But they, like the draasin, have been gone for centuries. When they still spoke to man, it was their teaching that allowed some of the most skilled shapings to exist."

"But the nymid are water elementals."

Roine nodded. "The nymid have never disappeared, not really, and never to those who knew how to listen. They're considered a part of the lesser elementals, more common and weaker than the great elementals. The lesser elementals have never been lost."

Tan frowned. "The nymid seemed impressive to me."

"If the draasin still live, does that mean that ara and golud still exist?" Amia asked.

Roine looked at her and frowned. "It's possible. Though the greatest scholars on the elementals claim they are gone. Much research has gone into this topic, as you can imagine. If they still exist, why have they have broken off contact?"

"Have they?" Tan said. "Maybe we only stopped listening."

Roine looked out over the lake and shrugged.

"Are all the great elementals as fearsome as the draasin?" Amia asked.

Roine shook his head. "Not from what I've read. They served as teachers, guiding the first shapers. The archives are full of accounts of early shapers guided by the elementals, taught the intricacies of their craft."

"You wish you could have learned from them," Amia commented, staring at him. Sensing him.

Roine frowned and she turned away. "There hasn't been a warrior so trained in over five hundred years. That was the last time warriors were truly powerful."

Tan looked at Roine with surprise. The man's shaping and skill was impressive enough, but several times he had commented on the fact that the ancient warriors outstripped him in strength and skill. Tan began to wonder how much greater the ancient warriors truly were.

"What is the great elemental for spirit?" Amia asked.

Roine looked at her and shook his head as he answered. "No one has ever discovered an elemental for spirit. Greater or lesser." He paused, holding Amia's gaze. "That doesn't mean it doesn't exist. Most of the archivists suspect they exist but have never been seen."

"Perhaps they have and were made to forget," she said.

Roine leaned back against the rock and startled them by laughing. "Years of study and you've offered the first argument that makes sense."

As his laughter died, he fell silent.

Tan rested, holding Amia, and neither of them spoke. They sat on the edge of the trail, quiet, drifting in and out of sleep, as darkness crept overhead, passing into night, and on until daylight cracked once more. Tan was not sure how much he truly slept—it was fitful and full of dreams of soaring in the clouds and hunting—yet when he blinked his eyes open to the breaking day, he felt rested.

Roine waited, watching them. "We should be off," he said quietly when he saw Tan waking.

"The lisincend?" Tan asked. He closed his eyes and searched outward. Within the rock, he felt nothing. There was no disturbance, no sense of the trees or insects, nothing of animals. Just solid stone.

Roine nodded. "They're back there. Probably trying to figure out the rock. The climb should slow them more than it slowed us. Still, we should hurry."

Tan woke Amia and she smiled at him sleepily before rubbing her eyes and stretching stiff muscles. "He let us rest."

"I think we all needed it. Perhaps me most of all." Roine waited until she stood. "Do we follow the trail?"

Amia closed her eyes briefly and nodded. "We are near."

They started down the trail and Roine's limp was less than it had been before. The trail wound around the mountain, presenting them with an amazing view of the trees and rocky slopes below them as it overlooked the lake. The ice that had been there had melted complete-ly. They followed the trail as it twisted, slowly winding up the slope. The path narrowed and, at one point, split. One way led them down the slope of the mountain while the other continued upward. Amia pointed upward.

It was late in the day when the trail ended at a huge cavern in the mountain face. The rock was carved with symbols. Tan recognized many of them from Roine's sword and others from the golden box he carried. Triangles with lines and squares interspersed with circles and carved figures. Words written in a foreign tongue arched over the opening. Around everything, Tan felt a shimmering energy. This was a place of power.

Amia looked into the cavern and pointed. "We must go in there," she said.

The darkness loomed and Tan shivered.

Roine looked at the cavern as well; turning to Amia and seeing her confirmation, he nodded. "So we will."

# CHAPTER 31
## *Key to the Artifact*

TAN STARTED TOWARD THE DARKNESS of the cavern, but Roine grabbed him by the shoulder, holding him back. "This is warded against entrance," Roine warned.

"Warded? What does that mean?" Tan asked.

Roine shook his head and frowned. "I don't know what all of these runes mean," he answered, looking at the carvings on the outer wall, "but I sense the warding. And it is powerful, unlike anything I've ever encountered."

Roine released Tan's shoulder and Tan stepped away from the entrance, staring at the carvings. He became aware of a low, sizzling energy hanging over the cavern, the rock, everything, and sensed a warning within. "What will happen if you can't remove the warding?"

"Then we can't enter," Roine answered. "Not safely, at least. I don't know what the warding will do. I sense a protective barrier, but it might be a defensive shaping as well." He stared at the markings, as if doing so would provide answers.

Roine paced outside the entrance to the cave, eyes locked on the lettering, his face pulled tight as he considered. "There is usually some type of key," he said, muttering mostly to himself, "but I see nothing in these writings that indicates what it might be."

"What kind of key?" Tan asked.

"For something like this," Roine answered, motioning at the cave, "it should be written on the stone. The method to safely bring down the warding. There is nothing. Of what I can read, there is only a warning."

Amia looked up at the writing, tilted her head, and frowned, but said nothing.

Roine continued pacing, his face drawn in concentration. He scrubbed occasionally at his hair in annoyance. He paused to finger the runes upon the stone, shaking his head as he did, and stepped back to reexamine the writings. At one point, he tossed his bulging pack to the ground near Tan's feet where it clinked.

Tan hadn't really paid much attention to the pack since Roine had returned. He toed it open and the gleaming metal box reflected the early morning light.

Amia knelt next to the box and pulled it out from within the pack. She stared at the inscriptions on the surface, then looked up and stared at the writing upon the stone. Her fingers ran over the carvings on the box until reaching a position only she could feel, and then she pressed.

There came a small *snick* as a lock released and the lid of the box opened.

Amia looked over to Tan, a small smile to her face, and turned back to the box. Roine paced, ignoring them. The interior of the box gleamed just as brightly as the outside did. Carvings were worked on its surface as well.

Tan felt a soft building pressure, the steady pressure of a shaping, realizing that Amia tried shaping something on the golden box. She pressed something else, and suddenly the five-sided box fell apart, lying flat upon the rocky ground with a loud *snap*.

Roine turned at the sound. He stared down at her with a look of shock. "What did you do? Why would you damage this?"

"Roine!" Amia said. The words surged with energy of a shaping.

He took a quick step back and away from Amia, eyeing her cautiously. "Do not shape me," he warned, his voice soft and his gaze fixed unblinkingly upon her. "I may not have the strength of the lisincend to defy you, but I warn you. Do not shape me."

"You need to learn how to remain calm." The words carried a soft energy and Tan knew she still shaped him. She smiled and Roine blinked slowly as he took a deep breath. "The box is unharmed. There was a switch inside that, when triggered, opened it like this." She flipped the box sides back up, locking them in place, to demonstrate.

Roine knelt before the golden box. "How did you open the lid?"

Amia shrugged. "There is a switch there, as well."

"Few have ever learned how to open the box," he began. "And none have ever realized there was another switch. How did you know?"

"I felt it," she said simply.

Roine shook his head as if clearing it. "Felt it? Or sensed it?"

"Are they not the same?" she asked.

"Not to me."

Amia just smiled. "You see the inside is marked much like the outside?"

"The outside of the box doesn't have much meaning, only symbols and runes for the elementals," he said, not elaborating. "That's why when you shaped the box you were able to detect a trail. The markings on the inside have never been clear."

252

Amia ran her hands across the inner surface of the box and it snapped open, lying flat once more. "Try again."

Roine looked at the sides of the box, turning it so that the longest side was first. "Great Mother," he swore. He looked to Amia and narrowed his eyes. "How did you know?"

She laughed. "I can read."

"This language is long dead!"

"Not to the Aeta," she said.

Roine nodded slowly and stood, holding the opened box carefully in his palms, and walked toward the cavern opening. Standing before it, holding the box in his hands, he looked at Amia again. "Then I'll need your help. Wait until I tell you, then send a shaping into the box."

Roine turned his attention upon the now flattened box. From the building pressure, he knew this to be a powerful shaping. Roine nodded to Amia. Energy built, this time from Amia.

And then a burst of stale air blew out at them.

Roine staggered back. Tan grabbed him before he could fall and lowered him to the ground. They let Roine sit while Amia snapped the sides of the small golden box back and closed the lid.

"What happened?" he asked.

Roine looked at the cave. "The box was more than a compass. It was also the key to the wardings. There was a shaping that could only be triggered by another shaper." He paused, looking to Amia. "Shapers."

Amia didn't look as spent as Roine, though her eyelids sagged a bit more than usual.

"How'd you know?" Tan asked.

"This writing is still taught to my people. There is the warning Roine mentions," she said, staring up at the writing overhead, "but there is also instruction interspersed. The warning is only for those who don't carry the golden key."

Roine looked at her again and shook his head. "It's fortunate you're with us. I don't think I could've taken down these wards alone." He shook his head again. "The ancient shapers…"

Roine slowly stood and walked toward the entrance to the cavern. There he hesitated, taking a deep breath before stepping into the darkness. Nothing happened.

Roine let out a pent-up breath and motioned for them to follow.

Amia grabbed Tan's hand and they followed Roine into the cavern. The path widened, hollowed into the hard stone of the mountain, and the walls, at least where still lit by daylight, were unnaturally smooth.

"Was this whole cave shaped?" Tan asked.

"I think so." He whistled softly. "Great Mother. I can't imagine the strength required to do this."

Soon daylight no longer reached far enough to light their way. He squeezed Amia's hand harder than he intended. She squeezed back, equally nervous.

"How will we see our way?"

"Watch," Roine said, somewhere in front of them.

Light bloomed all around them in small orbs attached to the wall. They were spaced regularly, like lanterns, and illuminated the cave as it stretched into the rock.

Tan walked over to one of the orbs, expecting heat, but there was none, only light. "How'd you know how to light these?"

Amia stared at the orbs in wonder.

"There are lamps like this in Ethea. And they're incredibly valuable. They were created by shapers long ago but their design has been lost. What few remain are owned by the greatest shapers." Roine smiled. "I saw one as we entered. I hadn't expected so many."

"How are they lit?" Tan asked.

"Any shaper can light these lamps."

"Any?" Amia looked away from the orbs on the wall and turned to Roine.

He laughed and nodded. "Any."

Amia focused on the nearest orb and it went out. She gasped before the light quickly came back on. "Amazing."

"We need to keep moving. I've no idea the length of this cave. Or where it takes us. But the entrance is no longer warded and I'd like to be away before the lisincend trap us here."

They walked quickly, Roine lighting the orbs as they moved through the cave, letting those behind dim after they passed. Roine's limp was more pronounced again. How much had the shaping to bring down the wardings cost him? Worse, in order to survive, they might need Roine to become Theondar.

The walls began to open and the ceiling overhead crept farther and farther away until no longer visible, lost in the shadows beyond the edge of the glowing lamps. A faint light glowed in the distance, brighter with every step. Soon the spacing of the lamps along the walls became greater and greater until they disappeared altogether.

Had they walked all the way through the mountain only to emerge on the other side?

But as they reached the light, he saw that it diffused from high overhead. A huge crack in the ceiling of the cave revealed light from the outside.

Thick, dark vines seemed to grow out of the stone and covered the walls of the cave. Tan thought at first that he might be seeing carvings along the wall, out of the stone itself, made to look like vines. Huge leaves sprouted from the vines and the occasional fragrant pale white flower grew on them. As they moved deeper into the cave, the walls progressively widened, opening into a huge cavern.

The vines twisted together, turning into something greater. Small bushes sprouted from the walls, stretching toward the light coming through the split in the rock overhead, reaching tendrils and leaves toward the light. With each step, the vegetation seemed denser, and soon the bushes turned to trees punching up from the rock as they grew toward the light overhead.

Purple and red fruits hung along the branches of the trees. Tan reached toward one, but Roine stopped him.

"Remember," he warned, "this cave, everything you see here, has been shaped to appear like this. These fruits, these trees," he said, motioning with his free arm, "may appear succulent, but I'd advise caution."

The ground itself now had a thin layer of fragrant grass and Tan could swear he heard the rush of wind and the soft burbling of a stream. The air around him was warm and comfortable, like a late spring day, and he felt at peace.

"How can all of this be shaped?"

"I keep telling you the ancient shapers were much more skilled than today. Many learned what they knew from the elementals themselves. A very different education than what I had at the university. I sense the underlying shaping and know this has all been artificially generated and is sustained. Great power was spent creating this."

Roine led them more carefully, looking from side to side as he moved deeper into the cave. Trees and bushes sprouted from the ground of the cavern as well, growing tall and high, stretching up toward the rock overhead. They blocked the light filtering down as they moved further into the cavern. Tan thought he heard the sound of birds chirping among the trees, but decided that must be imagined.

Roine turned to Amia. "Which way?"

She closed her eyes. "It's hard to tell. Everything feels different here.

I think—there." She pointed left, off their current path.

Roine allowed Amia to lead and she moved carefully along the soft greenery of the cavern floor. If Tan hadn't known better, he would have imagined they were in a warm forest, though none of the trees looked familiar. Neither did the flowering plants erupting along their path. The vegetation had the air of familiarity to it, but the trees, the flowers, and even the grass growing under his feet were unlike anything he had ever known. A soft sensation, almost an itch, beat at the edge of his consciousness. It took a while to realize that he *sensed* the strangeness around him.

Amia led them toward the soft burbling sound. As they approached, the towering trees stopped, opening into a clearing within the cavern. At the center of the clearing was a circular pool of silvery water, bubbling softly. An object hovered in the middle of the pool of liquid, suspended above it.

With absolute certainty, he knew they'd found it. "This is it." He started toward it.

Roine restrained him and pointed toward a huge stone pillar rising from the ground. Deep etchings marked its perimeter, carvings and runes similar to those on the cave entrance. A suppressed energy emanated from the pillar.

He let his consciousness stretch toward the pillar, trying to sense it. A painful crack within his mind sent his sensing snapping back to him. Tan dropped to his knees with the pain.

Roine reached to help him stand. "Tried to sense it?"

Tan nodded. Everything swam around him and spots danced in front of his eyes.

"It will pass," Roine said.

"How do you know?"

Roine laughed. "I've already done the same. My touch is gentler. Or weaker. So my response was less."

"What is it?" Tan asked.

Roine shook his head. "Some sort of pure earth, channeled and trapped, almost like an elemental." Roine stared at the towering pillar, hesitant to approach it. "Perhaps it is an elemental," he mused.

"Why?" The effects of whatever his sensing had done faded somewhat, but had not cleared completely.

"They create a barrier of some kind."

"They?" Tan asked.

Roine nodded, pointing to their right. He had been so focused on the pillar of earth that Tan hadn't looked around the clearing. A flame shot up and out of the ground, reminding Tan all too much of the fiery cage the lisincend used to trap Amia. The fire sizzled quietly, stretching toward the sky. Flames sputtered briefly before spouting higher into the cavern.

In front of the spout of flame, beyond the silvery pool, a wide stream of water poured from the ceiling of the cave, running straight down and out through an unseen opening in the floor of the cavern. There was a faint glow to the water. He knew without sensing there was an elemental power to the water.

Tan looked to the far left corner, expecting to see something there, another pillar of sorts, but saw nothing but the nearby leaves fluttering wildly as if in a heavy wind. Another elemental forming in a different sort of pillar.

Tan shook his head. "How is this possible?"

Roine looked at the four pillars surrounding the silvery liquid. "I would have loved to see the shaping of this."

"These are elementals, Roine." Tan felt certain of that.

The faint glowing of the water was almost certainly the nymid from the lake below. Tan began to wonder if the flames were once channeled from the draasin. That didn't explain the pillar of rock or of air.

Roine shook his head. "Not elementals. They can't be." He looked at everything in the cavern with a mixture of awe and disbelief.

"Look at how the water glows and how the fire sputters. I can't sense the nymid, but I suspect they flow through that water. And the draasin once created that fire," he said, pointing. "I don't know golud or ara, but they must be a part of this as well."

Roine stared, looking at the cascading water and then over to the fire. "They trapped the elementals here?"

Amia shook her head. "I don't think they were all trapped," she said. "I can't speak to them—not like Tan—but I sense the nymid offer themselves freely." She tilted her head, as if listening. "There is a deep presence within that rock, as well. I don't sense the anguish I felt with the draasin." She shivered from the memory. "I sense nothing from the wind."

"Nor would you," Roine said quietly.

Amia frowned at him a moment. "I think only the draasin had been forcibly held."

"Why would the ancient warriors trap the elementals? What could be so valuable to need that kind of protection?" Tan asked.

# CHAPTER 32
## Pillars of Protection

ROINE CLOSED HIS EYES, looking from each of the pillars before finally settling his eyes on the silvery pool at the center. Anguish covered his face, that and another emotion that Tan couldn't recognize.

"Perhaps there was no other way," Roine said.

"No other way for what?"

Roine pointed toward the silvery liquid, toward where the object hung suspended at the center. "To protect that."

"That's the ancient artifact? Just out in the open?"

Roine shrugged, squinting as he stared out past their barrier, trying to see what it was hovering above the liquid. "I don't know," he admitted. "The artifact isn't described. It's not even named. There are only vague references to it and what it does. I never thought to actually find it."

Tan looked from Roine out toward the silvery water. "What now?"

"We get past this barricade."

"How?" Tan asked. "If this barrier is powered by elementals, how can we get past it?"

"I don't know. I'm working on it."

Roine paced along the outer edge of the pillars, walking past each one, moving slowly and stopping, staring, as he came to the next. Tan and Amia followed him, watching, waiting for Roine to come up with the answer, but Tan wondered if an answer might not be had this time.

The power that stood before them was greater than Roine, perhaps even greater than the ancient warriors who crafted this place.

Roine approached the pillar of water and paused, staring at it briefly, before moving on.

Tan started to follow but Amia touched his arm and stopped him. "Can you speak to them?" she asked, pushing a strand of hair behind her ear. She looked at the water pouring out from somewhere overhead. It funneled down, hitting the stone without splashing before running out unseen below them. It created no spray, nothing but a solid sheet of water.

"I don't know. I'm not even sure if this is the nymid." He looked at the water, at the way it glowed as it flowed down. "What if this is the udilm?"

"Can you speak to them?" she repeated.

He took a deep breath and exhaled slowly, staring at the water, hesitating. The last time he had tried reaching for the nymid, he'd encountered the draasin. What if this was something different than the nymid? What if they were more like the draasin?

And if they couldn't reach the artifact, then the lisincend probably could not either.

"We don't even need to do anything. This protects it. Even the lisincend can't pass."

She frowned and looked toward the pillar of fire. It sputtered more than before. "Are you certain?"

The draasin likely had powered the pillar. And now that they were free, that connection would fail. Eventually the barrier would fail. Then the lisincend would reach the artifact.

Had they not freed the draasin, it might not even matter. The lisincend wouldn't have been able to reach the artifact. Now, because of what they'd done—what *he'd* done—the draasin flew free. And the protection around the artifact failed.

"This is my fault," he whispered.

Amia took his hand. "They deserved their freedom," she said, as if reading his thoughts. With the connection formed by her shaping him, perhaps she did.

"What if we fail?"

She looked at Roine as he limped around the outside rim of the pillars, the limp more pronounced than before. His shoulders sagged and his eyes lost some of their luster. Roine would not be able to help if the lisincend appeared.

"Then we fail. At least we'll have tried. And done right for the lisincend." Amia let out a soft breath. "These others serve willingly, but they grow tired. They deserve their release too."

Tan closed his eyes and focused his thoughts as he had when standing along the lake as he reached for the nymid. "I'll do what I can."

*Nymid!*

He sent the thought with as much force and energy as he could muster. He swayed in place. Then he waited.

Long moments passed. For a while, he thought he'd failed. A soft tickle came to the back of his mind, the sense of something else there, fleeting.

*Nymid!*

He sent the thought again with as much strength as he could manage.

Again the soft tickle came to the back of his mind. Tan felt a definite presence, soft and gentle, settle into his mind. He took a deep breath, easing the tension he'd held.

*Who calls the nymid?*

*I am Tan.*

*He Who is Tan. You know the nymid?*

Tan nodded and then sent the answer. *Yes. You helped me once.* He held up his arms and lifted the shirt Roine had lent him, revealing the burned and charred shirt below. *You healed me once.*

*You wear our armor.* The nymid fell silent for long moments. *We know you, He Who is Tan.* There was a pause. *You released True Fire.*

*We did. The Daughter felt their pain.*

He sensed sadness from the nymid. *They felt much. If we had known, we would never have agreed to the plan. They were not to have suffered. Once we knew, there was nothing that could be done.*

*They are free now.*

The nymid seemed pleased. *You have done well. Why do you call?*

*We must reach the artifact.* Tan sent an image of the object at the center of the pool.

*That is protected by the Mother,* the nymid said. *Only one blessed by the Mother can touch the object.*

Blessed by the Mother? *We can't pass even this barrier.* Tan created an image of the pillars for the nymid.

*The barrier is weakened,* the nymid said.

*It may be weak, but we still cannot pass. What is it?*

*A bargain. And one made freely.* There was a pause. *Nearly freely. And made to protect these lands, this place.*

*Why?* Tan asked.

263

There was something more to what the nymid had agreed to than simply protecting the artifact. He got no answer.

The nymid were silent for long moments and Tan worried they were done speaking with him.

*What would you do with the object?*

*We protect it from Twisted Fire.*

*Twisted Fire cannot reach the object. We protect it well. The Mother protects it well.*

*There is one among Twisted Fire who is powerful. We fear that in time he might succeed.*

Tan sent an image of Fur and his battle with Roine.

The nymid seemed to consider. *That cannot happen.*

*No.*

*We have protected the object for countless cycles. Those who created the object saw its danger and tasked us with watching over it.*

*Why?*

*It provides great power.*

*What does the object do?*

*Only the Mother knows for sure.*

Tan decided to try a different approach. *Did releasing the draasin weaken the barrier?* The sputtering pillar of fire had him wondering how much of this he had caused.

*It is possible. True Fire did not remain to participate in the protection.*

*What effect will that have? Can Twisted Fire now pass through the barrier?*

*You reason well, He Who is Tan,* the nymid said. *And may be correct. The object must not be possessed by Twisted Fire.*

*Let us protect it.*

The nymid fell silent for long moments and Tan again thought that they had broken off communication. He turned to Amia, uncertain, when he heard the nymid's soft presence once more in his mind.

*You may pass. The armor granted you will allow you to move through the barrier, but know that the object can only be possessed by one blessed by the Mother.*

The nymid receded from his mind, leaving him. He shook his head, clearing the sensation, though felt none of the pain as he had with the draasin. Fatigue nearly overwhelmed him, leaving him weakened as Roine after a shaping.

"The nymid state I can pass."

Roine had come behind him. "We can?"

"They said I can pass. I think that means just me. I'm still protected by the armor they granted me during Amia's rescue. They said it will let me move through the barrier."

Roine looked at the water streaming from the ceiling and forming the faintly glowing water pillar. "You still will not be able to reach the artifact." Roine pointed toward the silvery pool. "I've been considering what that liquid represents. If each pillar represents one of the elementals, or *is* one of the elementals," he continued, though his tone seemed unconvinced, "together they form this barrier so immense I can't pass. It's a protection unlike anything I could have imagined. It might be enough to protect the artifact from the lisincend."

Tan considered Roine a moment. "Were you going to use it?"

Roine looked toward the center of the silvery liquid where the artifact hung suspended, unmoving. "I don't even know what it does. But I think we'd have to try."

"You said great power is trapped inside."

Roine nodded. "And I could do much good."

"More than the ancients who created it?" Tan asked. "Why do you think they hid it? Why create such elaborate protection?"

"I don't know. Few records of that time remain. They suggest the ancient warriors knew a time would come when this artifact would be needed."

Tan frowned. "They saw the future?"

"Perhaps a prophecy," he said. "Perhaps nothing so exotic. Many of the ancient shapers were scholars first. Many spent their time studying the world around them." He looked at Tan. "Many used their ability to speak to the elementals in their studies." He stared at the pool of silvery liquid. "Though much of their records survived, not everything did. Most who know of this artifact think the ancient warriors anticipated a time when its power would be needed."

"And you think that time is now?"

"The kingdoms have fewer and fewer shapers. Without this, we might fall. Perhaps to Incendin. Perhaps to someone else, but our greatest weapons have grown scarce."

"Why don't you think I'll be able to reach it?"

"The pool of silver. If that's spirit, you won't be able to reach it."

"But I can," Amia said.

Roine shook his head. "I'm not sure you can. What if you need to be able to use all the elementals to reach the artifact?"

"If we don't, the lisincend will try. Fur will try."

A conflicted expression passed across Roine's face. "I thought only you would be allowed to pass through the barrier."

Tan turned to Amia. "Everything the nymid did to help me, they did because of you." He thought he finally understood. "They know you, don't they?"

"They knew my Mother," she answered quietly.

"They pulled us to them," Tan said, remembering the presence after Roine had sent them on a shaping of wind. "Did your Mother ask them to help?"

Tan couldn't remember. So much had happened when they first faced the lisincend that he couldn't be sure. Had she stepped into the stream? Could she have communicated with the nymid?

Amia shook her head. "I don't know."

"She could speak to the nymid?" Roine asked.

"She nearly drowned when she was young," Amia answered. "She, like Tan, was saved. It was then that she learned to speak with them."

"Where?" Roine asked. "This same lake?"

Amia shook her head. "I don't think so. You called the lake a place of convergence, a place of power. My people would have felt that power and simply stayed away." She shook her head again. "But there are many rivers and streams feeding this lake. The nymid follow the water."

"Could she speak to any of the other elementals?" Roine asked, looking at Tan.

Amia shook her head. "She felt as you did. That the great elementals were gone."

Tan looked at the pillars forming the barrier. "No. Not gone." Of that he was certain. "Please, will you help?" he asked Amia.

She looked at the artifact where it hovered above the liquid. A fleeting concern flickered across her eyes and then was gone. She nodded.

They neared the pillar of water when they heard a low humming of energy, so different than the rush of water. Tan removed the shirt Roine had lent him, exposing his burned and ruined shirt beneath. Hope surged through him when he saw a very faint glow from the shirt where he'd rubbed the nymid armor upon him so many nights ago.

Wrapping his arms around Amia, he backed toward where he felt the barrier. Each step slow. Deliberate.

Roine watched. Tan felt a shaping build that went skittering back as it hit some unseen wall. Roine's face flashed in irritation and he rubbed his temples roughly.

The barrier parted like thick mud. Resistance eased slowly with each step. Amia kept herself stiff as he held her, protecting her as much as he could with his body and praying she would come through the barrier unharmed.

And then, suddenly, the resistance disappeared. Tan went flying past the barrier, holding Amia in his arms.

They fell in a tangle at the very edge of the silvery pool. Thick liquid burbled softly, almost murmuring to them. The edge of the cloak Amia wore—his cloak—had dipped into the liquid. She pulled it out, shaking the liquid from the cloak, but it would not come off.

Where it touched the cloak sizzled. Hazy shimmers of steam rose from the cloak.

Tan rolled back and Amia went with him. "How are we going to get through that?"

"Not 'we.'" Amia started to pull off her maroon pants and bright blue shirt.

Tan flushed and looked away. "What are you doing, Amia?"

"What must be done."

He felt her quickly building a shaping as pressure behind his ears. There was no subtlety to how it built, and it was not gentle. The energy raced to a peak, searing into his head, stabbing through his skull with needles. His ears felt like they would explode.

Tan looked at Amia. She stood, breathtaking.

Facing away from him, she stared at the pool of silver liquid, nude. Tan couldn't look away. Her pale skin nearly glowed from the energy she shaped. The ends of her hair curled outward, as if pressed by the energy swirling through her.

And then she took a step forward.

"No!" Tan lunged toward her.

He couldn't reach her in time. Her foot touched the surface of the thick liquid and she sank softly into it. Amia did not cry out or make any sound.

Instead, Tan felt a surge in the energy she shaped. She stepped forward, deeper into the strange pool. As she pulled her foot from the liquid, the thick substance clung for a moment before oozing away, dripping back into the pool.

Her skin was unharmed.

His tension eased, if only briefly.

He couldn't take his eyes off her as she walked forward. The dark liquid soon reached her knee, then her thigh, and then rolled over her rounded buttocks. Still she pressed forward, never faltering with her steps. The energy she shaped never waned. Soon the liquid reached the middle of her back. She still had a dozen paces to reach the artifact.

Tan couldn't look away. When it reached her neck he felt a flutter of fear, and, without meaning to do so, sent a warning thought. *Careful!*

Amia faltered. As she did, she sank a hand's width deeper into the pool. The energy she shaped fluttered at the same time.

The energy of her shaping roared through his mind again, nearly so painful as to blur his vision. She took another step forward.

He struggled to find calm, to focus on his breathing, to simply watch her, afraid that he might unintentionally startle her again. When the liquid passed over her eyes, Tan almost looked away.

And then her arm reached from the thick liquid and grabbed the artifact.

She clutched it and turned, sliding forward. Tan felt a triumphant surge from her.

Slowly she made her way back. At first only her arm was visible. The thick liquid covered even the top of her head. Then, slowly, her eyes were free, then her face, and then her neck. With each step, the silvery liquid clung to her before oozing away, leaving her unmarked and unharmed. Tan stared unabashedly as her bared breasts were freed and then her belly, and then, slowly, her thighs and legs. She stepped out of the pool, the last of the liquid dripping from her, and fell forward into his arms.

The energy she'd been shaping disappeared suddenly. Tan felt it as a pop in his ears. She held the artifact in one hand, her knuckles white, and shivered.

Tan carried her away from the pool and grabbed her clothes, quickly helping her dress. She was unable to help much, weakened from the effort of whatever she had done to tolerate wading through the pool.

Amia smiled weakly at him. "Did you like watching?"

Tan flushed but did not look away. Through their shaped connection, she'd know how he felt anyway. "Yes," he answered.

She laughed and handed him the artifact.

It was a long cylinder, about as long as his forearm, and covered in the same carvings and shapes as the golden box and Roine's sword. Unlike the box, it was not gold. Rather it was nearly black, almost as if made of the same silvery liquid Amia just walked through. It shone dully, absorbing the light of the cavern rather than reflecting it.

Tan helped Amia to stand and she wobbled toward where Roine stood watching, a stunned expression to his face. Tan wrapped his arms around Amia when he felt the barrier and surged through it more confidently this time, knowing that they would come through unharmed.

Roine reached for the artifact. Tan handed it to him and he took it slowly, reverentially. He stared at it, trying to understand the wording written into the strange dark surface.

"So many years," he whispered. Roine looked up at them. His eyes were haunted. "I've spent so many years searching for this. Many were lost. And now I hold it in my hands."

"What now? What will you do with it?"

"I don't know. I think once I would have tried to use it. Now," he shrugged and ran his free hand through his hair. "Now, after seeing what the ancients did to protect it, I don't think I dare. This must reach Ethea and King Althem." Roine looked to Amia. "How were you unharmed?"

"I am blessed by the Great Mother."

Her comment mirrored what the nymid had said. "What now?" Tan asked.

"Now we return to Ethea, somehow keeping ahead of the lisincend and the hounds."

Tan laughed. "Sounds easy when you say it."

Roine laughed and started to say something more, but an explosion overhead interrupted him.

The rock around the ceiling fell toward them. A sudden swirling wind tossed debris around the cavern, whipping the leaves and branches of the shaped forest. Then a crack of lightning split the sky overhead, shooting through the rock to end nearly at their feet.

When the dust settled, Tan heard a hard cry.

"Theondar!"

Nearby, Roine closed his eyes and took a deep breath, his hand clenching into a white-knuckled fist. "Lacertin," he said softly.

# CHAPTER 33
## Chased by Fire

THEY COWERED BACK from another surge of swirling dust and flying rock. Roine clutched the artifact in his hands. Tan felt the sudden building pressure of Roine shaping.

Roine tried to use the artifact.

A powerful blast of wind hit them, pressing them back. Roine turned to Tan. "Take this," he said, handing the artifact to him. "I'm not strong enough to use it. You must protect this, get it to Althem. Tell him I sent you. Go! Do whatever it takes."

Tan took it from him carefully, holding the ancient device gently. "You don't think you should—"

Roine cut him off. "No. If Lacertin defeats me, he must not have the artifact. The other shapers can help, but only if you reach the capital." Roine looked over his shoulder and into the buffeting wind now growing with a dry heat as well. "Take this too," he said, unbuckling his sword and strapping it onto Tan's waist. "I will not need it for this." His eyes were intense, fierce, and flashed with a hot anger.

"Roine," Tan protested.

"Tannen!" he said. "Now is the time when you must serve your king. Take the artifact and get yourself and Amia out of this cave. Head for Ethea."

He turned away from Tan and called into the blowing wind and dust, standing within the chaos as if unfazed. "Lacertin! Have you come to answer for your treason?"

The wind died briefly and a tall, lean figure stood surrounded in shadows. He was dressed all in black and seemed to crackle with lightning. "Treason?" Lacertin repeated and laughed. "Strange that you would be the one to make such an accusation."

"You have hidden yourself for nearly twenty years. Now you choose to make your allegiance known?" Roine asked.

Lacertin laughed. "Hidden? No. Prepared, Theondar. Now I am ready to take what is mine."

"It was never yours!" Roine roared. He raised his arm and a streak of lightning seemed to jump from his hand, racing toward Lacertin. The other warrior made a simple gesture and the lightning turned, arcing overhead, and leapt from the cavern harmlessly.

"Theondar," Lacertin chided. "How little you have learned."

Roine raised his other arm and Tan felt the rapid buildup of energy and then a blast of wind and water shot toward Lacertin. Lacertin waved his hand in front of him and this seemed to part, splitting and sparing him, leaving him unharmed.

"Time, it seems, has not changed some things," Lacertin spoke. "You never were very creative with your shapings."

He flicked a finger and Roine went rigid, his arms held to his sides. Roine's mouth worked to speak or scream, but no sound came out.

Another flick and a wire-thin streak of flame raced toward Roine.

It swirled around him, pressing toward his flesh. Sweat beaded on Roine's face with the effort of pushing it back. Flame inched closer and closer. Lacertin laughed.

"At the least I should thank you for finding this. You saved me much searching." He looked around the cavern. "I must say the ancient warriors, though, *were* creative. This," he said, waving his arm around him, "is impressive. I would ask you how you managed to reach the artifact, but you seem predisposed."

He smiled, watching Roine struggle. The flame sank closer to his flesh.

Roine closed his eyes and inhaled deeply. Tan felt the huge surge of energy followed by an explosion. The fire circling him disappeared. His arms were free. Hatred dripped from his gaze as Roine opened his eyes.

Lacertin only smiled.

"Theondar. Perhaps I *should* give you a bit more credit."

Roine shook his head. "I would rather you underestimate me."

Lacertin took a step forward, still cloaked in shadows. "The device. I will have it."

"You will not be able to use it," he said. "It was crafted by the ancients and only one with their gifts can access its power. For all that you may be, even you are not gifted like the ancient warriors, Lacertin."

Lacertin only laughed again. It was a dark sound and haunted. "You cannot begin to know what I am capable of doing, Theondar," he answered. "Now. Give me the device."

"You know I will not."

Lacertin took another step closer. His hands twisted in a complex pattern and Roine fell backward, pinned to the ground. His face twisted in pain as unseen lashes struck him over and over, too fast for him to avoid and too powerful for him to hide the painful effect.

Lacertin stepped closer, nearly upon Roine. "Know, then, that I will simply take it."

Something changed on Roine's face. "Come and try," he whispered.

The cavern erupted in thunder. A huge bolt of lightning streaked down from the sky, striking the ground where Roine lay. When it passed, Roine was gone.

Lacertin looked up through the crack in the cavern exposing the daylight and a dark smile twisted his shadowed mouth. "Theondar," he whispered. He turned, eyeing Tan and Amia, and then another bolt of lightning shot down from the sky, striking Lacertin, and he disappeared.

Overhead, the sky thundered. Lightning ripped through the bright sky, tearing it apart with repeated blasts. Tan was forced to look away.

"What now?" Amia asked.

As much as he hated it, Roine was right. They needed to get the artifact to the king. Whatever else, Incendin couldn't have it. He slipped the artifact into one of the pockets of his pants. It was heavy and felt awkward, but he thought it safe. "We need to leave. Make for Ethea."

They both heard something then. It was a low and quiet, barely more than rustling leaves.

Tan sent out his awareness, questing toward the trees and grasses around them. He could almost see them in his mind and sensed the disturbance, knowing what they'd heard.

"The lisincend," he said.

Amia's face showed no sign of fear, just firm resolution. "Then we must go."

They stepped quickly away from the clearing, sliding away from the pillars and the barrier and into the trees. Tan was vaguely aware that something about the barrier was different, weaker. When they reached the protection of the trees, he turned to look.

The huge stone pillar, the most physically solid of the pillars, sank into the stone, slowly disappearing. Where the pillar of wind had blown, whipping the leaves and branches of the nearby trees, now was very little movement. The pillar of fire had stopped sputtering and was completely silent, blowing itself out at some point during all the commotion.

Only the pillar of water remained. The nymid still held their end of the bargain.

Water flowed from an unseen opening in the ceiling of the cavern, cascading down and through the floor of the cave. The water held just a hint of a pale green light, only noticeable because Tan knew what to look for.

In the center of the clearing, the pool of the thick, silvery liquid also receded, slowly draining away from the edge of the pool. Tan didn't know where it went.

"What was in that pool?"

"The power of the Mother."

"How could the ancient warriors trap the power of the Great Mother?" he wondered, not expecting an answer.

"They couldn't. That power was given freely." Amia watched the disappearing liquid. "I think it's but a tiny drop of her power. Maybe no more than a drop of a drop."

Three lisincend burst into the clearing. Fur was among them, sliding confidently from the trees, radiating heat that made the shaped forest wilt from its presence. In spite of the haze surrounding them, Tan saw them clearly. He wondered if the power of the cavern allowed them to be seen.

They reached what was left of the barrier and paused. Fur sniffed, sensing something amiss, before shoving one of the other lisincend through. The creature slid through the barrier with a hiss, then turned and stared at Fur with fiery eyes.

"Nothing," it said.

Fur nodded and he and the other lisincend slid across the barrier. Once inside, they looked around, smelling the air. "She was here."

Then the power of the barrier surged.

Tan was not sure how he knew, but it strengthened. Nothing like it had been before, but enough that the lisincend would be trapped within it.

Could the nymid be helping them again?

With the thought, he heard a soft command whispered in the back of his mind, like a gentle touch, a gentle rain, different than the nymid.

*Go,* the voice commanded.

Tan pulled Amia and they hurried around the edge of the trees, keeping the clearing in sight as they moved. When they were partway around the clearing, the lisincend saw them.

"There!" one of the creatures hissed.

Tan looked back as Fur threw one of the lisincend forward, into the barrier. The creature hit the unseen wall, pressing forward for a few steps with a triumphant look upon its face. Then, suddenly, it dropped to the ground, screaming and hissing. Steam rose from its thick hide. It crawled forward, trying to get through the barrier. By the time it reached the other side, much of its hide had peeled back, leaving it bloodied.

Fur screamed. The horrible sound echoed off the walls of the cavern.

Fur turned toward the pillar of water. With a furious shaping, he threw energy toward it. The water was no longer a match for the fury of the lisincend. Twisted Fire turned the flowing pillar of water into a trail of steam.

Tan felt the barrier fall.

The injured lisincend staggered back toward Fur, flailing its arms, and tripped, sliding into the remnants of the silvery pool, only to disappear with a loud hiss.

Fur roared in anger, splitting the cavern with his furious cry. "I smell you, girl," he hollered. "I know your scent and can find you wherever you go. I will enjoy the hunt."

Amia turned to Tan in fear. He grabbed her hand, not sure where to go. Tan quested out with his mind, searching the cave for the way out. He tracked the cave entrance as he once would have tracked deer or a wolf, letting the subtle changes to the air and wind flow serve as his guide.

They ran. Tan followed what he sensed. Trees thinned and became more stunted the farther they moved, soon growing no taller than shrubs. When he saw the strange vines upon the walls, he knew they went in the right direction.

"They're behind us."

Tan let his senses search behind him. The two remaining lisincend were near the edge of the trees and they headed toward them.

"They're frustrated," Amia said.

"Can you do anything to make it worse?" he asked.

"I can try. I don't know if it will work."

"We only need a delay."

She nodded and Tan felt the building pressure as she worked her shaping. He felt it slip slowly, subtly, into the trees. He sensed the lisincend struggle, wandering off course a bit.

"They may not even know you did anything."

She narrowed her eyes at him, biting back a question. "That was my intent," she said. "How can you tell?"

He led her down the cave at a quick jog. "Since you shaped me," he started, "I've been able to feel it when you perform a shaping. I feel the energy. I don't understand, not really." He glanced at her. "With that shaping, I felt you slowly release the energy and knew it was a gentle touch."

"Can you feel others shaping?"

"It is different. Each shaper has a different energy, almost like a signature. I think it started when you shaped me. Does that mean anything?"

She shook her head softly. "I don't know. It's unusual, I think."

The cave grew darker the farther they got from the cavern. Tan sensed behind him again. The lisincend had found their way once more. Fur tore the strange vines from the wall in his rage and some of his muted shouts echoed through the cave.

"I can't see anything," Amia said, reaching toward one of the lamps.

Tan grabbed her wrist. "I don't think we should let the lisincend see us."

"They see fine in the dark," she answered. "They sense our heat. We've never known how good their eyesight is during the day, but we've always known they have an advantage at night."

They ran down the cavern with Tan leading, sensing his way through the darkness. He was able to feel the pressure off the walls and the ground and used it to keep them roughly in the middle of the cave. Occasionally he would sense behind them.

The lisincend were gaining.

He said nothing to Amia, only urging her faster.

Then in the distance he saw the hint of light. They were close. They couldn't follow the same path they'd followed up from the lake. The climb down the sheer rock face would be too slow and the lisincend would be upon them in moments. Which way would they go?

As they emerged into the bright light of day, the sky thundered ceaselessly, like a heavy drum. Frequent bolts of lightning attempted to tear apart the sky. The air sizzled with the energy of the lightning, almost crackling with it.

Roine and Lacertin battled.

Tan could not pause to watch, but wished that he could. Overhead, an epic battle between two powerful Cloud Warriors raged, and he was witness to it.

They reached the split in the trail. Tan hesitated before pulling Amia off the main path, veering to the left and down. If they could reach the lake and the nymid, they might find safety.

Behind him, Fur roared as he left the cave.

They wouldn't reach the lake in time.

"We need to hide," he told Amia.

"Fur will find us."

"You have his sword," she said, motioning to Roine's sword hanging from Tan's waist.

"I've never used a sword. And my bow…" Had he not lost it in the lake when Fur nearly killed him, he might be able to try something, anything. Instead, Fur would catch them. They would die.

Amia squeezed his hand. "Neither have I. We make quite a pair."

Tan laughed in spite of himself.

They half stumbled down the path, practically sliding. The trail was steep and more than once, Tan reached for a handhold to catch himself or Amia as they slipped, sensing danger at the last instant.

At the bottom of the trail they reached a grassy base. A wide river ran through here. Tan hoped it ran around the mountain and into the lake. Maybe even the one the nymid had widened to slow the lisincend. If that was the case, could he reach the nymid?

He glanced back. The lisincend were close. "We have to jump."

He squeezed her hand and jumped into the river with her. When ld water hit him, the air left his lungs. Amia flailed in the water, struggling against the current. He pulled her forward with powerful kicks then he dipped underwater, letting the current pull them along.

He sensed the opposite shore close by. Another kick and they reached it.

Tan pressed his head above the surface of the water, turning to look for the lisincend as he did. Amia came up from the water at the same time, gasping for air. They kept low in the water, not daring to show themselves.

The lisincend stood nearly a hundred paces across the river and down the shore. They hadn't seen them yet. A particularly bright bolt of lightning split the sky. Tan used the distraction to pull Amia from the water and they stumbled toward the trees, moving quickly and keeping as low as possible.

Once hiding in the cover of the trees, he peered out at the lisincend. "The water won't stop them," he said, remembering what Fur had said to Roine.

"No," Amia agreed, "but it may slow them."

The first lisincend stepped into the water, sniffing the air. Suddenly it motioned in their direction. Fur smiled. It was hideous and unnatural and full of venom.

"You will be mine, girl," he hissed.

"Tan—" Amia started.

Tan didn't answer. He closed his eyes, focusing his mind as he reached for the nymid.

*We need help!*

He sent the thought as a shout, praying the nymid would hear.

No answer came.

Both the lisincend were in the water now, moving toward them, unfazed by the water.

They needed to move—to do something—or else the lisincend

would reach them. But even if they ran, it would not matter. Not now. The lisincend were too fast. Too powerful.

Without the nymid for help, they would be caught. Tan would be burned, like Amia's Mother. And then the lisincend would be free to do whatever they wanted to Amia. The artifact would be theirs.

*Please! We need your help.*

He sent the plea with the last of his fading energy. His vision blurred from the energy required sending the thought and he sagged toward Amia.

"Just run," he began weakly, staggering into the trees and falling. "I'll hold them as long as I can. Take the artifact. Get to safety."

She shook her head. "I'll not leave you, Tan." She squeezed his hand.

He met her eyes, sensing the lisincend nearly upon them.

*Protect her*, he sent with the last of his energy.

The lisincend were close enough to feel the heat rising from them. Steam rose around them as they walked, the river evaporating in their advance. Fur led the charge and a powerful shaping built as he neared. Tan wouldn't survive the attack this time; he'd been lucky to have the nymid save him the last time.

And now? He'd failed. He'd failed his mother asking him to help Roine and the king. Now he'd never be able to travel to Ethea as she'd wanted. He'd failed Roine; the lisincend would take the artifact back to Incendin and all that power would be theirs. With it, they would attack the kingdoms and there weren't shapers enough to stop them.

And he'd failed Amia. The lingering plea to protect her still tickled his mind, only now he couldn't do anything more to help her. He'd failed.

Amia squeezed his hand again, as if knowing his thoughts. He couldn't look at her.

1 then there was a presence in his mind. Huge and rough,

nothing like the nymid. Had it ever really left his mind? Had the connection ever been broken?

*Who calls?*

The draasin. Tan shook from pain or fear, he did not know.

*Tan*, he said. *Tan, who freed you.*

He sensed irritation from the draasin.

*We need your help. I need your help.*

*Why should I help you? I hunt now.*

*For the freedom you were given.*

*You took freedom away. You limit what I may hunt.*

*I released you from the ice and pain. I ended the suffering.*

Tan barely had the energy to send the last thought and sagged into Amia.

The draasin was silent. They would not help. Nothing would.

The lisincend stood barely ten paces away. Fur pointed toward them.

Amia pulled at his arm, trying to get him to come with her, but Tan resisted. There was another thing he could try, if only he was strong enough.

*Hunt near the river*, Tan suggested, sending an image of where they hid, using what was left of his energy.

The draasin finally answered him. *You forbid us to hunt man, little warrior.*

*There is more to hunt than man near the river*, Tan said. *Come. Help me. Hunt.*

*I will help. This time, little warrior.*

"Tan!" Amia yelled.

Fur was nearly upon them. "I hear you now, girl. I will enjoy tearing you apart. And the other with you, as well."

"Tan?"

He pulled her back into the trees. They couldn't move, not fast enough.

The building shaping was earsplitting. Tan could barely tolerate it, shaking with its power.

Then there was a cry like nothing he could imagine. The sound pierced the sky, overpowering the thunder rolling through the air. The sound of a predator the world had not seen in nearly one thousand years. And it hunted.

Instinctively Tan cringed, and he felt a satisfied laugh from the presence in his mind. Tan steeled himself, sending the image of the lisincend.

A huge shape erupted above the trees, blotting out the light, and flying hard and fast toward them. The lisincend stopped to turn and see what was coming.

The draasin attacked the smaller lisincend first, swooping out of the sky. It grabbed the lisincend from where it stood in the river, chewing it quickly and swallowing before twisting and turning skyward again.

Fur moved toward the center of the river, less certain than before. He watched the draasin, his eyes widening. The energy Fur had been building erupted as a huge bolt of fire toward the draasin.

The fire struck the creature in its abdomen and disappeared.

The draasin roared.

Not in pain, Tan realized. Fire would not hurt the draasin. Not a fire elemental.

No, the draasin roared in anger.

Tan shivered at the sound. Amia squeezed his hand. She smiled at the enormous creature hovering above the river, a pleased looked to her face.

*You dare use fire against the draasin!*

1 heard the words as a shout within his mind and realized from

Fur's expression that he did as well.

Then the draasin struck. Its head darted toward the water quickly, striking at Fur. Fur grabbed the huge jaw and twisted, thrusting it back and away from him, ducking from underneath a barbed tail darting toward him.

Then Fur ran.

He jumped out of the river in a single leap. Once on the shore, he ran quickly into the trees and disappeared. The draasin flapped its huge wings once and was above the trees, flying low over the treetops. Hunting.

*Hunt well*, Tan said.

*Always*, the draasin answered.

Tan felt its mind grow distant as it flew away, following Fur. There was a sense of satisfaction from the creature. Faintly, Tan knew they'd done the right thing in freeing the creature.

Though the draasin's mind grew distant, Tan was still aware of it.

"Are we safe?"

He looked around the forest. Could they be safe?

But the lisincend were gone. One dead in the cave. Another eaten by the draasin. And Fur, running, hunted by the great elemental. Could the hounds still be out there?

He sent his sensing out and around the forest. Pressure built within his ears and let out slowly as his sensing washed over the forest. Birds and squirrels and even a fox roamed the forest. Cool wind gusted from the north. But nothing else. No sign of the hounds.

He smiled. They'd survived more than they had a right to survive. "I think we are."

"You protected me," she said.

"Not me. I needed help."

She still smiled and squeezed his hand. "We all need help at times."

Tan looked toward the sky at the small black spot that was the draasin. Overhead, the sky still thundered and lightning crackled.

After resting for a moment, they followed the river, heading south. Toward Ethea. Tan felt the artifact as a heaviness in his pocket. Was everything they'd been through worth it? After losing Nor, the Aeta, and even Velminth, did keeping the artifact away from Incendin matter?

After seeing how little the lisincend cared for others, their fiery violence, he had to think it was. He hoped his mother would have been proud.

Amia touched his arm and a wave of peace washed over him.

Finally, when the thunder died and the last of the lightning went with it, he looked up to the sky. "I wonder who won."

"There were no winners in any of this."

"No. But I met you. I spoke to the nymid. And the draasin were freed from ages of suffering. I think some good has come from this."

Not enough to make up for what was lost, but it was a start.

Amia pulled him close. Then she kissed him. He was startled at first, but he let her full lips envelop his and kissed her back, and felt hope for the future for the first time in as long as he could remember.

# EPILOGUE

THEY FOUND ROINE near the lake.

Tan and Amia had followed the wide river, walking along its shore as it meandered through the forest. Their hands were entwined and he felt reluctant to let her go, enjoying the sensation of her hand in his.

The forest around them gradually returned to life. Insects buzzed, squirrels climbed on trees, and the sun shone brightly overhead. Tan felt more and more relaxed with each step he took, knowing the normalcy of the forest meant the lisincend were truly gone. And the hounds.

He smiled.

Amia looked up at him and smiled back. He sensed her growing ease. There would be grieving later for both of them, but for now, they simply enjoyed each other's company.

The river crested a small hill before running down and toward the lake. They followed it, moving casually. When they reached the lake, Tan felt a sense of warmth, of welcome, as if the nymid greeted them. He didn't reach for them.

The bright sun reflected off the calm water of the lake, glittering and reflecting like a thousand stars. They stopped by the edge of the water and took a drink. The water tasted cool and refreshing. Not far down the shore was the cluster of rocks where so many horrible things had happened. The first attack when Tan had nearly died. Roine's attack on the lisincend. And his rescue of Amia.

Amia saw him staring at the rocks. She squeezed his hand and he squeezed back, letting the sudden tension leave him. Neither spoke.

They found him near the rocks, lying half in the water.

He lay still, motionless, though his chest rose and fell so they knew he still lived. His face was torn and bleeding. His dark green clothes were tattered and stained with blood. The water washed some of it away.

They knelt next to Roine and Tan touched his forehead. Roine opened his eyes, blinking against the bright light.

"Did you defeat Lacertin?" Tan asked.

Roine shook his head weakly. "No." But he smiled. "I managed better than I thought I could. For now, he's gone. Chased away. And we have the artifact." Roine glanced at Tan, closing his eyes when Tan nodded, patting his pocket. "The lisincend?"

"Gone," Tan answered.

Roine blinked his eyes open again. "Gone? Even Fur?"

"For now," Tan answered and smiled, baring his teeth. He didn't know if Fur managed to escape the draasin, but it didn't matter right now. "The draasin helped. Fur is now the hunted."

Roine nodded slowly. "Good. I still wonder if we did the right thing freeing them. The world hasn't seen their kind in centuries. We can't know what price we'll pay."

"They needed to be freed, Roine," Tan said. "They suffered. And \n't joined the barrier willingly. Not like the others."

Roine looked at Tan, slowly shaking his head. "Perhaps you're right," he said with a sigh.

"What now?" Tan asked.

Roine pushed himself up and looked down at his tattered clothes streaked with his blood, staring out into the lake before turning his attention to the south. "Now we need to reach Althem. Now we travel to Ethea."

"You think the artifact will help?" Tan asked.

Roine shook his head. "I don't even know anymore. It wouldn't work for me. Perhaps too much time has passed since its creation. The ancient warriors are no more." He shook his head again. "But I have to think we've done well. The lisincend are defeated. And Lacertin has been outed. No more can he hide his plans."

Tan pulled the artifact out of his pocket and thrust it toward Roine. The silver surface was dull, lifeless, and reflected none of the bright sun. "You should carry it."

Roine took it and, turning it in his hands, he stared at the surface as he ran a finger along the markings. Slowly, he pulled his attention away from the artifact and handed it back to Tan. "No. You carry it. If not for you, none of this would be possible."

Tan took it back and held it in his hands, feeling the soft weight of the device. The markings on the surface were meticulously done and he ran his finger along them as Roine had done. A soft pressure built and he looked up, wondering why Roine or Amia would be shaping. Neither gave any sign that they were.

Tan stood and Amia followed. They both helped Roine to stand. He trembled for a moment before steadying himself. And then they started off, walking along the shore of the lake, toward Ethea.

Amia took Tan's hand and her dark eyes studied him. She brushed her pale hair back from her eyes, tucking it behind her ears. He closed his eyes a moment before letting himself be led, feeling the soft breeze on his face, the earthy scent to the ground, the warmth of the sun, and felt a brief spray of water strike him as well. And he smiled.

Tucking the artifact into his pocket, he didn't see it begin glowing faintly, pulsing, as they started off toward Ethea.

DK HOLMBERG currently lives in rural Minnesota where the winter cold and the summer mosquitoes keep him inside and writing.

To see other books and read more, please go to www.dkholmberg.com

Follow me on twitter: @dkholmberg

Word-of-mouth is crucial for any author to succeed and how books are discovered. If you enjoyed the book, please consider leaving a review online at your favorite bookseller or Goodreads, even if it's only a line or two; it would make all the difference and would be very much appreciated.

# Bound by Fire
## The Cloud Warrior Saga, Book 2

The powerful draasin – elemental creatures of fire not seen for a thousand years – have returned. Not all are convinced they should have been freed.

As Tan struggles to learn earth shaping, he discovers dangerous fire shapers from Incendin have come to Ethea. When the city is attacked by the draasin, Tan must use his connection with them to learn why. Doing so leads him from the city and forces him to once more face the terrible shapers of Incendin, but this time bound to the draasin for help. If he fails, much more than his life is at stake, for Incendin has stolen the artifact and plans to use its power for unknown destruction.

# CHAPTER 1

## *The Master Shaper*

Tannen Minden sat at a long, faded oak table, leaning forward as he waited for the instructor to arrive. Only a week in Ethea and already he longed for the forests of Galen around him. Had he been able to find Amia, he wouldn't have bothered coming to this lecture, but he struggled to find her the last few days and when he did, she seemed anxious. How much of the anxiety came from the strange and massive capital city and how much from losing everyone she knew?

After how the lisincend destroyed his home of Nor, he understood that anxiety well.

He rubbed his neck. The aching he'd felt since reaching the city throbbed with more intensity this morning. At first, he thought it the change in altitude—Nor sat much higher than Ethea—but now he wondered if it had to do with the connection he'd made while there. Could the distant sense he still had of the draasin be giving him the pain?

The girl at the end of the table glanced at him again. She had brown hair cut short and a thin face. A green dress several sizes too large draped over her. A thick book rested open on the table in front of her, but she kept looking up from it to him.

Another boy, built like a blacksmith, sat down the table. He kept his eyes fixed straight ahead, as if he feared looking around too much. Tan watched him, waiting for a crack in his focus, but none came. He wore a thick wool jacket dyed a dark blue and his hair was cut short. His skin was deeply tanned.

And then there was a man near the window. He stared out, fingers drumming across the stone as he stared through the opaque glass. He shifted from one foot to another, his boots the only part of him visible beneath the long gray cloak he wore. Even his head was covered, hiding his face.

As far as Tan knew, these were all students at the university. And he was older than each of them.

Since arriving in Ethea, Tan had seen people from all over the kingdoms. It had surprised him how different each style of dress was, and he hadn't been here long enough to know where each style came from. Amia might, since she was one of the Aeta, traders given the freedom to wander without concern for borders, if only he could find her.

Like usual, no one spoke. Tan had attended few classes since arriving in Ethea. When they had first reached Ethea, Roine encouraged him to attend as many as possible, especially those with an earth-sensing focus. He remained convinced Tan could become an earth shaper, but how would he ever even sense anything within the walls of the university? At least in Galen, the trees and grasses and life around him gave him something to sense. Here, all he sensed was the vast expanse of stone that comprised the university.

The girl looked up at him again. Tan frowned at her and she looked away, burying her face in her book once more.

He didn't want to be here. Not only this room, but in this city. This had always been his mother's dream for him, never his. If he had his choice, he would have remained in Galen, climbing the hills around Nor.

The man near the window stopped drumming his fingers on the window and turned to face them. The hood of his cloak fell down to his shoulders, revealing curly brown hair. "This is all who choose to attend?" His voice sounded low, thick and gravelly.

The girl pushed her book aside, closing it slowly. The thick boy turned to face Tan.

Now that Tan could see the man's face, he saw he was older—much older than Tan. Not a student, then. The man grunted and looked around the room, flinty eyes stopping on each of them before they settled on Tan, widening slightly as they did. His nostrils flared briefly as he sniffed.

"A waste of time," he muttered. He flicked his gaze to the boy. "You. Where in Ter are you from?"

The boy blinked and swallowed. "Keoth, sir."

The man grunted and the corners of his eyes twitched. "Keoth? Does that make you a farmer or quarryman?"

The boy's back stiffened slightly. He looked at the man, unblinking. "Farmer, sir."

The man sniffed, his nostrils flaring again. His eyes narrowed and he pursed his lips as if he might say something, but then he looked over to the girl. "And you. Where in Vatten are you from? Too slight to be a fisherman's daughter. A weaver?"

The girl glanced at her book and then looked up and past the man, nodding as she did.

The man shook his head, not bothering to hide his annoyance. "And then there's you," he said, turning to Tan. "You're too old to be a new student—" he regarded Tan's age with derision "—but I haven't seen you in other classes."

"I've only been—"

The man cut him off with a wave of the hand. "From your build, you could be from Ter or Vatten, but you don't have the right coloring. Your hair is too dark for Nara. That leaves Galen."

Tan nodded. The way he spoke of Galen put Tan on edge, his tone making it seem like he wished he could exclude Galen from the kingdoms. Already, he didn't like this man.

"Not many come from Galen anymore. Fewer will come now that Incendin attacks." The girl sucked in a quick breath and the man turned to her. "The rumors are true. Best not to hide from them. You empower them with your fear. Besides, there's no reason to fear Incendin here in the university. You're safest surrounded by our best shapers."

"But their shapers—" she started in a whisper.

"Are no different than me. Fire works no different than earth." As emphasis, the stone around the window peeled away briefly before folding back into place. Tan's ears popped as it did.

The boy's eyes widened, the most reaction Tan had seen from him. The girl smiled and pulled her book up to her chest, clutching it to herself.

"A skilled shaper can hold back the fire shapers of Incendin, and isn't that why you're here?"

The Master shaper dismissed Incendin's fire shapers so quickly, but Tan knew what they were capable of. He'd seen their destruction first-hand, had witnessed how they destroyed his home as if it were nothing. "It's not only fire shapers to fear."

The man's eyes narrowed slightly and a tight smile pulled at the corners of his mouth. "So, you *are* from Galen."

Tan nodded.

"Don't scare the others with stories. The truth can be awful on its own."

Had he not lost everyone he knew to those *stories*, Tan might have been more forgiving of the comment. Instead, other than Cobin and Bal, only Lins Alles survived and Tan had no interest in seeing him again, not after seeing him working *with* the lisincend. And he hadn't seen Cobin or Bal since reaching Ethea. For all Tan knew, they'd gone somewhere else, away from the danger of the capital. Knowing how Cobin was an earth senser, Tan would understand him not wanting to return to Ethea. Likely, he wanted to get as far from Incendin as possible to keep Bal safe, someplace like Ter, where there would be other earth sensers and where the threat of attack was minimal.

And Lins? If Tan saw him again, he didn't know *what* he would do. He'd spent years fearing his temper; now he wanted nothing more from him. After helping the lisincend, had he gone to Incendin? Or had he faded into obscurity within the kingdoms?

"You don't think we should fear Incendin? After what they did?" Tan asked.

The man sniffed again. He kept his hands in the pocket of his cloak and fixed Tan with a hard gaze. "Their attacks have grown stronger, it is true, but the barrier protects us from a more direct attack."

"The barrier didn't keep the lisincend from passing through. The barrier did nothing to stop my home from being destroyed."

Tan realized he'd raised his voice and took a calming breath.

The girl looked from him to the man standing at the front of the room. The smile faded from her face, and with it, all the color in her cheeks. Her wide blue eyes made her look younger than Bal.

The other boy simply stared at the man. He didn't look over at Tan, as if taking his eyes off the shaper at the front of the room would get him into some sort of trouble.

The man leaned forward, resting his hands on the table as he stared at Tan. A dark expression flashed across his eyes. "You speak of rumors as if they are true. Few enough know of the lisincend. I would like to know how you learned about them."

Tan shook his head. He should leave. There was nothing this man would teach him that he wanted to know, but he was new to the university and he owed it to his memory of his mother to at least try. "I've seen them."

The man laughed. "Then you would be dead. Instead, you sit here and argue with a Master of the university." He paused and started to turn before catching himself and turning back. "Had the lisincend attacked, there would be little to slow them until they reached Ethea."

"Only a warrior shaper," Tan answered.

And even Roine had almost not been enough. Had not the draasin—the great winged fire elemental—come when Tan called, what would have happened with Fur and the other lisincend? Tan wouldn't have survived, but more than that, they would have captured the artifact, the one thing that might be able to help the kingdoms push back Incendin.

"There no longer are any warriors," the man said. "So be glad you have not seen the lisincend."

"The ashes of my village would say otherwise. And if you need further convincing, seek out Roine. Ask him what happened to Nor."

Tan started to stand. He wasn't in the mood to listen to the Master anyway. He would have to come another time, perhaps find another earth shaper to learn from, though Roine said the Master instructing this class was more skilled than most.

"Why would one of the Athans have been in Galen?"

Tan sighed and looked up, wishing he were back in Galen, back beneath the trees and following some unknown trail as it wound into the mountains. At least there, he knew what to do. He could sense his way along, so he knew where he needed to go. In Ethea, surrounded by all these people that he didn't understand, he never felt fully sure of himself.

But if he could learn to be a shaper—an earth shaper like the Master—wouldn't he take that opportunity? It required his allegiance to the king, but shapers were gifted with much power, abilities he'd only glimpsed while traveling with Roine. How much better would it be if *he* could do some of the things he'd seen Roine do?

"Serving the king," Tan answered. "And protecting the kingdoms from Incendin. More than that, you'll have to ask him."

"And you claim you encountered one of the lisincend while with Roine?"

Tan nodded.

"Where is it now?"

"Two were killed. Fur might still be running back to Incendin." Or eaten. Tan hoped the draasin had caught him but suspected Fur might have been strong enough to escape and survive. If he did, how long did they have before Incendin sent more of the lisincend into the kingdoms?

If he dared embrace the connection with the draasin, he might learn, but doing so meant pain and fear. Regardless of how it had saved them, the great fire elemental was dangerous to Tan.

The Master shaper blinked. "You faced more than one of the lisincend?"

Tan nodded again.

The Master studied Tan for a moment, gray eyes seeming to stare through him before taking a shallow breath. Without another word, he turned to the door and hurried out, pulling the hood of his cloak back over his head as he went.

Tan frowned. What had just happened?

So much about Ethea was strange. The last time he'd seen him, Roine tried offering suggestions about the university and promised to help in any way he could, but as Athan, he had other responsibilities. Tan hadn't seen Roine since their second day in Ethea.

The thick boy got up slowly and made his way to the door after the Master. He left quietly, making his way down the narrow hall and out of sight.

Tan sighed and started to leave. A gentle tug at the sleeve of his jacket caused him to turn.

The girl stood looking up at him. She barely came to his shoulder. Up close, her short brown hair looked uneven and ragged, as if she'd cut it with a dull knife. One hand gripped a handful of fabric, holding her dress off the floor so she didn't trip. The other held a stack of books she somehow didn't spill as she pulled on his sleeve. A serious expression furrowed her brow.

"Is what you said true?" Her voice sounded less meek than when she'd spoken to the Master shaper.

Tan nodded.

"You saw one of these creatures?"

Tan stiffened. "That's what I said."

"You said it was Fur?"

Tan frowned. "You know of him?" The Master shaper had been right that few knew of the lisincend. At least in Galen, he hadn't heard of the lisincend before they attacked, and Galen shared a border with Incendin.

The girl swallowed, her head bobbing in a nod. "My grandfather—" She took a deep breath and met Tan's eyes. "My grandfather fought in the Incendin war. Barely survived. When I was younger—" Tan snorted and she frowned "—he wouldn't talk about it. I knew he lost friends during the war. But as he's gotten older, his mind started to wander. Sometimes he speaks about the nightmares he saw. Only one of them ever had a name. Fur." She shivered, as if a breeze suddenly gusted through the window. "Always said his name in a whisper, and usually after having too much wine. He's real?"

Tan understood the reaction. Nearly dying at the hands of the lisincend did that to him. "He's real. And as terrifying as your grandfather said."

The girl shook her head. "He never said much other than a name, but not much scared him. A water shaper—and strong, too—so anything of fire that frightening…"

Tan nodded, remembering the way Fur had nearly burned away the lake. Had the nymid—the water elementals at the heart of the lake—not been there, Fur might have been strong enough.

"You plan to study at the university?" she asked.

The sudden change took Tan aback. He nodded.

"You're older than most students," she commented. "You know, most come to the university when they learn they're sensers. If you can sense the elements, some learn to shape as well."

"I never wanted to come in the first place," Tan answered.

"Never wanted to come? Why wouldn't you want to come? Don't you care to learn if you can be a shaper?"

Tan took a deep breath before answering. He'd never cared before. Not that he didn't think the idea of shaping sounded impressive, just that he didn't want to commit to what came with it: service to the king like his father—and his mother, he reminded himself—bought by learning. Service that claimed his father's life fighting Incendin.

But he'd seen what the lisincend would do. He'd seen the lengths they went—the mindless destruction they inflicted. How could he refuse to help if he had the ability?

"There's more to it than wanting to be a shaper," he said.

She looked at him skeptically. "What more can there be? Either you want to learn or you don't. And if you're here, it means you have the ability to learn."

"How did he know you're from Vatten?" Tan asked, changing the subject. He didn't know this girl at all, and here she was, pressing him no differently than his mother had.

"How can you not know?"

He shrugged. "I can't tell where anyone is from."

She laughed, the sound smooth and light, betraying a cloud that came over her face. "You should probably learn, especially if you're going to stay here. Everyone is like that Master. Once they figure out where you're from…"

Tan sighed and glanced at the window. Another reason for him to wish he was out of Ethea and back in Galen. At least there, he understood how things worked. As long as he didn't upset the manor lord—or his son—he was fine.

Maybe he needed to find Amia and see if she would leave with him.

Finally, he shook his head. Standing here changed nothing. "I need to get going," he decided.

Tan started out of the room, and the girl trailed after him. She kept her dress bunched in one fist to keep it from dragging on the floor. The books were pressed against her chest. A single lantern lit the musty, narrow hall outside the room. Rough stone shifted with strange shadows. Even here, Tan had little sense of anything.

"So what are you?" the girl asked as they reached a stair leading down.

He paused and looked at her. "What do you mean?"

She sniffed. "Well, you're *here*, right? So what kind of senser are you?"

He nodded. "Earth senser."

"From Galen?"

He nodded again.

The girl frowned for a moment and then shrugged. "I'm a water shaper. Pretty common in Vatten, you know."

He didn't know but didn't say anything as he continued down the stairs. At the bottom, a door led out into a wide courtyard. Grass and a few trees grew tidily here, though the center of the courtyard was cleared. There, stones were set in a circular pattern.

The girl said something but Tan missed it. Pressure built in his ears, the sensation familiar to him. Someone performed a shaping nearby, and a powerful one at that.

The sudden rumble of thunder followed by a loud crack of lightning made him take a quick step back. Tan had felt this shaping before.

When it cleared, Roine stood at the center of the clearing. Dried blood smeared on the top of his brow from an open wound and he held a slender sword clutched in his hand. He took a deep breath and then collapsed.

CPSIA information can be obtained
at www.ICGtesting.com
Printed in the USA
FSHW011251071020
74574FS

9 780692 309322